FLIGHT RISK

FLIGHT RISK

E.L. DEPINTO

Columbus, Ohio

Flight Risk
Published by Gatekeeper Press
2167 Stringtown Rd, Suite 109
Columbus, OH 43123-2989
www.GatekeeperPress.com

Library of Congress Control Number: 2021942034

ISBN (paperback): 9781662906749
eISBN: 9781662906756

Playlist

Heart of Glass- Blondie

Breaking the Girl- Red Hot Chili Peppers

Artificial Sweetener- No Doubt

Dancing On My Own- Robyn

Water Me- Lizzo

Feel So Close- Calvin Harris

First Date- Blink 182

Lay It on Me- Vance Joy

Send My Love (To Your New Lover)- Adele

If I Ever Feel Better- Phoenix

Ghosts of Beverly Hills Drive- Death Cab for Cutie

Sunday, Bloody Sunday- U2

Gypsy- Fleetwood Mac

Lovesong- The Cure

Out of the Woods- Taylor Swift

How's It Going to Be- Third Eye Blind

Renegade - Styx

I Wanna Grow Old with You- Adam Sandler

Chapter 1

Persephone

A t the end of the day, we are just an accumulation of all our decisions, for better or for worse. That puts a lot of unfair pressure on us, doesn't it? Can we get a different scorecard? Perhaps a new rubric to judge us on? No?

Seems like someone in Heaven is pawning off all the work onto us humans.

Most decisions we make are split second decisions.

Do it.

Don't do it.

Go.

Don't go.

Sing this song in front of strangers even though you are tone deaf.

Drop it low, then pick it up slow.

Take a shot of tequila.

Don't take a shot of tequila.

I've made some good decisions in my life. Like going to work for my dad and his company, which gave me the opportunity to spend more time with him before he died. Or deciding where to go to college, choosing a great apartment in NYC, and even purchasing the shoes I'm currently wearing, which are extremely comfortable for a long night out.

But the singular decision of singing karaoke in a crowded bar in Savannah, Georgia because a bachelorette party took me under their wing and begged me to go up next? It felt like a good decision fifteen minutes ago when I signed up, but it swiftly turned the corner to "bad decision-ville."

I stumble on stage, mumble the first verse, then pick up wind and start seductively twisting my hips, blitzed out of my mind, while crooning a poor rendition of "I Got Friends in Low Places" by Garth Brooks. It was a tough visual for an equally tough song, but it's been a rough few days. Hell, it'd been a rough few months, so this train wreck performance was pretty par for the course.

The bar was a mix of college kids and smaller subgroups of older adults like myself trying to squeeze out the last of their youth on a Saturday night. Up front is the all-star girl squad I met while sulking on a barstool earlier tonight. The girls were from Dallas, TX, here for a bachelorette party and all but recruiting people to join in on their good time. I begrudgingly obliged out of politeness, and look where that got me? Singing, badly I might add, on a stage in front of strangers.

The first few shots were necessary purely to acclimate me to the Southern charm of these ladies, but not the last five. These girls took advantage of my amiable mood and got *me* drunk along with them.

Once I took my pathetic bow and the karaoke DJ moved on to his next victim, I declared myself an honorary bridesmaid while finding my lady birds again. The six girls and future wifey are fun loving, charming southern belles, and truly electrifying to be around. They're a black hole of merriment and they keep irresistibly sucking people into their orbit, myself included.

I had noticed earlier in the night the bridal party were wearing their engagement rings and wedding bands. They had no idea my own diamond was currently in the change tray of my rental car. But these women didn't discriminate when deciding who to pull into their circle. No man, woman, or child was safe from their manic allure tonight.

There's something truly enthralling about a bachelorette party; the rules of social etiquette don't apply to them. They're allowed to scream as loud as they want, interrupt any conversation, cut the line at the bar, and apparently, dance with anyone. It's one of those unwritten rules of life: bachelorette parties can do no wrong.

The girls circle me, taking a break from our dancing to rapid fire questions at me.

"Is your hair real?"

"No, is yours?"

Cackling breaks out, but they keep on. "Your dress is cute. Where did you get it?"

"Revolve." Heads nod and they all mumble in response.

"Where are you from?"

"New York."

"Do you have a boyfriend?"

"I just walked out on my fiancé."

Audible gasps. Four different versions of "Oh my God, honey, are you okay?" shootout at me.

"Yeah, he sucked. I think he was cheating on me."

The group gasps again, then breaks out in unified mumbles ranging from "fuck him" to "you deserve better" to "but you're such a hot blonde."

"How do you know?" Haley from the back asked shyly.

"Sarah!" Louann slapped her friend for her lack of propriety.

"It's fine. I found some incriminating evidence, if you know what I mean," I exhale to the group, my lips loose from all the liquor. My gaze was swimming from eye to eye to catch their shocked reactions. I hope my vague response won't elicit more questions, so I continue on, "I'm fine, honestly. Good riddance." The words are hollow, reverberating out of my drunken mouth. They say fake it til you make it, right?

"Of course, you are fine, you're with u-us. D-Don't worry we'll, we… will get you on your w-way," the bride slurred her comforting words, eyes rolling in the back of her head with each stutter, but in my own inebriated state, I accepted them as gospel.

Trixie, one of the bridesmaids, has an innate ability to make any person smile. I catch her flash her own bright smile, take a flirty sip of her drink, and bat her eyes before flinging out compliments to a few strangers.

"Aren't you all finer than frogs' hair split four ways!" She croons to a group of college aged males.

Louann, Sabrina, and Haley all barrel over, giggling into their cups.

"Can I trouble one of you sweet angels for your belt? I happen to have a great game in mind, but I lack the *proper equipment.*" Trixie motions to her killer, one-year-post-baby-body, tucked tightly into a black bodycon dress.

The three young men preen under her compliments, then practically fight each other to hand over a belt first while the rest of the girls bat flirty lashes and create small talk in between.

"Thank you! Oh, thank you, you can be the first to go!" She snatches the belt and Sabrina instinctively grabs the other end while yelling, "LIMBO!"

The patrons around us balk at first, but ultimately can't resist the gravitational pull of their drunken enigma and people begin lining up to take their turn to shimmy under a makeshift limbo stick.

Who even thinks to do something like this in the middle of a bar with strangers?

Not many people are open to the excitement of a night like this, a night where you're more likely to end up kissing the porcelain throne than a hot stranger. But I am one of those people, always ready to take the night. I lost myself these past months. I'm ready to find that fun side of me again, so once I hop into the mix, slam that 7th shot of tequila, and make my way under the make-shift limbo stick to receive my obligatory, albeit drunken, round of applause from the bystanders.

Sabrina and Louann are bopping from group to group, all watching adults do limbo in a crowded bar, all while dragging me by the wrist when they thrust me into the arms of a devastatingly handsome man I currently see two of.

"Are you single?" They giggle up at him.

"Uh… yes?" he says while I'm still fumbling in his arms.

"Perfect!" Sabrina chirps, then turns to me, "You're welcome!" Then the girls squeal and run away.

"We just love love!!!" I can hear their voices trailing off as they push further into the center of the bar.

The hottie who's currently helping me stand straight by steadying my shoulders had been with a group of guys I had seen prowling around the whole night. They looked my age, which is the "I definitely still try to drink but wake up with a two day hangover now" crowd, just based on the quality of their shoes. Twenty-three-year-olds don't wear Cole Haans to bars with crisp dark jeans and untucked button downs.

"Hi," my drunken gaze floats up to meet his eyes. They look dreamy enough, as a set of four. He's tall, so much that my chin hits his sternum when I meet his gaze. From what I can see from behind the gaze of my drunk vision, he seems extremely handsome.

"Hi there, little lady." He chuckles and helps me straighten myself out after being physically thrown into his arms. His very nicely shaped arms that my drunken hands find themselves slithering up to squeeze to find out just how strong they are.

"Sorry, my friends think you're cute. I'm… I'm apparently the messenger," I joke and nod towards the direction where new friends scampered off, dropping my hands.

There comes a point in everyone's night where you stop caring about if you should talk or not and just decide to let your lips flap free. I've been past that point for hours now and I've never been more glad to have a massive burst of drunken bravado as I have right now, talking to the first handsome man in a single state for years.

"I promise I won't shoot the messenger," he replies with an encouraging smile back.

A very drunk girl slams into my attractive stranger, spilling his draft beer all over my chest. Since I am also a *very drunk girl*, my reaction is delayed by several seconds.

"Oh jeez, I'm so sorry... I. uh. That girl..." He's stammering and reaching into his back pocket to grab a handkerchief to dry me off. *Only in the South do men carry those*, I think to myself. I love it more than I should. It's not until he's dabbing my chest that I fully realize he's touching me. I am way drunker than I thought. Damn that bachelorette party.

"It's s-okay, not the first or the last to spill beer on my chest," I slur with a giggle, sounding oddly sexual accidentally.

He returns the laugh and hands me the semi-soiled cloth to finish the job he awkwardly started. Our fingers brush on the pass off and I feel my flushed face heat up another notch from the standard level of drunken rosy cheeks.

I force a demure smile instead of a goofy intoxicated one, a feat worthy of an Olympic medal. "So, are you enjoying your night? Or are you planning on spilling more of the good god's nectar?"

"I was enjoying it, you were a vision on stage singing earlier," he says and slants his head to the side to crack a lopsided smile.

I lightly smack his chest in jest, a bold move for a new acquaintance but my drunken strength knows no bound. I toss my arms out wide and give my best Russell Crowe in *Gladiator* impression, "'Were you not entertained?'"

His eyebrows shoot up to his hairline then he throws his head back in hysterical laughter a full three seconds later. A delayed reaction. I can't tell if it's because he's drunk or infinitely surprised by my *excellent* impression.

His lack of verbal response makes me uneasy and prompts me to keep talking over his residual chuckles. "Hey! There was definitely worse up there! I don't see you going up and embarrassing yourself for the sake of this entire bar's entertainment!"

"A cute girl like you being an *entertainer* and knows one line in a very mediocre movie, color me impressed."

"Would you be able to *entertain* the bar as well as I just did?"

"Ah, well, no. I do not have the hip mobility to be honest. You got me there. I think I need a few more of these to loosen up the vocal cords through," he lifts his glass which is practically empty now and jerks it to the side in a false cheer. "I would ask you if you wanted another drink, but it seems like I already got you one," he motions to my chest in reference to the beer he spilt there not long ago.

"Grab me a Coke, please, kind sir. Nothing like a fountain soda to help sober you up! I have no idea how those girls got me so drunk so fast! I don't even know them!" I confess half talking to myself.

He's smiling at me like I'm the most adorable thing here, despite feeling like a ball of disgusting drunkenness covered in beer. We make our way to the bar and he orders us our new drinks. I feign a motion to my wallet and he shoo's my attempt away with a jerky hand motion.

"Who are you here with then?"

"Myself," I shrug and break our locked gaze. "Just enjoying a long… sabbatical" my mouth answers before my mind allows it.

"Sounds adventurous. What's the plan?" He's curious.

"I don't tell *strangers* where I'm headed, safety thing, you know," my body is now the one deceiving me as I lean closer to his chest and purr back at him. It's a sexy taunt to make my acquaintance so we're no longer strangers. It worked when I was single, but it's a line I haven't used in years, and definitely not under these circumstances.

He takes the bait and rakes a slow gaze from my eyes to my lips while he responds,

"Well that's fine by me, I'm Brooks. Now we're not strangers."

"Seph," my hand juts out to shake his, even though we're barely a foot apart. He smirks while placing his hand in mine, shaking it slowly before raising the back of my hand to his lips to kiss. The act itself would have made me cringe had it been any man in New York City, but there's something so wildly bewitching with his faintly southern accent and dark locks. His eyes glint in the glow of purple, blue, and green lights of the bar, I can hardly tell what color they truly are. He's so far from NYC handsome that I wouldn't be able to even compare the two. "Nice to meet you, Steph," he mispronounces my name, but I don't bother correcting him. I'm far too mesmerized by the way his lips curl at the corners when he's amused by me.

"Charmed," my voice is a whisper in his hand since the music blares on around us. We spend another hour or so exchanging flirty pleasantries, making small talk, and gently rubbing up against each other pretending to dance along with the crowd. He's a gentleman. He's actually two gentlemen, since I am still seeing double. His hands never travel lower than they should and his eyes only drift occasionally to my lips, despite my very skimpy outfit.

His hand on the small of my back has been sending electric shocks up and down my spine as it shifts up, down, and side to side. The gentle tug to press our hips closer together is welcome, but he only uses the move sporadically, as if trying to give our bodies space to breathe while we swap favorite movie titles and tv shows.

The packed outskirts of the dance floor work to my advantage, squeezing us in closer proximity, forcing my hand to his chest while his arm wraps further around my tiny waist. Lust filled eyes look down on me in a moment suspended in drunken time.

The gentle kiss is exploratory, slow and soft but transforms into heavy and passionate. Our lips act out a night's worth of chemistry, locked in more time than I can account for until he breaks off for us to both catch our breath. We both smile, pressing foreheads together, mouths drifting back to find each other's lips again.

· His lips graze over mine, tempting and teasing while I keep my eyes closed, enjoying one sense at a time.

I can feel lips traveling up my cheeks and to my ear, blazing a trail of soft kisses on the way there.

"Steph, do you mind if I get your number? I'd love to see you again sometime before you leave, perhaps in a less crowded room," his mouth is almost entirely pressed up against my ear, shooting chills down my spine.

Then I realize what he's asking for.

My number.

I stiffen in his embrace.

The number I just got, that no one knows. Heat crawls up my neck and lights me into a nervous fire. I went off the grid for a reason, to be unattainable, to make sure no one *could* contact me. By giving him my number now, it would be distracting and frustrating. He'd either call me to hang out, which maybe I'd be many miles away by the time he did, or he'd never contact me and leave me annoyed for days. Lose-lose situation, even drunk me can grasp that concept, and I tense up before I answer.

"Sure."

He grins and slides the unlocked iPhone into my slender hands to input a number that will never call him back, a number tied to a phone that I threw off a bridge yesterday. I'd feel more guilty, but he is not my future husband and this is not my final destination. I'm not in Savannah for a long time, just a good time, just tonight and maybe a few nights after that.

Oh, and that good time? It's come to a nauseating end. Almost immediately after handing his phone back, my stomach churns, and in perfect timing, his friend grabs his shoulder to motion they're leaving. He turns back to me to say goodbye, but I cut him off at the pass.

"I have to go too, don't worry. Call me?" I say, knowing he may, but also knowing I won't pick up. Maybe the fish from the bottom of the river will answer for me.

"Believe me, I will," Brooks looks longingly at me before slowly leaning in to drop a quick parting kiss on my lips. It's short and sweet and makes my toes curl. I feel ten times more guilty about giving him a number, but it's for the best. *He's better off without me*, I rationalize.

Once he turns to leave, I take a step back, burp up a little vomit, then lean down and throw up under my barstool.

Chapter 2

Persephone

———————

Waking up in the hotel bed the next morning is the complete opposite of fun. Hungover and sad, my mind drifted from the night's debauchery to why I'm lying alone in a Georgia hotel room sucked dry of every ounce of hydration.

My dad is gone. I woke up every morning for the past few months thinking of him, but today is a little different. Today I feel irrevocably broken and alone. Coaxing my hangover to secede a little, I chug the bottle of water from the nightstand and fall into a memory.

"Ughhhh, daddddd!" I groaned into the hotel suite from the center of my very comfortable king size bed. I heard commotion and internally sighed in relief knowing he was enroute to my room, hopefully with breakfast. Or coffee. Or both.

"You look like you've seen better sunrises, my peach," he chuckled and tossed a loosely wrapped bagel into the sea of white hotel covers.

"And you are an angel sent from the heavens above!" I dove into the treasure, finding it plentifully filled with cream cheese.

"I know it was your 21st birthday, and you had never drank before you were legal…" He paused to smirk and wink at me, both of us knowing how many encounters with alcohol I had even in high school, nevermind the three years of college I had already been through.

"But since you are now legal, I bestow upon you the most sacred of family secrets. The Kline Hangover Cure."

Dad's eyebrows arched up and he revealed a small glass bottle with an amber liquid inside. His mischievous gaze bestowed an even more mischievous smile as he tossed the bottle to me again, allowing the covers to catch his gift.

"What is this?" My brows pinched together with a dull ache as I popped the cork off to smell.

"Eh, I wouldn't smell it," my dad shifted on his feet and gave a vague wave of his hand before nodding at me to drink up.

I quirked an apprehensive eyebrow and paused. While I trusted my father to never steer me wrong, he was known to play a prank. Not just mild pranks either.

He'd let a farm animal run wild in your yard, tin foil your office, stuff packing peanuts in your car, or go as far as slowly steal every spoon in your house slowly over time. Nothing was off limits. No prank was too small or too long. He lived for the moment when you realized it was him. The slow grin that inevitably found your face when you realized he was fucking with you.

So, to say I did trust him would be fair, but I also knew the devious mind of the man who sired me.

"My heiress, goddess divine, I would never deceive you," he chided.

I rolled my eyes and conceded to the fate that awaited me within the bottle. As I drained the small vile, dad waited with bated breath for my reaction. A trick, I thought.

But with a suck of air, I realized this was no 'cure'. It was the poison itself.

"Fuck! Dad! Shit, that's so gross!" I coughed and wretched while a shit eating grin formed on his worn in but handsome face. The wrinkles in his skin were light but suited him well with his salt and pepper hair.

"Hair of the dog, my darling. Not much of a secret, I must admit, but very effective," he shrugged and laughed at me.

My disgusted face painted the picture of my appreciation, one that didn't miss my father's notice.

"Okay, okay. Don't be so dramatic," he rolled his eyes and tossed me a red Gatorade he had procured from his back pocket.

"Oh, thank god," I breathed, and chugged half the contents in one go, ate more of the bagel and finished the bottle. He watched me and smiled.

"Happy Birthday, Persephone," he said with a fatherly tone. "Get your rest, round two starts at 4pm. Your uncles are about to drink you under the table," he flicked a wrist and waltzed out of the room.

Dad made the Hangover Cure many more times for me, too often to count or keep up with. In recent years when my partying years were in full swing, in jest, he would ship boxes of small vials to me, claiming he couldn't keep up with the demand, so he wanted me to have a bulk stock.

I laughed every time I saw the box show up at my doorstep. It was equal parts fatherly and gag. Always the jokester.

I hadn't drunk enough in a single night to be this hungover since he left, so the memory had stayed buried under the thousands of others that occupied my mind most days. They played over and over like a movie on repeat, details sometimes hazy, but half the fun was trying to remember all the details. Trying to recall the reason behind his playful madness. Whether it was flipping a table, throwing food, or diving into a pool fully clothed, my dad always had a reason to do so.

It could have been the way one of his friends looked at him or a halfhearted dare, my father was a man of intention. It made him intoxicating to be around, but his absence irrevocably noticeable from any gathering.

I push out of bed to pad my way to the bathroom. My entirely naked body is every indication of how intoxicated I was last night, since my pajamas were perfectly laid out on the foot of the bed, completely ignored.

Washing up, my eyes lift to my haunted reflection in the mirror. They linger over the finger sized bruises still decorating my arms, over the healing gash that laid the length of my back left shoulder.

The night after I met Harrison, I was hung over in more ways than one. I had accompanied my dad to a Christmas party to help rub elbows with potential clients and met his stockbroker. Harrison's cool demeanor was the opposite to my father's fiery one.

He was charming and refined, the way a salesman ought to be.

"Your father is a very funny man, I enjoy our dinners together," Harrison's eyes flickered towards my father's, enhancing the compliment with a genuine grin.

"He's a real comedian, alright. Did he mention how he filled my room with water cups last week? The entire floor, covered with red solo cups filled with water! Like I didn't have a single thing to do but find a way out of that mess!" My tone was chastising, but I couldn't hide the grin. While his pranks were often ill timed, like, on a weekday morning before work, they were often frustratingly humorous.

"It's not my fault you didn't prepare for the unexpected. Every morning you should wake up early, just in case," my dad joked back, the man was never early a day in his life.

Harrison chimed in, *"Your daughter is a charmer like you, old man,"* and clapped a palm to my dad's suit-covered arm.

"Much more so with spirits," my eyes locked on my father. *"And not as much when my father is impeding on my night,"* I said through clenched teeth. I inclined my head with mock cheers of my champagne glass and my father's eyes flashed with understanding.

As if on cue, my father mumbled about seeing a friend on the other side of the room and bowed out of our little circle, leaving the lane open for Harrison.

We spent the night talking over cocktails about New York City, clubs we'd been to, overlapping friend circles, and favorite restaurants. When he invited me to his hotel on the next block, much before the party was over, I immediately said yes. If nothing else, I'd be in and out before my dad even noticed I was gone.

I was mesmerized by a man so equally matched myself in social status and interests. It was like staring at a mirror of myself. A party girl meets a party boy, a tale as old as time.

From that moment on, I couldn't imagine a day I didn't talk to him, and I never had to. I went up to his hotel room that night, he called me a car, then texted or called every day after that. Every day for an entire year.

So, what led me to the moment of pouring my heart into a microphone in a Georgia bar? It's a great question and one that has a simple answer. Last night may be foggy in my mind, but my tale of woe was clear as day, finding its insidious way to blanket every corner of my mind.

Harrison and I tried to keep our love alive, tried to ignore the problems, despite his incessant need to go out without me. We sat through silent dinners, allowed our sex life to roll over and die, and anticipated every other day meltdowns over expired milk. His last straw was me asking to postpone our October wedding.

For as long as I live, I will never forget that fight. The vases being rocketed across the living room, the dining room table being flipped on its side, the escalation of our screaming to physical pushes and shoves, and then subsequently, him leaving me for four days alone at the apartment after grabbing my arm too tightly. He was a vortex of pain and suffering, livid about having to wait longer and sick of my "inability to move on" from my father's death.

"I just don't think I can do the wedding this year, Harrison. It's too soon after and I just can't handle thinking about it, never mind actually going through with it."

"How could you even say that to me? Do you not love me? Do you not want to be with me? After everything I've done for you. You want to punish me and make me wait; you want me to be as miserable as you."

I couldn't entirely disagree; I wasn't being a good partner or even a decent friend and I wasn't thinking about his feelings. My lack of interest in life was draining to him and ultimately my drab presence in the apartment exhausted him, too. The woman he signed up to love was not the same woman living in his apartment or sleeping next to him in bed.

Harrison was all I had, no real people in my shallow life. My 'friends' were people of the night, only there to hold your hair back while you blow chunks, then talk shit about you the next day. My father and his friends were the only acquaintances outside my social group, but I wasn't about to bore a bunch of 65-year-old men with my self pity over a game of cards.

Deep down, I knew this wasn't normal, that feeling trapped and scared in my own home wasn't right for either of us. I knew my father would have never done this to my mother, but I didn't know what else to do, where to go, or how to stop it.

Work acquaintances noticed the change in my demeanor. I was sad for months, but lately I was broken and timid. I barely came into the office to hide my own physical condition, having some flexibility in my "work from home" ability being the owner's daughter. They kept asking if "the happy hour queen retired for good" or not. How do you tell a coworker you can barely leave your bed every morning to brush your teeth, nevermind think about going to happy hour?

Surprisingly, it was my assistant, Aisley, who eventually called me out. She's a natural talker so when she sat down for our morning one-on-one to go over the day's agenda, I didn't think twice about her lingering in my office to chat longer. She didn't mince her words as she laid into me.

"I… need to talk to you about something," she said before leaving. *"I'm just going to come out and say it Ms. Kline, your staff is worried about you."*

I thought I hadn't heard her correctly, "I'm sorry, Aisley, repeat that for me?"

"You heard me; we're worried. I know you're going through it right now, but you're different… You flinch when doors slam, your dark circles are more like under eyebrows. You've lost a lot of weight and I

don't think it's related to your father anymore..." She started out strong with her convictions, but towards the end, she must have noticed how uncomfortable I was hearing this from her and she puttered out while looking at me nervously for my response.

"Under eyebrows?"

"Yes, your dark circles are so thick they're like eyebrows under your eyes!"

I blinked at her in shock instead of laughing, something I would have done months ago.

"Things have been… tough the last few months, I agree. But that doesn't mean there are any… issues at home," I treaded lightly with my verbiage. "Harrison and I are just not seeing eye to eye on everything right now…" realizing I'm all but confirming her suspicion while I only mentioned Harrison.

She looked at me concerned, almost like she was drinking my response, but it wasn't going down easy and had a bad flavor. I could see the sourness on her face. Uneasy eyes stared back at me for a few moments, and it made me squirm in my seat.

Trying to fill the void, I go on, "I appreciate the concern, Aisley, I really do. But… I'm fine, or I will be fine eventually." With another long pregnant pause, there is no indication she will be leaving after my last assurance. She wasn't buying it, and I couldn't blame her.

"You're not, and you won't be. But that doesn't mean you will never be… You can leave Persephone; you can leave him. You don't have family here; you don't have anything tying you here other than a lease he can afford on his own. You can disappear for a while, if you want to," she rattled out quickly, worried I will cut her off before she makes her full point. "You can leave here and not ever have to look back. Most people don't have that luxury."

It's not lost on me that she used my first name instead of Ms. Kline, which she rarely does in the office, or ever. She's sincerely concerned for my well being, her eyes fixed on mine searching for my acceptance. We *sat in silence until she broke the moment and shot out of her seat to leave.*

"I know that was a lot and it's really not my place to say anything especially at work, but your whole team is concerned about you. We love you as a boss and a friend. I just couldn't keep watching you wither away like this." She's reading my utterly shocked face and backpedaling, "I'm sorry if I overstepped..."

I can't find it in me to lift my gaze from the desk, but she takes the hint from my glassy eyes that it's time for her to leave. She props open the door and I sneak in one last word, "Thank you Aisley, that will be all for now," just in case anyone is lingering outside the door in earshot.

Aisley is a sweet girl, one of the few coworkers that came to my dad's wake, sent flowers, checked in on me regularly, and never pried or asked too many questions. She let me breathe in the months following, didn't judge, and offered a helping hand when it came to deadlines I was trending to miss. She kept my schedule open and as free as possible and for that I couldn't thank her enough. Less meetings meant more time to myself, which I desperately craved.

For her to suggest I leave my relationship not only crossed the line of professionalism but was inappropriate as a friend. She knew better than to come in here and tell me what to do with my life, she knows me well enough to understand how poorly that conversation could have gone if I wasn't operating at half-mast.

That's why even suggesting it forced me to consider it.

When the door closed, the tears building in my eyes dropped to the desk. I started fighting my anxiety about the entire office thinking I was being physically abused by my fiancè and the shame that accompanied it. The tension rolled over my shoulders, tightening my chest, and closing my throat on itself from my normal airflow. My heart ached.

It was 9:34am on May 19th, sitting at my desk in my office, trying to suppress a panic attack, where I decided to *consider* leaving Harrison Montgomery.

It was 6:32pm on May 19th, sitting on Harrison's home office floor, hugging the trash can after regurgitating my dinner, where I decided to actually leave Harrison Montgomery.

I was bored and alone, aimlessly wandering our apartment when I decided to creep a little bit through my fiance's things. There wasn't much to sort through, no pictures on his laptop, no messages from girls that I didn't already know, and no extensive porn history to be concerned with. I was clicking out of the internet window when a file that said "Delete" caught my eye on the desktop.

Curious, I clicked in and saw multiple video files dated from a few days ago. Clicking into the first one, I saw my fiance in a suit, fixing the camera to stay in place. My eye naturally saw the tie he was wearing, and I distinctly remember the day. It was only a few days ago, the day after another big argument we had, and I brought home a tie as an apology. He wore it the next day in a show of an accepted apology.

Once he backed away from the camera, he shrugged his jacket off, and I took note of the room around him. It was a swanky hotel room with a large king size bed in the middle with the bedspread still made perfectly.

It was familiar, one I've definitely been in before, but couldn't put my finger on when or where. He kicked his shoes off, then his pants, then plopped on a chair to work on his shirt. Then the girl walked in. Completely naked.

I knew what happened next and the pain it would bring to my chest, but I couldn't stop watching. The moans were loud, the sound of skin slapping together rang through the office walls and I sat there with my mouth open watching every second of adultery.

They switched positions multiple times, he was rough with the transitions, pushing her down a little harder than any man should, but every time he forced a new position, her face was perfectly in frame. It was as if he planned it that way.

He found his own pleasure, discarded the condom, and kept kissing her for a while after, as if she was more than just a casual lay. Unable to withstand the sudden change of intimacy, I shuttled forward at least 10 minutes until I saw her skuffle out of the room and Harrison walk towards the camera to turn it off. The screen cut to black, and I grabbed the trash can to hold my vomit once again.

After retching a few times, I put down the bucket and called the only person I knew who could help me at this moment.

"Aisley?"

The rings stopped but silence filled the line.

"Aisley, are you there?"

"Ms. Kline? Uhm, Hi. Is everything okay? Did I forget to lock your office?"

I pause, unsure if *not* locking my office door is a regular occurrence for her to immediately jump to that conclusion.

"No, nothing is wrong. I, uh, need your help," I admit.

"Oh! Of course, what can I do for you? I just left the office, but I can come back if you need…"

"God, I'm sorry to call after work hours. I'm just a bit all over the place right now," I pause to gather my thoughts, which are flying a mile a minute through the airways of my mind. "This is a personal favor. You can log it as overtime though."

"Sure, no problem. What can I help you with?" she asks back curiously. It's a bizarre request and an even stranger phone call, so her inquisitive tone is unsurprising.

"I need you to clear my schedule for the week and the rest of the month." I pause for her reaction, but she remains silent, waiting for more instruction or a reason.

"I need a rental car booked for 5pm tomorrow afternoon, preferably a larger SUV, for an indefinite amount of time. Get me a meeting with Carter first thing tomorrow morning, tell him it's urgent. Get a storage unit then order a moving crew to get to my apartment at 9am tomorrow morning, they need to be able to deliver it all to the storage unit, then ship a few pieces of furniture to the address I'll provide later. I also need a new phone and new phone number. Bring in Safrina if you need help with any of this."

I take a breath and wait for her reaction, but my nerves get the better of me and I snap, "Did you get all that?"

"Yes, yes! Got it. Car, Carter, storage unit, phone, I can do that," she's nervous and I can hear papers shuttling as she's scrambling trying to write it all down.

Aisley must understand by now what I'm planning on doing, but she doesn't ask and my tongue refuses to form the words to confirm.

I'm leaving my fiancè. Those words never pass my lips, so I settle on the next best, which are equally as accurate. "I am not coming back to New York City…" I swallow hard trying to vocalize my decisions as if it makes it more final, "...anytime soon. If you think of any other loose end I'm missing, please help me tie them, I'm going a million miles a minute here."

"Of cou-"

"And Aisley? Please make all the calls you or Safrina need to make tomorrow from my office and my office only. Use my desk if you must and close the door. It's imperative that this stays a secret from the rest of the office until 7pm tomorrow when Harrison might get home."

Aisley exhales harshly out, "Absolutely, you have my word." She was silent again on the other side, but this time it was to wait for more instruction.

"That's all for tonight, I think. Text me tomorrow if you have any questions. Email all the confirmations to my personal email," I swallow. "And Aisley?"

"Yes?"

"Thank you."

Chapter 3

Persephone

"The hair looks so good, seriously, amazing," the young girl behind the counter gushes.

"Thank you, it's quite a change for me. I've never been a brunette before." I shuffle nervously and fish through my purse to find my card.

"You got a cut and color, right? One hundred and fifteen dollars is your total," she says as I hand her the card and rake my hand through my much shorter hair that falls just past my shoulders. It feels so much lighter without my extensions sewn in.

I hand her a signed receipt with a sizable tip.

"Thank you, have yourself a nice day ma'am," I wish her a good day in return, toss my card back in my oversized bag and waltz out. I feel like I am a whole new woman, a more natural version of myself and I've never felt better.

It's been three days since I met the Bachelorette party girls in Savannah, and I sucked the face of a devastatingly handsome man.

It's been four days since I chucked my phone into a river. I had forgotten to dispose of it and it housed all the missed calls from Harrison. I couldn't keep looking at it. I couldn't keep the last shred of my life in NYC buried at the bottom of my purse. I also couldn't risk it if he tracked it.

Having a new phone number is a new sense of power I needed. No one can contact me unless I allow them too. I had a mini freak-out when that devilishly handsome man had asked for my number at the bar, but I did well to keep my composure while intoxicated and entered my old number instead. I wonder if the fish picked up his call. I wonder if he even called.

I am completely off the map, off the grid, not a single soul on this Earth knows where I am now, and I'd like to stay that way. I didn't even tell Aisley or Safrina what *direction* I was heading. They both gave me a quick hug, wished me luck, told me I was doing the right thing, urged me to give them updates along the way so they know I'm alive and said goodbye. I agreed but only via Facebook messenger. I couldn't risk anyone from my old life knowing my new number.

I left Harrison *this time* with no explanation, no note, and not even a single strand of hair of mine could be found in the apartment now. He probably came home that day and found half our living room empty with me completely wiped from every room, shrugged, and poured himself a whiskey. There isn't so much as a single comb or piece of lint that is mine in that place anymore.

Truthfully, I didn't even want to take anything we bought in our time together. I didn't last time I left him, I only took a weekender bag, but I hadn't anticipated staying away forever that instance, but it was a thought in my mind.

This time, I planned to never go back. I took the furniture that was passed down to me from my late grandmother, packed a few large suitcases, and left.

It's not that I wasn't scared of Harrison's response, I was on some level, especially since he was terrifying to deal with when I left before, but I just wanted to start over without the possibility of him showing up on my doorstep. I wanted a new life without the strings of my old one. I wanted nothing to do with New York anymore, it only housed painful memories of loss, betrayal, and heartbreak.

Driving out of New York City on the George Washington Bridge was like escaping Alcatraz. It felt like an impossibility that I only envisioned in my wildest dreams, not a reality of my creation.

What the fuck am I doing?
Where the fuck am I going?

Seeing a Facebook message from Aisley for the first time since I left jolted me out of my thoughts, giving me a small heart attack.

Hey… Hope you're doing okay wherever you are. We are thinking of you. The whole office knows now. It was quite the gossip this morning. Carter must have told everyone you 'resigned'. I called Harrison's office pretending to be a client and his assistant said hasn't been in since you left either. Let me know if you want to be kept in the loop or if it's easier to not talk about him at all… Let us know if you're safe.

- Aisley & Safrina

Phew. Okay, that wasn't bad. A sick part of me was glad he was at least upset enough to not show up to work, but I'm not sure how much more information I'll be able to handle in the future. Dipping a toe in feels like going backwards to the past and I'm on my own trail now into the future. A future free of Harrison.

I'm in Savannah, ready to go to my final destination at some point, but unsure what that destination even looks like. Big city? No, not again. Normal suburban city? Perhaps? Small town? Sounds quaint.

Where do I go?

It's at that moment I notice a billboard coming up on the right, it reads, "Looking for a sign? Here it is. Maggie's Diner. Exit 33".

Welp. That seems like Pops might be trying to tell me something from heaven, like he knew I was looking for one and placed it right in my sights. It feels too obvious to not at least check it out.

Exit 33, here I come!

Pulling off the highway at Exit 33, I turn my phone's GPS off and drive slowly into a town that looks straight out of a romance movie. There's a downtown with all local family-owned shops and small restaurants. It's cute and harmless, maybe even inviting to an outsider like me.

At the end of the long block of businesses, the tin can that doubles as a diner has a bright red neon sign that reads, "Maggie's Diner", as depicted on the sign from the highway. I was hoping for something a little *more*, but I now believe I was expecting too much. I park, walk in, and plop myself down on the first bar stool I find, regardless of the few patrons in the diner for a late-afternoon lunch or early dinner. Most people, I hope, are at work, and that's why it's so dead here.

"Hey suga', you look like a new face. What can I do ya for?" A large chested, red haired woman comes from the kitchen with a pot of coffee in her hand and a bright smile to light up the place. Name tag reads Celia. "Coffee maybe?" She raises both eyebrows and gestures to fill my empty cup when I hesitate to reply.

I smile tightly and nod, then exhale dramatically through my nostrils and into the menu to say, "What's good?"

"Well now, that's a loaded question. You're after the lunch crowd but before suppertime. Do you wanna eat an early dinner or overeat a late lunch?" She asks with a smirk.

"Great question," I grumble. "I suppose an early dinner, then a lodging recommendation too, if there is one."

"Another loaded question, are those the only kind you ask?" She laughs and sets the coffee jug down. "We're known for the grits, but the burger is divine. Just don't tell the cook I said so."

Her eyes cast into me, and I can feel the weight of those blue irises stare into my core. She's trying to be kind and welcoming, but I can sense the defensive nature of her avoidance in the lodging question, like I shouldn't even think about sticking around here. I nod to acknowledge her response but don't repeat the question.

"I guess I'll take the burger then, thank you."

She nods and writes it down quickly, asking me the normal slew of burger related questions. I like my burgers rare normally but at a diner in the middle of Georgia? I think I'll opt for medium as a precaution.

She pauses before turning to hand the ticket over to the ticket window and says, "As for lodging, depending if you're here to stay or looking for a quickie..." she glances up then over my shoulder and her whole face brightens and she forgets whatever information she was about to pass on to me, completely transfixed at whoever has walked in. Trying to not be intrusive, I stay with my back to the person who walked in and wait for their approach. I pick up my phone and start scrolling on Instagram, as if I'm busy with my own life.

"Hey there, good lookin'. What on God's green earth are you doing here before dinner? Dishin' out your daily smiles to all your angels? I am glad to collect early," she maneuvers down the counter out of my direct line of sight and into the man's behind me.

Out of my peripheral vision, I can see she drops both elbows on the counter to push her already large chest up into a beautiful bed of boobies. I can't help but glance quickly to see her flashing a smile too bright to be anything but open flirtation.

A familiar raspy voice flows from behind me and the sound of it makes my chest tight. His voice is like a nice cut of wood, smooth but rugged. I can't even imagine the body attached to it, but by the looks of Celia over here, I assume he looks as delicious as he sounds. I can't help wondering if I've run across him from my very short travels in this area.

"Well, hello there, gorgeous girl. Just picking up my order as always. I'm a bit early, have to run to the courthouse today, then a client meeting right after, it's okay if it's not ready. I can wait a few minutes," he plops down into the chair two down from me and it takes all my willpower to keep looking at the menu, even though I already ordered.

"Course, suga. Let me check with Phil," Celia picks her titties off the bar and slowly saunters back into the kitchen, sashaying her hips all the way through the swinging doors.

From under my eyelashes, I spare a quick glance. Curiosity killed the cat. Surely it wouldn't kill a 30-year-old woman who hasn't had sex in months and is wondering what the body of a man attached to that voice looks like.

I shouldn't have looked.

"You're a new face," he turns on his swivel barstool and grins at me. "Just passing through our charming town?"

He's talking to me? Why?

I peek up at him through my lashes and almost fall out of my chair from shock.

It's him.

It's the man from the bar that I gave the wrong number to, that has haunted my dreams the last three nights, the man who sent a shiver down my spine from whispering in my ear.

Oh my God.

Oh, my fucking God.

I instinctively shove the hair in my face behind my ear in a desperate attempt at casualness, trying to calm myself from this awkward night after encounter, but I immediately notice he doesn't seem phased.

Jutting my chin out with a hint of courage, I appraise the man my mind kept a hazy photograph of and realize he's much more attractive than previous day dreams.

His perfectly chiseled jawline is more like a celebrity than a small-town citizen, with just as fine features elsewhere. The straight but perfectly sized male nose leads to his impossibly hazel eyes, rimmed with dark lashes and quaffed hair.

He could have just stepped out of a GQ magazine, and I wouldn't have known the difference.

God, a man in slacks and a button down with the sleeves rolled up to his elbows… nothing more tantalizing in the world, except maybe when they do that one-sided smirk, like he's doing to me now as I find my words.

I clear my throat and drop the menu. "I… uh… ya I suppose," I flash a quick smirk and finally pick my eyes off the counter to get a real look at God himself. He's beautiful, more beautiful than I cared to remember. Tall, dark, and handsome, longish locks combed back and gently popped over the back collar of his button up.

"Welcome to Dorian. Where ya headed?" He cocks his head, and his eyes look actually interested, despite the awkward small talk with a seeming stranger.

He doesn't recognize me! I cannot believe he does not recognize me!

Then I remembered my hair appointment from yesterday. Not only did I go from platinum blonde to a dark brunette but it's also at least 8 inches shorter from the long mane that nearly grazed the top of my butt when it was straight. The pounds of make-up I had on that night have now been reduced to a thin layer of foundation and light mascara. To be fair, I look like a different person, one that I hardly recognized waking up this morning, one that he thankfully does not recognize. I'll keep the facade up, no need to go backwards in time.

"Not sure to be honest. Guess I don't really have a final destination right now…" I'm not sure what else to say, but I already know I've disclosed too much that this conversation is going to continue whether I want it to or not.

"Passing through with no place to go? Sounds mysterious. Staying in town for the night?"

"I don't usually tell strangers where I sleep, to be honest," I quip with a humorless laugh and turn towards him.

His eyes twinkle at my response, like a flash of familiarity ran through them but were extinguished instantly once he took in the color of my hair.

"Touché. Apologies for overstepping, it's smart of you to keep yourself protected when traveling alone. Information is valuable. I'm Brooks Dawson, the town lawyer," he leans over the barstool in between us to lend his hand for our introduction.

Wearily, I grab his hand to shake it back and purse my lips at the contact of our skin. Soft hands, just like I remember from the other night.

"I never said I was traveling alone."

"Oh, I just assumed. Here for work or pleasure? I assume pleasure if you don't have a destination," he rambles.

Is he nervous or does he always talk this much? Does he recognize me?

"I'm here for… researching purposes. It's a long project with, uh… a lot of complicated facets." It's not a complete lie. I'm here to figure out what to do next, where to live next and my life is very complicated at the moment.

"I see, sounds like you're not going to give me much more detail on that account," he chuckles to himself. "You never told me your name."

"I know," I say with a sassy smile and quick eye contact. Who am I in this conversation? Wow. I am impressed with myself for not having a complete meltdown yet! I gave him my real name before, albeit he misheard it and it was a shortened version of it, but I did say my real name. Will he put two and two together?

With both brows arched and his hands up, my very animated new acquaintance laughs softly and says, "I hear you loud and clear. No personal information disclosed until further review. It's a safe play for an attractive single female traveler, but I promise the people here are not out to get you. I would know, I am the town lawyer. The worst someone will do is run you off the road for driving too slow out on 87."

Attractive? Single? Oh yeah. I forgot; I *am* single now. I glance down at my bare ring finger where my 4-carat pear shaped engagement normally sat. Not that I missed that monstrosity, but it was odd not to have it on.

"Noted. Sounds like my best chance at survival is walking," I joke.

He grins and turns his attention to a bouncing Celia. She's carrying his takeout bag, my burger, and a big smile. He thanks her and glances up at me to say something else but stops himself.

I cut him off regardless, "My name is Persephone." With a tight grin, I turn to my food and begin to prepare my burger with ketchup.

"Persephone," he chews on my name for a second under his breath and I hold my own hoping he doesn't make the connection. "I hope to see you around again soon, Persephone, that is, if you are even staying overnight." I heard him get up and walk towards the door. Before the ring of the door, he adds over his shoulder, "There's a Hyatt a mile away, but if you're interested in something more unique, I suggest Baxter's Bed and Breakfast. Louann makes a great quiche every morning."

I nod my appreciation for the recommendation before he turns to leave, watching one of the most beautiful males I've ever seen walk out the door.

Chapter 4

Persephone

———————

With Brooks' recommendation on my mind, I find myself in front of Baxter's Bed and Breakfast trying to muster up all the courage in my pattering heart to enter the damn building without passing out in a state of panic.

Hotels feel more comfortable to me because they all *look* the same. It's basically tricking my mind that my environment really hasn't changed. If I stay at a Marriott or a Hyatt, I could very reasonably be in New York City and convince myself that much as well. The white linen that feels both stiff and comfortable, the mass-produced artwork on the walls, the standard bathroom set up that would be wonderful in any house is what you get from a hotel.

Baxter's will be…. Quite the opposite.

With a deep breath and a half, a dose of Xanax, I walk into Baxter's with my overnight bag hoping to get an open room. From the outside, the Inn looks like a plantation manor with a big porch and dual floor columns. It's unfamiliar for a lifetime New Yorker, as most of the real estate I'm used to are walk-up brownstones and penthouses in skyscrapers.

The inside reminds me of my grandmother's living room, old and ornate, but timelessly decorated with deep cherry woods and antique furnishings. It's the mismatched patterns, butterscotch candies in thick glass bowls, familiar scent of heavy floral perfume, and flower pattern rugs that make my brows shoot up in astonishment. It's as if I stepped into every single grandmother's house on the East coast, wrapped into one home. It's not an explicitly white linen, sterile hotel room at the Hyatt, but I supposed there's always time to turn around and...

"Hi, welcome to Baxter's Bed & Breakfast. Are you checking in with us today?"

I spin around faster than a top to find a lithe blonde poking out behind the mahogany counter.

"Hello, uhm, I don't have a reservation, but was just inquiring if you had any vacancies for tonight?"

"Oh! Of course! Let me just take a look in our log!" I see her pull out a physical book, which is when I notice there is not a computer at the desk. Oh god... "We have a beautiful Queen room with a fireplace for $150 a night, a Double suite with a shared bath for $115, and a King master room and is... $200 a night. I'm sorry, usually we have a few more options."

Shared bathroom?! "The King master is fine; it has a private bathroom right? When will that room be vacant?"

"Great! Let me check, usually that room is for our VIP guests, it doesn't get occupants very often," she shrugs and flips the page to skim the logs for the next tenant. "It doesn't look like anyone is staying in that room until next weekend, so about a week from today," she peaks up through her lashes tentatively to gauge my reaction, unsure if that is what I wanted to hear or not.

"Hmm." My thoughts wander to my intended length of stay, a week seems like too long, but I'm tired and travel sounds equally as exhausting as staying put.

Mid-thought, my eyes catch on myself in the mirror behind the girl. My face is stoic with my lips in a natural frown. There's no sense of kindness on my face, only unabashedly bitchiness stamped across my forehead. It's a resting bitch face if I've ever seen one. It makes me cringe to see myself so hollow and cold, even if that's exactly how I feel on the inside. My hair color fits me quite well, but the look seems so unnatural to me.

Immediately feeling guilty for stressing this young lady out and being a bit standoffish, I force a tight-lipped grin in response. I forget how New Yorkers come off, so direct and cold, despite whatever feelings we harbor on the inside. My outward reflection of self is not indicative of me as a person, it's quite the opposite. Many people have initially described me as self-assured, intimidating, impassive, and refined. A resting bitch face, private schooling, a designer suit, and an introverted personality will do that for a girl, I suppose.

It's not me though.

I've always thought of myself as thoughtful, introspective, insecure, and out of place, almost entirely opposite of what I portray.

I finally replied, "A week is perfect. Do you mind if I pay in full now?"

Rifling through my purse, I dig out my wallet to grab my license and credit card, silently thanking myself for never financially tying myself to Harrison, despite him wanting to combine our accounts before my father died. I have money saved for myself, I have my own finances in order, even if they have been slightly neglected over the last few months.

"Sure! Oh Mrs. Simpson is going to be thrilled to have a week's reservation! Usually, we only get weekend travelers! She's our cook and head of housekeeping. You'll see her fussing about the house, I'm sure!"

The squeaky blonde runs my cards through a very old fashion credit card press and snaps a picture of my license on what looks like a very outdated iPad. I wonder if they enjoy living in the 90's and that's part of the charm, or they just can't afford the computer and updated resources.

"Thank you, Miss…" she glances at the credit card with squinted eyes, "Kline. Happy to have you staying with us! Allow me to give you the grand tour!" She perks up and motions me to follow her down the hallway.

We've walked through the whole house, besides my room, and I haven't seen an electrical device made in the last decade. What did I just get myself into?

Settled in my "King Master", which should barely qualify as a master in any house I've ever seen, I'm oddly relaxed by the modest nature of the house. It's quaint and lovely despite lacking any modern touches. Small updates could really elevate the grandiose of the house, especially with such a spectacular front of the house. With its old fashion charm, it reminds me of every grandmother I've ever known.

Delighted that an inn with outdated everything has WIFI at least, I log into my email to check my messages for the first time since leaving and I notice an email from Harrison dated Tuesday, the day after I left. It's been 6 days and 5 nights since I packed my shit, abandoned my ex-fiancè, and cut all ties to the only home I've ever known.

It's my own stupidity that let me forget to block this particular mode of communication from him after tossing my phone. The swell of anxiety is like rising seawater in a sinking boat. The inevitability of it capsizing and filling every crevice is demoralizing and relentless. It's difficult to breathe, the air is leaving the room at an exponential rate. Where's my Xanax?

A tight chest, tears pricking at my eyes, and bile rising in the back of my throat, I sink into the King size bed, which is surprisingly comfortable, and brace myself for the email that will slice open my heart.

P,

Where did you go? Come home, we can talk about it. This is all very embarrassing... I'm sorry if I pushed you away. I know it's been a tough couple months for you, but I want to work this out. Did you block my number? Call me.

-H

Choking on my own saliva, I jerk up and scrunch my face. Really? That's it? That's your desperate plea for me to come home? Some half ass arbitrary apology, a quick 'I want to work this out"? Are you kidding me?

Ha!

I'm not sure if I'm more pissed or upset, but neither emotion bubbles up. It's laughter that comes pouring out of me like a broken faucet. Thundering laughter fills the overly decorated colonial styled room, and I can't stop. It's one of few times I've truly laughed in months since before pop died and I have no idea why I am laughing so hard.

Dad was everything to me and I never expected him to leave me so young. I didn't get enough time with him, or my mother. She died when I was younger, leaving my father to figure out how to raise a teenage daughter.

He had no clue, neither did his friends, none of which had a woman in their lives long enough to make a difference for me. I saw women come and go, some would leave departing advice, others would leave nice dresses or shoes. I appreciated the bother either way.

He might not have had a clue how to help his teenage daughter become a woman, but he raised me how to be a good person.

How to give without expecting anything in return.

One time he brought me on a shopping trip, told me to pick out all my favorite winter jackets and gloves, however many I wanted. He picked out a few himself as well. Instead of driving home, we drove them all to shelter, dropping some off on the street when we saw someone in need.

I remember feeling devastated that I wasn't going to be able to wear anything I picked out.

"Daddy, why would you make me pick out all those jackets and then not even let me keep *one*?"

"Do you need a new jacket, Persephone?" He said sternly.

"Well, no, I have plenty at home…" I replied back, confused about the question.

"Wouldn't you rather everyone had what they needed instead of you hogging it all to yourself?"

I pondered it for a minute, then nodded my agreement. It was a roundabout way to teach a fundamental lesson in gluttony and greed, but one I'd never forget.

Dad always had a weird way to teach me a lesson, whether it was an anecdote or saying, I learned everything I know through him.

That's why when he passed away, it left such a gaping hole in me, I couldn't bear to face the day without him. I couldn't imagine a world without him in it, so I let my own collapse around me.

You don't know how bad it is when you're in it until you're *out of it*. Until the veil is lifted and the colors go from grey to bright. I learned that the hard way, looking back at the months I let squirm by me, as I grieved the greatest man I ever knew.

Chapter 5

Persephone

B rooks and the perky blonde at the front desk were right, Mrs. Simpson's breakfast quiches were divine. I have been in this cute little town for almost two days now, though I've hardly left the Baxter's. Exploring isn't exactly something that interests me, nor does it stroke my anxiety.

I've been reading over the terms of my father's estate quite thoroughly, which I've conveniently ignored for months now. There's more liquid cash than I actually know what to do with, nevermind the assets locked up in stock and his company. My company, now.

What should I do? What do I do with a company that I have no interest in running, but is my father's legacy? I ran the HR department, managed a bunch of stuffy highly paid employees. It wasn't rocket science or anything. It was pushing pennies around. Harrison managed real money, where they retained, acquired and grew revenue and clients. He would have made a better successor to my father. My namesake was the only reason I even had a high-ranking job at that company at all.

So now what? I'm supposed to re-explore my old interests? What interests? Going to club openings? Re-organizing the living room and excessively buying from Restoration Hardware? Tagging along with my dad to his friends' weekly poker night? Avoid social interactions by drinking a bottle of wine before Harrison comes home so I'm 'too drunk' to meet friends after dinner? I had some awesome hobbies, huh?

Shuffling through more papers that I've neglected with stifled grief; an unopened letter pops out and catches my attention. My name is scribbled on the front with my father's longhand. That demonic friend, anxiety, is batting at the doors, forcing all the blood to rush into my heart at once. I had never seen this letter, I barely got out of bed every day. It must have been buried under all the paperwork and mess without regard.

I tear it open and immediately dive headfirst into the last words my father will ever speak to me.

Sweet child of mine, Persephone,

If you are reading this, I am so sorry to have left you in the mortal realm, however I did... Hopefully I went out with a bang and didn't die peacefully in my sleep. That's too boring for my liking.

Please know, no matter where I ended up, whether it be the gates of heaven or hell, I love you beyond measure. You have always been the sunshine on a cloudy day for me, the pot of gold at the end of every rainbow, the lucky penny on every street corner. My love for you knows no bounds, so I will not begin creating those boundaries in death.

You know me, Sephy, I will never leave you. If ghosts exist, I will find a way to pay the Lord himself off to let me haunt you forever.

I started to chuckle at the ridiculousness of the note; he was exuberant in life and still left me smiling in his death.

I know one of my poor health choices probably put me in an early grave. Too much booze, cigars, women, and red meat, but please know I died happy, whichever took me. Happy to be your father and friend, happy to be in good company all these years, and happy to have (hoped to) left you an estate in which you'd never have to work again. You're welcome by the way. :-)

I rolled my eyes at that line.

If I know my Sephy like I think I do, you're feeling adrift, maybe a little lost without your troublemaker of an old man to take care of and that's okay. I want you to feel every emotion, every high and every low that comes with living your life and that includes mourning losses too. It's not about the money you make or the decisions you own, but the way in which you hit the pitches life throws your way. You will swing and miss more times than you swing and make contact,, you will lose more times than you win, you will be sad but not more than you are happy, and my only regret in life is not letting you fail more. But at the fork in every road, I implore you to take the risk, take the road less travelled, do what your heart says and not just your brain.

With success comes happiness, which I always want for you. It provides us with a feeling of confidence and satisfaction that no human alive could manufacture on their own. But with failure... ah yes, with sweet failure comes growth.

With my dying breath, I want you to fail more. I want you to try and fuck up, I want you to take a chance and get burned (but not too badly), I want you to work at a job you suck at and figure out how to do it better. I want you to live to know both success and failure because they both teach us so much. But you can't have either without putting yourself out there, and I know you're in shell mode right now with me gone.

Take the risk, Sephy.

You've lived a comfortable life under my wing and maybe I made it too easy for you, not let you fail enough, but you're ready to fly, my girl. You're ready to take the plunge and fall without Pops swooping in and helping you out like my big lug of a dummy self always did. I should have let you fail more so you learned to get back up easier without me. I'm sorry I handicapped you like that, but I couldn't help it. Don't bring my grave flowers for a month as punishment.

I know your anxiety is probably biting at the bit to come out and control you. Know your anxiety doesn't work against you, it works for you. You think your options through so you always make educated decisions. Your overactive imagination has actually taught you to see beyond the four confines of the box while conjuring up every possible situation in the world, you just usually assume the worst case. Start assuming the best case. I'm sure with my untimely death, you are feeling as bad as when Mom died (not a competition but I hope I won), but please don't. Don't waste your days mourning me, Sephy. I lived my life, I got to watch you grow up and become one of the most incredible women I've ever known.

I am sorry for dying on you, my plan was to live forever, but nothing ever goes to plan, no matter how hard you try. Take this advice from a dead guy- do whatever makes you happy and take as many risks as your heart allows. Make some better friends too... It will be weird to have a dead father as a best friend.

You're funnier than you give yourself credit for and you're a crackerjack of a poker player. I'm at peace knowing you won't beat me ever again. Was that joke in poor taste? I'm sorry, I can't help it. Ending this letter is harder than having to say goodbye in person, I imagine.

I love you always, my baby girl. Fly too high. Learn how to make coffee, for god sake. Skip work. Take long vacations. Lose your keys. Fall in love. Keep your head high.

Always yours,

Pops

A sharp inhale and sobs come pummeling out of me. I had valiantly avoided crying the entire first pass of the letter to make sure I didn't miss a single space from blurry eyes. I've read the letter six times over since, digesting every word like the first time. My dad was a weird guy, always joking around and couldn't help but be sarcastic. His death letter was no different, riddled with funny moments, derision, and surprisingly good advice. That was my father though, the greatest and most insane man I knew.

We once spent five hours playing a single game of chess because neither of us could make a decision, so we drank, got distracted, made a drunken dinner of microwave chicken nuggets, and ordered a pizza. It wasn't until I nearly tripped over a thrown chess piece in the hall that we remembered the game was still set up as we left it. We didn't mind the minor excursion in the middle, we welcomed the pause like it was a natural progression of the game.

We sat one night on the outside on his boat, splitting a bottle of Zinfandel and a sleeve of Oreos, throwing marbles at the other yachts in the harbor, trying to see how far we could throw them. Why the man had a large bag of marbles on his own boat, I had no idea and never asked, but it drove the other slip occupants crazy when they found them rolling around on their ships days later. We had played dumb when other boat owners asked us, confirming we also found marbles on our deck. Our lies were meant to divert suspicion from us, but the fits of laughter we broke out into moments later gave us away.

I spent the rest of the day and night analyzing every paragraph and contemplating the ways in which I could honor his last wishes for me. What did he mean by failing? Did he genuinely want me to fail at things I tried? Did that mean he knew I wouldn't be at the company after his death?

My life was especially cushy, aside from the complete mental breakdown after dad's death, so I understood all his sentiments there. I understood the whole letter, except for the end.... Well, I took that long vacation... Lose my keys though? I know my dad was a little eccentric but no need to make life more difficult.

I had spent hours envisioning my father speaking the last words he had ever written to me. The mindless dribble had me falling in and out of consciousness all night, which led me to a 10am wake up for the first time in ten years. I didn't sleep in, but the peace that came with Pop's letter must have milked at my melatonin for the night. Uncurling and stretching, I naturally untangled myself from the sheets, flopped on the floor and started the process of leaving the building to explore the town.

An hour later, I'm outside in the sunshine of Georgia, walking down the street eyeballing every storefront, in search of something to catch my eye. Silently pleading for a sign. I venture into a little soap store, an olive oil tasting stand, a farmer's market, a cute clothing boutique, and finally stop in front of the town's coffee shop.

The sign on the window says, "HELP WANTED - PART-TIME", but I was positive my father was playing tricks on me. "Learn to make coffee", he said explicitly in the letter. What an odd coincidence.

Standing like a fish out of water with my jaw slightly slackened open, a voice behind me startled me.

"Are you going inside or just staring in for a little longer?"

Brooks.

I turned around to him to confirm the identity of the sultry voice I already knew. Yup, it was Brooks alright. "It's a free country and all, I might choose to stand here a bit longer."

He chuckled and it's something heavenly. A dark husk but there's something childlike about it. "Loitering is illegal in most public places," he poked back.

"Guess it's time to move now that an officer of the court is here."

"Can I buy you a coffee instead? Or tea? I have a small break between clients, and you look like you could use a lawyer with all your law breaking this afternoon," his eyes light up with amusement from our flirtatious banter.

My gut reaction is "absolutely not, I'm engaged", but in a split second I remember my circumstances and re-evaluate the request. An extremely hot guy just asked to buy me coffee during his lunch break, even my anxiety doesn't come up with a viable excuse for such an innocent diversion from reality.

Not wanting to sound too overzealous, I reply smoothly with a sly smile, "Is your retainer fee a cup of joe?"

His smirk widens into a full grin that reaches every inch of his face, even the small crevices near his eyes. "Yes. A coffee is all I ask for. Not a bad deal, right?" He pauses to wait for my response, and I just shyly nod with a thin-lipped smile. "After you then," he opens the door and gestures for me to walk in first.

Inside is your standard cute coffee shop. Lots of natural wood, cozy nooks, pillows, and a big counter filled with pastries and utensils. We ordered and he paid, despite that polite offer for his retainer fees we joked about before.

We stand by the counter to wait for our drinks, and I take a look around to scope out a spot, but only see one secluded nook available. It's cozy but small. The spontaneity of this date doesn't allow for me to plan a seating arrangement. I have no idea how intimate Beau planned to get on a quick coffee date.

When the iced coffees come out, he snags both along with straws and strides towards the nook with confidence, like it was his plan all along. I follow like a little duck following the momma bird. I let him set the placement of the cups before sliding into the booth accordingly.

"So, Persephone, I see you're still in town. Did you take my suggestion for Baxter's or did the Hyatt win out?"

"I told you, I don't provide my sleeping arrangements to strangers," I tried to be polite while shutting his small talk from our first meeting down again but reconsidered after thinking of my dad's letter. Take a risk. I took a big gulp of coffee and continued, "But yes, if you must know, I ended up at Baxter's. You were quite right about the quiche."

"Ah yes, I forgot I told you about the quiche! The woman knows her way around the kitchen. I suppose since you were so secret about the nature and length of your visit to Dorian the first time we met, that hasn't changed?" He's poking at me in the most gentle and funny way, I can't help but play back without being too curt in avoiding an answer.

"I'm not a closed book, it's just that my plans are interchangeable and flexible at the moment. I'm a bit like a plastic bag in the wind right now, if you know what I mean."

"American Beauty. Good movie. I like the reference. Are you a movie buff?" He asks and eagerly awaits my reply while waiting for praise for catching my movie reference. I seem to have his undivided attention and he took the hint of not wanting to talk about my vague explanation of circumstances.

"Definitely a movie lover, maybe not a 'buff' or a cinephile. You?" I volley back.

"Big time movie guy, though I don't watch them nearly as often as I want to. Work gets me home late then it's off to bed or the gym."

"You work a lot?" I ask inquisitively.

"I work too much, yes, but I don't have much else going on right now so it's better to work too much than play too much I suppose. Keeps me from loitering outside businesses," he teases me.

"I actually just got the opposite advice today. Play a little more, work a little less, I'm trying to follow suit, but I've been itching to read my work emails since I left the office." The truth that fumbles out of my mouth surprises me and the look of amusement on his face tells me he noticed my admission shocked me.

"Where do you work, or is that a big secret too?"

"A company. It's… family owned."

"I see. Around here? I know most. What do you do?"

"I work too much," I smile and play stupid at his question, then give him more of a real answer to quell his invasive questions. "My position is subject to change soon. That's a bit why I'm here now. I'm looking for other options." It's all true, but it's just not the entire truth.

"I'm sorry, sounds like either you're getting fired or promoted, but by your description, I can't tell which," his brows knit together a bit confused how to proceed and still keep the conversation light.

I send a reassuring grin across the table and take a sip of coffee. "Promotion of sorts, but it's too much responsibility and not enough of a pay off for me. I'm trying to figure out how to… get out of saying yes without making too much of a mess, if that makes sense."

He nods and stares into my eyes with concern, "It does. You seem like a smart woman, I'm sure you'll come up with a creative solution for yourself." He pauses when I smile and nod then continues, "You have a slight accent, not a tick of Southern in ya, where are you from if you don't mind me asking?"

I appreciate the soft edges to the question. He's learning me quickly and a sensation of gratitude warms my belly. It also encourages me to not fight him back so hard this time. "New York City, born and raised," I preen.

His eyebrows shoot up and juvenile excitement crosses his face, it's beyond the point of adorable. I fail to understand how this man isn't fighting women off with sticks every moment of the day.

"My sister lives there now, I think she's in the Upper West Side, or maybe it's the East. She's got herself a rich boyfriend and a nice apartment. She's quite the overachiever of the family," he laughs.

My natural reaction when I talk about neighborhoods in NYC kicks in before I can guard my own words, "Ah yes, either is nice. I lived in the Upper West Side, near Central Park." Shit. Did I just refer to myself living in NYC in the past tense already? It hasn't been much more than a week…

"Really? Small world. Lived you say?" he curiously tries to peck away at more.

I make a mental note that nothing I say will ever slip past him. His inquisitive expression shows he's dying to know more about where I live now and where I work if not for the Upper West Side. I let a crumb fall in front of his face and he picked it up all too easily.

"I assume you no longer live there? Can't imagine what would make you give up a location like that."

He's joking but it hits a nerve and I clam-up. Being cheated on by my ex-fiancè is what would make me give it up, but I don't want to dive into that rabbit hole.

I force a closed lip smile, "I found a nicer place away from the city. Are you from here, or Savannah?"

"Grew up right here in town. Never left, except for college," he says quickly.

"Love the town so much you couldn't bear to leave?"

"Every town needs a lawyer, plus every newly widowed mother could use her son living down the street," he shrugs, like not moving out of your hometown for the sake of your mother is a deed any decent man would concede to.

His father is dead, too. What are the odds? I glaze over it, not wanting to draw attention to my new orphan status any more than I want to talk about our dead fathers.

"That's... nice of you. You ever want to, like, actually leave though? Or are you happy to stay put?" I'm not sure why I keep asking. He clearly doesn't want to talk about this topic. His responses are polite but succinct and short.

"I don't like change much, plus not everyone needs to take a road trip to make a change," his voice lowered an octave and picked up a brush of sandpaper to it.

It was a bit of a low blow meant as a joke but landed like a rock in a pond. Had I hit one of his triggers? Adonis lawyer who never left his small hometown and never plans to?

He studies my face which has completely hardened, I think he senses the shift in my mood and glances at his watch. "It's been delightful getting to know you more Persephone, but I have to run to a client meeting now." He pauses and tries to catch another read on my face, which naturally finds itself grinning like an idiot even though his last question annoyed me.

"If you're still in town tomorrow night, I'd love to see you again. Maybe we upgrade to alcoholic beverages and food next time? Sans loitering."

Again, I think of my father's letter before answering. *Take more risks.*

"Sure, that would be great."

He reaches into his pocket to take out his phone, assuming to ask for my number.

I freeze. This feels like deja vu, especially with this man and this phone. No one has my new number. I barely even know the damn digits. I don't think I'm ready to give it out yet, just like I wasn't when he asked me the first time last weekend. How can I get out of this?

I dive to my phone that sits on the table face down next to my hands and thrust it in front of him to add his number before he can successfully do the same to me.

He pauses at the sudden movement but stops his own hands' descent to grab my phone and plug in his number. But then, he does the unthinkable, the unfathomable, the most obnoxious thing of all. He calls his own phone from mine.

"There. Now we both have each other's number." He hands me back my phone and I must have lost all the color in my face because he looks at me strangely and smirks before saving my contact in his own phone.

I glanced away into the coffee shop for the first time since this little date started to hide the emotions plastered on my face, the painful apprehension and concern. In my peripheral vision, I see him lifting his phone and snap a picture of me.

I whip my head back to him and narrow my eyes to say incredulously, "Did you just take a picture of me?"

"Yes. Quite a good side profile as well. Very artsy with the pillows and lighting," he jests, waving his hand in description, clearly trying to make light of his invasiveness.

My lips press into a flat line, and I furrow my brow in disapproval until he turns his phone around to show me the picture. It's actually quite a lovely picture of me. I look youthful and slightly concentrated, despite where my head was at the moment. It highlights the slight curve of my nose and the lighting plays well with the strength of my bone structure.

"I'm only letting you keep that because it is a cool picture and I look okay in it," I chastise him with thinly veiled anger.

"No, you don't look okay, you look incredible. And it reminds me of what I got to spend the last 20 minutes affectionately looking at while she deflected any and all personal questions."

With a flash of his pearly whites and a wiggle of his brows, he gets up to walk out. Before he clears the table, he says, "I'll call you about tomorrow," and then leaves my line of sight.

Damn. He has my goddamn number. Now what the hell am I going to do? Can I change it again?

Chapter 6
Persephone

———————

Brooks called just like he said he would later that evening. He asked for my "availability" which was hilarious. He had no idea how wide open I truly was when it came to appointments these days. I've actually never been so insanely *available.*

It didn't take much convincing for me to say yes, but my father's lasting words kept lingering in the back of my head. *Take the risk.* Brooks was a handsome man, sweet, funny, quick witted, and friendly. Plus, I had already spent a night with him. A drunken night of dancing he clearly was so drunk he forgot, but a fun night, nonetheless.

If nothing else, it was nice to have something to do and a familiar face to do it with.

I start getting ready for my date with Brooks a whole 4 hours beforehand, since there is absolutely nothing else going on in my post-runaway life. I pick out a little black dress that hasn't been worn since one of my first few dates with Harrison. My ex fiancè had brought me to a steakhouse but ordered a filet mignon, which was a pet peeve of mine.

I hate when people just order the filet assuming it's the best steak money can buy.

It's a safe choice, since it's a more tender part of the cow, but it's not the *only* delicious cut of meat. Harrison once ordered me one, too, without asking first, which annoyed me to no end. Not only did he arrogantly order my meal for me but ordered me my least favorite cut of steak.

Double bogey.

Flitting around the room fixing my hair, I was concerned about the attire for the restaurant Brooks would take me to tonight, but then finally conceded that nothing near here could possibly be fancier than a suit jacket requirement, therefore, my simple black quarter length sheath dress would be either perfectly appropriate or slightly overdressed, either of which suited me fine. I could blame overdressed-ness on being a New Yorker.

Three taps on my door startled me, but I quickly recovered and went to collect my purse. I open the door, but before I could shift out of the room, Brooks stops me, smiles, and with big bright eyes, he says, "You look beautiful tonight, Persephone."

I squeeze out a smile and slide by him, still so uncomfortable to be on a date for the first time in almost two years, nevermind accepting compliments from a man I had already drunkenly tongue wrestled with.

"Thank you, you look quite dapper yourself," I reply as I glance back around to meet his eyes for the first time. He's wearing a blue button up with a white collar, a patterned red tie, navy suit, and camel brown shoes. He looks incredible.

"Thank you. Unfortunately, still in court attire, but shall we?" Brooks holds out an arm for me to take and we make our way outside in the darkening evening.

"Where are we going? Are we walking?"

Brooks was prompt and on time. He actually allotted a few minutes to schmooze with the ladies' downstairs at the concierge desk and still left room to *be* at my door by 7pm sharp. I only knew because I saw him come in while I perched at the window at 6:45, anxiously waiting for his arrival. He didn't make it to my door until exactly 7pm, 10 minutes after he walked into the inn, and when we passed the front desk on our way out, they told us to enjoy dinner. His forethought in the matter impressed me the most. The kindness for chatting with the working women at the desk was a close second, though.

Weirdly, the promptness barely registered, which normally would have been my cornerstone make or break moment.

I guess the loser in my past set a precedent that I no longer cared for.

"Are you opposed to strolling down the street with me, Persephone? Am I that embarrassing to be seen with?" He teases.

"No, no, just most guys would drive on a first date, that's all," I pause, confused at my own words. The bulk of my dating career was meeting at bars after taking trains or Ubers to get there alone. I must have been channeling deep seeded Harrison aggressions. Harrison wouldn't even walk a block, he called town cars all the time, never a cab or Uber, unless it was an Uber Black. "It's a nice change of pace to walk."

"My sister always calls a cab, I hate it. You miss the buzz of the city around you. Sounds dumb when I say it out loud though," he remarks while seeming a little embarrassed by his admission. The "town" was a few people walking around, a car driving by, and a single buzzing streetlight.

I try not to grin, he's cute when he's not trying to be. We walk silently through town to the restaurant, enjoying the 'nightlife', my hand nestles into the crook of his arm. We stop outside an awning for a restaurant, not a bar.

"I believe I okayed drinks, not dinner," I glance up at a nervous man wincing, but also holding back a smile. "Did I miss negotiations?"

"Apologies, I thought I said *food*, not specifically dinner though. 'Suppose that's okay with you? Assuming you haven't eaten already?" His eyes turn from playful to weary in a heartbeat with his question, and I couldn't help but feel sorry for poking fun at him for inferring dinner. I was expecting we'd be going to dinner and not just drinks because of the time of day.

"Just drinks" are either typically a 9pm or later affair, at least in NYC.

Relief dripped through his expression while he acknowledged my assuring smirk. We were seated in the intimate back corner of the outside patio. The restaurant was cute with old time southern charm met with string lights and lush greenery. I didn't notice the type of food until I saw the vast array of steak options on the menu, then confirming as such when I noticed the name on top, "Ron Black's Steakhouse".

I stifle a sigh.

The waiter comes to take our drink orders and we continue some small talk and back and forth light banter that I enjoy much more than I should for surface level conversation.

Now down to the pinnacle of the night, the make or break moment. What was this man going to order for dinner?

Not only does a meal choice tell you a lot about the type of person someone is, but it also tells a lot about who they *aren't*. A man who goes to a steakhouse and orders anything, but steak tells me they are not ruled by logic or reason and can be irrationally concerned about the opinions of others. They care about going to a nice restaurant, but don't even enjoy the place's *specialty*. It's a weird flex. Red flag.

Order a $30 salad? Red flag. Too much to spend on a salad, clearly, they're delusional.

Order plain chicken, they're probably a plain person. Yellow flag, which I consider a "warning flag." Warning flags are for situations that may originally seem odd or off, but not enough to halt all involvement. It's more a "proceed with caution" in my book. Chicken breast is notoriously average at most places, and I find it only enjoyable when it's a thigh, a wing or fried. I question any man who orders a chicken breast.

With an unfortunate disadvantage for Brooks, a warning flag will be thrown if he orders a goddamn filet mignon, since Harrison always ordered them. It's a pet peeve as well, perhaps originally stemming from Harrison. My thought process for it isn't super logical, but I judge so heavily on meal choices even prior to Harrison, that the rule made sense in my head.

With bated breath, I wait for the waiter to come back over and take our meal order.

"Are you all set to place your orders?" The very attractive female waitress purrs at Brooks.

"Yes, I believe so," Brooks replies and looks towards me for confirmation and waits for me to start the order. Plus one point for not ordering for me. Off to a good start.

"We are, I'll have the New York Strip, please," I force a smile at our waitress who clearly wants to be on my date.

"Great, how would you like that cooked?" She replies flatly, but polite. I notice Brooks put his menu down like he's judging my desired meat temperature in the same silent way I am judging *his* menu selection.

"Medium rare, please, thank you," I say brightly, confident in the way I take my steak.

Steak should be eaten medium rare or rare, anything else is blasphemous. If he doesn't agree, that could be an automatic yellow flag for questionable taste. Everyone knows the steak is juicer and more flavorful when it's done medium rare. I hand her the menu and look to Brooks for the most anticipated moment of my night.

Honestly, maybe even my entire week.

"Cindy, right?" She nods emphatically. I love that he uses people's names, it's very personal and shows he really listens, even to the small details that people often forget, like a name.

"I'll have the same, NY Strip, medium rare. Do the potatoes and brussels sprouts work for you, Persephone?" He glances at me for approval, which my stunned self blinks and nods back. "Thank you," he hands over the menu while looking at me and grinning. The server takes the hint to leave and shuffles away without another peep.

Plus another 5 fictional points for not checking out the waitress as she walks away. Brooks is doing very well in the fake point system I have running as a tally in the back of my mind.

Brooks chuckles after we locked eyes for a few pregnant moments and asks, "I feel like I'm on trial, am I on trial?" I blush at his accusation and try to laugh it off, but he presses further, "What's the judge's ruling?"

"Yes, but the charges have been dropped due to the prosecution discovering new evidence." Our flirtatious sarcasm has been enjoyable, so it's fun to keep it going. He seems to like it as well and volleys back.

"I must have missed the arraignment, what charges were being held against me, Judge?" His eyes study me like I am a puzzle to piece together. If he only knew that half the pieces were locked away in the drawer...

I drop my teasing face to commit to my joke.

"Oh this can't be good, give it to me straight, I deserve the truth…" He says, prodding me more, playing farther into our game.

"You can't handle the truth!" I blurt out the movie line like it was a part of the fabric of my soul.

Brooks breaks character for a moment to whisper, "Love the *A Few Good Men* reference, but go on."

A giggle escapes me before I can redact back into seriousness. Solemnly I utter, "Treason and then first-degree murder."

He surprises me with a full belly laugh and a happily confused face, "I think I need these charges explained to me in a bit more detail."

I keep my straight face to go along with the ruse and try not to crack. "Treason for potentially ordering anything but a steak at a steakhouse, and then first-degree murder for how you like the steak cooked. Thankfully for you, the court found both to be made in error and you were cleared of all charges." I let a coy smile slip onto my face while my gag is finally fully unveiled.

Brooks' amusement was exploding now, completely enthralled by my teasing. I see it in how his eyes light up and the crinkles under his lids scrunch. It feels good to be appreciated for my extensive sarcasm again. My father always did, but Harrison found it tiresome, thus, I could never truly be myself.

"I can't express how pleased it makes me to hear the court found that the evidence was insufficient, but I'd love to be present at the arraignment next time I stand trial for *murder or treason.*"

"Sounds like you need a better lawyer," I quip. We were both almost bursting at the seams with laughter from our banter.

"Ha! I sure do," he said before switching back into normal conversation, "I can't deny that hearing you order your steak medium rare checked off a box for me in my head, though I didn't even think about the possibility of you not ordering a steak and what that could mean for your overall character. That might be something to add to my standard date checklist."

"It's an important quality, ordering food at the right time and right place. It shows a level of logic, sensibility, and social awareness." I pause to gauge his response to my snarky, judgmental mindset.

He leans in, squints incredulously, then says, "I need to hear more about this. Apparently, I've been judging people wrong for quite some time," his hand waves out toward me, palm face up, as if he's giving me the floor to speak my piece and defend my statement.

"Logic… because you should know what the restaurant specializes in and order that to truly get the most out of the meal. Sensibility… for when you're on a date and don't want to order something difficult to eat and look like a buffoon," he chuckles at my word choice, and I continue while trying to hold back my own laugh. "Then awareness… for reading the table and environment. You never want to order too much, whether it's price wise or in quantity."

His amazement didn't die down, but he shook his head slowly before answering, "You're wise beyond your years. What would have happened if I ordered chicken or salmon?" He's still playing, but intently curious about my response.

"Red flag, immediate termination of future contact post-date," I say nonchalantly with a sip of wine to make it ambiguous if I was actually serious or not. I am serious, but even I know that I'd sound crazy if I admitted to it.

"Wow, didn't realize how important this was, well what about if I order my steak well done? Would I get a lethal injection?" His lips twist in a wry smile that I couldn't help but to match with my own.

"Pretty sure Georgia still has the death penalty, so be careful there, Brooks," I hum. His brows quirk along with his lips, and I drag the joke on, "Overcooking a steak *should* be illegal. Anything cooked more than medium is an abomination," his mouth drops open, but I go on and defend myself. "I don't make the rules, I just follow them, counsellor."

He laughs again, face lit up with pure merriment, "I have to be honest with you, I have never laughed this much on a date in my life. We haven't even gotten our dinner yet and I already know I want to see you again."

I smile and nod, "I'd like that too, I think." The compliment heated my face and sent a spicy tingle down my spine. I haven't enjoyed a date so much either. The server came back over with both entrees in each hand. The wine continued to flow and our cheeky ribbing lit up the rest of the dinner, though moving towards less serious matters like television show choices and favorite classic rock songs.

"Bohemian Rhapsody is easily the greatest song ever written, it's almost indisputable," Brooks dropped his fork on the plate, jokingly frustrated with my dissent.

"*Stairway to Heaven, Hotel California, Free Bird*?! Do none of those ring a bell to you? How can you just immediately, without thought, say for sure it's Queen?" I'm flabbergasted our first argument is about a song, but my face is heated listening to him deftly defend his choice.

Must be the lawyer in him.

"It's the best song, those are all great songs too, just not the best," he says matter of factly while driving his spoon into our delicious half eaten brownie sundae.

My mouth is cocked open in shock. Staring holes into his face did nothing while he casually licks his spoon clean and goes back for another bite.

"You gonna eat more of this? It's very good," he is hardly holding back his smile. He notices I haven't taken another bite since we started disagreeing on the greatest classic rock song of all time. With my mouth still ajar, he breaks off a perfect scoop of brownie to ice cream to hot fudge to whip cream ratioed spoonful and plops it into my Venus fly trap of a mouth. I clamp down and he pulls the spoon out like you would while feeding a toddler, then he goes back in for his own perfect bite.

I break the stare once I chew and swallow, "Okay, agree to disagree, Mr. Lawyer, as long as you can agree on who is the greatest rock band of all time." He nods with an interested flinch of his eyebrows, egging me on to continue our game. "We'll say it on three, yeah? Greatest rock band on one, two…" I paused and gave him a scolding mother look, as if to will him to say the band in my mind. "Three."

"The Beatles," we say together in almost perfect unison.

"Oh, thank god," my breath catches, and my hand lifts to my brow in a very serious expression of relief while his boyish chuckle bounces towards me.

"I feel like I just dodged a reg flag and potential indictment!"

I blew out a breath, "Yes, Brooks, yes, you did."

"For scientific purposes, what would you have done if I said The Rolling Stones?" He's teasing me, but since I'm past heart attack concerns and my heart rate has leveled, I entertained it.

"I may have let you argue your cause, Mr. Dawson, but I think you would have found your jury on the prosecution's side."

His face scrunches as the busboy comes to clear off our table, "Do you mind helping us settle an argument?" The young man is a little startled and nervous but responds once he realizes Brooks is talking to him and looking for an answer.

"Uhm, sure. What can I help you with tonight, sir?"

"My lovely date and I are in a disagreement. I'd love for you to weigh in," the man looked uncomfortable as his eyes darted back and forth from me to Brooks. I give him an assuring smile. Brooks doesn't skip a beat once the kid gives a quick nod.

"Who is the greatest rock band of all time?"

The busboys' eyebrows knit together while he thinks, "I don't know, like The Foo Fighters maybe?" He answers nervously and looks to each of us for confirmation he helped settle our disagreement.

"Thank you, that was very helpful," Brooks smiles at the young man as he scuttles away then looks at me amused. "That didn't work to my advantage, and now I feel old."

We both giggle wildly in agreement.

"No, all you proved was you are in the proper age bracket to date me," I quipped back. "Let's try the waitress though, she seems like she could be around 30."

Brooks takes a casing of the room trying to locate her, she finds him looking for her and zips over in a hurry.

"Sorry to bother you, but just have a debate going on that I think you could help settle," he pauses and waits for her flirtatious and agreeable simper.

"Of course," she purrs, and I roll my eyes blatantly since I knew she won't see it. She won't waste a minute looking my way.

"Who is the greatest rock band of all time?"

She looks confused, blinking rapidly as if the question was "What is the first 30 decimals of pi?"

I smile at her pause, like the busboy, she's not sure how to answer, but not for a lack of knowledge. She doesn't want to disagree with him, she wants to please him.

"Hm, well what did each of you say? Perhaps I can help and weigh in that way."

Smart.

"Well, let's hear your answer first, then I'll tell you what each of us said." Brooks was not flirting back; he is genuinely curious of her answer and has no interest in playing her game while *our* contest is still on.

"Okay, well, I'd say maybe Aerosmith?" she looks from under her big fake lashes at Brooks for affirmation.

Not wanting to hurt her feelings, he smiles, thanked her, then says, "Good choice." He turns his gaze to mine to answer the waitress' initial question, "We both said The Beatles."

"Oh, right, them. I suppose they could be too," she mumbles. "Did you want anything else tonight? Or should I bring you the check?"

Brooks looks at me while he answers, "I think we'll finish our drinks and sit a while longer but bring the check whenever you're ready. Thank you," and with that, our tie breaker sauntered away.

His stare captures me and holds me in its thrall, affectionately creating a bubble around us no one else could penetrate, even a cute waitress.

Brooks is a slippery slope, but I don't intend to fight against slipping on my ride down.

After closing the restaurant and our casual stroll back to my room, it was hard to not admit the date was perfect by all accounts. Brooks is funny, charming, and the most gentlemanly man I had ever met. On top of those accolades, he is also impossibly quick witted and a great conversationalist, always asking thoughtful questions instead of falling back into small talk.

We stop in front of the bed and breakfast instead of him walking me inside. He is respectful and not assuming, which adds quite a few points in my book. I feel myself come alive with him, especially when we playfully argued, but I still wasn't healed enough to have someone in my bed again so quickly.

My emotional scars will take time, but it was actually my physical ones I was more concerned about. The big bumps and bruises are always easier to explain away, but the little bruise clusters around my thighs would be cause for alarm.

Brooks is intensely astute to details, so I know I wouldn't make it 5 minutes naked before he would piece the whole situation together. How the fingerprint sized bruises connect to the other larger bruises, my ambiguous intended destination, and the true intention of my "trip". He was too smart to not.

A kiss would be all I'd allow, and even then, it terrified me to no end to wander down this path with him. He'd remember the feel of my lips and piece together the other secret I was keeping from him. The one where we made out all night, then gave him a phone number that never texted him back. For all I knew, he had texted me the next day trying to see me again. How could I explain my ridiculousness of giving my old number? It was either that or lie and say I miss typed it.

Even if I wanted to come clean now, how would I even begin that conversation?

"Hey, I met you the other night, but I looked like a club nymph with blonde hair. I recognized you from the diner but didn't want to bring it up on the off chance you were mad about me giving you a bogus number."

Yeah, I think I'll just stick to what he doesn't know, won't hurt him.

Brooks wraps both hands around my waist to pull me closer, but I catch his sloppy tipsy smile he acquired sometime after the fourth glass of wine, before he nuzzles into my neck.

"Tell me when I can see you again," he hums into my hair and all the goosebumps on my body perk up at once.

Not wanting to sound too available but still flirty, "Tell me when you *want* to see me again, and I'll tell you if you can."

"Tomorrow," he says instantly. "And the day after that."

I can't help but adore his eagerness. "Tomorrow it is then," my voice drops to a whisper as both our heads drew closer together and our gazes lowered to each other's lips.

Encased in the moment, his words floated into my ears, "I'm going to kiss you now if that's okay."

My nod only bounces once before his lips catch mine and we lock in a soft probing embrace. We break apart a few seconds later only to latch back on and press into a series of long open mouth kisses spanning an inordinate amount of time. I could taste the wine from tonight on his lips while we momentarily got lost in each other's touch.

At some point, his hand travels up into my hair and behind my head as the other one explores the curves of my hips and back. My own pesky hands have a mind of their own and make their way to his chest, slide up his neck to eventually descend into the nest of gentle curls around his nape.

We break apart again and I immediately put myself back together from the pile of mush I am currently in.

"Goodnight Brooks. Maybe I'll see you tomorrow?" I ask with my brows raised and slightly panting.

Brooks is still reeling from our kiss, his eyes wildly searching mine before he computes my goodbye and responds.

"You *will* see me tomorrow, same time? Dinner will be involved, but not the main attraction. Wear something comfortable, like jeans and a t-shirt. Does that work?"

I nod and turn to leave. I appreciate the heads up on apparel. He snags my arm and twirls me back into a soul searing kiss, as if the one before wasn't enough, as if that one before didn't alter my world's axis. If the one before didn't, this one surely did.

We break apart, exchange wordless and toothless smiles, then headed in opposite directions; me inside, him back down the same way we came from.

Chapter 7

Persephone

The next morning catches me off guard with its bright sunshine and chirping birds. It's not the alcoholic hangover that's hitting me hard but the regret and shame of last night. Am I seriously ready to get back into it with someone else after literally fleeing the only place I've ever lived from an abusive ex-fiancé?! It's only been 9 days since I've left my whole world behind.

I've had good days and bad. Yesterday was one of the best days I've had in years, but with a man I hardly know. I can't use our strange undeniable connection as an excuse for my momentary loss of control. I'm not trying to get involved with someone so quickly after Harrison, but everything about being around Brooks feels so right.

I reach for my phone to instinctually check my messages, a habit I've had a hard time breaking despite the lack of incoming *anything*. Only one person in this world has my number so it's no surprise my heart flutters at the notification sitting on my lock screen. A text from Brooks.

Brooks: Hey there. I would have texted you last night, but I walked into my apartment and collapsed into a dreamless slumber. I woke up thinking of you and our date last night. Looking forward to doing it again. Arraignment included.

It's not a love poem but it's insanely sweet and thoughtful as well as brave. A man owning his feelings instead of playing some dumb game of cat and mouse is rare and should be *coveted* whenever encountered in the wild, like an endangered species. Brooks is a real man who freely admits how he feels about the woman he went out on a date with, and I couldn't admire him more for it.

Harrison was never this sweet, even in the beginning when he was supposedly "wooing" me. Sure, I'd get a cute "Good morning" text, but nothing explicitly honest or complete. Looking back, it felt like Harrison was checking boxes when it came to our romance.

He'd call when he was supposed to, after dates, feigning thoughtless texts like he was supposed to, but the women's bar is so low for men. All they have to do is *text back* and it's inferred the man is interested. The 2 seconds to rifle off a text shouldn't be an indication of interest, yet an entire population hangs to see the dancing dots on their iPhones like it's a prize to be won.

Harrison was much better in person, though still robotic in ways. Always a gentleman, opening doors, picking up checks, and bringing home flowers. I didn't know any better, that there should have been more sizzle between us. That we should have had more than just fulfilling a need, a space.

Brooks and I have our banter, our back and forth. We have the laughs, the common ground of likes and interests. He didn't need to fill the gaps of silence with gentlemanly gestures because we were too busy laughing our night away.

As Brooks' reward for a thoughtful text, I replied immediately instead of playing the game and waiting half the day.

Persephone: Me too ;-)

Purposefully vague, I thought myself to be very coy in my reply. I didn't expect a response any time soon, it was 9:30am and he was probably at work, but my phone pinged a few minutes later.

Brooks: Which part are you 'me tooing'? Falling asleep before you could text me, waking up to thoughts of me, or looking forward to tonight?

Persephone: Wouldn't you like to know?
Brooks: Yes, I would, that's why I'm asking, silly girl.

I couldn't help but smile at the affectionate name calling. Apparently, we were there now. I didn't mind.

Persephone: Guess you'll have to wait and see, my friend.
Brooks: Friend? Do you kiss all your friends like that?
Persephone: What if I said yes?
Brooks: I'd ask you to forgo seeing them for a while.
Persephone: Haha. Then, no.
Brooks: That's good, I'd rather laugh with your friends than fight them.
Persephone: Who says you'll even meet them?

The pain of that truth twists in my stomach. I have no friends right now, there is no one to meet. Maybe one day, my dad's poker crew, but they didn't even know I left New York yet.

Brooks: Wishful thinking? I already got a third date, so I'm hoping to keep em' coming, for however long you stick around.

I paused, started to type a few times and stopped. Nerves flash through me, and I sit up. Did he finally remember our first encounter? Does that count as a date? He's probably watching the bubbles appear and disappear, but I can't find the words to say.

Persephone: Third date? I thought dinner was date #1?

Brooks immediately replies, as if waiting for my response from before.

Brooks: Coffee was date #1, so you could say I tricked you into a second date, but let's not get into semantics.

Relief washes over me, and I let out the breath I had been holding in.

Persephone: They say never to trust a lawyer (eye roll emoji)
Brooks: Oh boy. I'm going to stop while I'm ahead. Tonight at 7pm?
Persephone: See you then, in jeans apparently.
Brooks: Can't wait ;-)
Persephone: For me in jeans, the food, or the date in general?
Brooks: The food... wait, the jeans. Ah, no... All three.
Persephone: Sure, sure.
Brooks: Hah, see you then, silly girl.

Short and sweet, our text exchange brightened my day and it had hardly begun. He brought out my combative, sarcastic side I really only ever displayed when around my dad and occasionally my co-workers. It was refreshing and empowering to talk to someone as interesting as Brooks. Easy going and playful, I couldn't help but start to feel excited for our third date this evening.

Dressed in a pair of stylish, boyfriend fit, ripped jeans and a cute black quarter sleeve t-shirt, I fish out a pair of white sneakers from my car. Most of my clothes were still in limbo, but I had a closet full of things in the trunk that I didn't care to bring into my room at Baxter's yet. I wore my now shorter brown hair in a curly ponytail tonight, as opposed to the blown straight look I had going on last night. My makeup was lighter and less dramatic as well. My look was polished but comfortable, I looked nothing like any date I had ever been on with someone in NYC, and I loved every second of checking my reflection in the mirror.

I am calm, relaxed even, despite the symphony of single cell combustions singing across my chest. My skin prickles in anticipation for his knock on my door.

Three light raps on my door pop an instant grin to my cheeks. Like last night, Brooks is perfectly on time. Snagging my small brown crossover bag, I open the door to find an Abercrombie & Fitch model standing outside. His dark hair is mussed up, almost purposefully, and he has light colored jeans on with a distressed salmon colored V-neck t-shirt, and white soled, navy cloth Polo sneakers. It seems I was not the only one who looked entirely different from last night's attire.

'Dressed down Brooks' is equally as sexy as 'straight from the courtroom Brooks'. He does casual just as well as refined, which is no easy feat. Most men reside in one of two categories, looking comfortable in a suit or more so in casual attire. Harrison was always a master in a suit but looked strange and uncomfortable in anything less than a rolled sleeved button up and slacks. I don't think I ever saw him in a t-shirt, except for before bed.

Brooks' eyes light up in tandem with his smile when I open the door, and he catches a glimpse of "casual" me. I adore the crinkles that hug around his eyes when he smiles.

"You look great. I like the pony," he reaches around and tugs my brown mane gently. I laugh and step out to close the door.

"Thanks, you look good in or out of suit," I compliment back, really just expunging my thoughts more than anything.

"I do what I can," he hums and extends his hand to hold mine as we walk on the street to our destination. Hand holding wasn't necessarily foreign territory for me, but usually only used, when necessary, at events or moments where cameras would capture me from any angle, never for just a useless public display of affection.

We leisurely walk while Brooks asks me what I did that day.

"I've been reading, walking a bit around town, and… watching a ton of Netflix," I laugh at myself for binging so many trashy rom coms.

"Sounds a hell of a lot nicer than reading depositions and talking to clients, which is all I did today," he gives me a quick wink coupled with a lift of the corner of his lip.

Rocking with a new sensation of walking downtown with a man holding my hand for his own pleasure, I begin contemplating where he is taking me. We walk past all the restaurants and all the store fronts until we end up at a dock. That's when I see the boat.

The pontoon boat has its table popped up, a cooler, a few blankets, and string lights wrapped around the overhead bar. The small tabletop isn't set, but I notice a large brown bag next to the cooler. Fascination and appreciation swells inside me. He planned this sweet, romantic night for me. My lips twist up, unsure if I was holding back a smile or some tiny tears buzzing in the corners of my eyes.

The shock and adoration on my face must have come across as contempt, because Brooks squeezes my hand and says, "I should have asked if you were afraid of boats, it's okay if you are, we can do something else."

I spin quickly and grab his other hand, "No! No… I am just… surprised at how thoughtful and sweet this is. Seriously, Brooks," I smile affectionately at him and tug him by our interlocked hands towards the boat. "Are we eating on the docks, or do you know how to drive this thing too?"

He laughs and his mood shifts from unsure back to excited.

"Yes, I know how to drive my own boat, thank you very much. There's a firework show later tonight on the other side of the lake."

He hops on then extends his hand back to me to help me step onto the boat. "I figured dresses and suits were a little too aggressive for a night on the bay."

"Good call, what can I do?"

"Sit on the captain's lap and relax," he taps his lap, and I give him a feigned disapproving look. "Okay, okay, you can sit where you'd like," he shoots his hands up showing his surrender.

We cruise softly and silently into the middle of the lake I didn't even know existed in this town until tonight. He settles the boat, drops anchor, then puts on a classic rock playlist for background noise and walks back to the cooler to offer me a drink.

"I don't have a wine list like last night, but I have beer, red, white, vodka, or just water."

I'm already outside of all normal date comforts, why not keep it going?

"Beer me, please."

His eyebrows raise and I catch the corners of his mouth creeping upwards before he turns to grab us both a *can* of beer.

"Didn't take you for a beer woman, but then again, everything I've learned about you has surprised me," he says then notices my mock offended face. He adds in quickly, "in the best ways possible, of course." My fake anger subsides while a pressed quirk of my lips appear.

"I like to keep people on their toes. Seems like you do as well, I never expected a third date boat ride, very clever," I compliment. There are no marbles, and this isn't the ocean, but I feel my dad with me tonight.

"The Thursday night fireworks worked in my favor. I brought different pastas from Luongo's. I should have asked if you liked Italian, but it completely slipped my mind during our sparring match today via text."

"Pasta is great, I'm not picky, just judgmental of other people's food choices," I huff, referencing our dinner conversation from last night. He joins in and pulls out the containers.

"I kept you in mind when I ordered and didn't get any spaghetti or twirl pasta, only ones you can easily stab with a fork. Easy to eat, sensible is what I believe you'd classify it as?" He looks to me for my approval in his decision, like I'm truly the judge and the jury on all thing's dinner date related.

Laughing back, "I think you're fine." I pause dramatically and turn a strange shade of seriousness, "assuming you got bread."

His dark eyes turn into saucers, like a deer caught in headlights and he rifles into the bag to try to see if they gave us bread. I feel a little bad for giving him a scare, but the look of relief on his face when he finds a small loaf wrapped up at the bottom of the bag was priceless.

"Got the bread. Scared me for a second there, though."

"Don't worry, bread wouldn't have been making or break, more like a yellow warning flag," I poke back at him assuring but his face doesn't light back up to his normal brightness.

"Seriously, Brooks, this was super thoughtful and sweet," I turn in my seat to look at where we were, in the middle of a bay in a boat lit up with twinkly lights. "I've had a… tough few weeks, actually months, and this was such a nice gesture. Thank you."

He nods and starts assessing my face, looking for more details in my vague innuendo of a difficult recent past. He finally releases the breath he was holding in and says, "I was waiting for the "I can't keep seeing you" part of that speech. I have to be honest; I am thrilled it never came." He laughs into his beer can before casting his head back, taking a swig then looking back up at me.

"No, court hasn't adjourned yet," I tease.

"I'm not sure what's been going on, but if I can offer free legal advice, let me know. I am happy to help," Brooks turns a bit more serious but genuinely concerned and helpful. I appreciate the gesture of help more than he could realize and allow my tall wall to lower an inch.

"No, nothing you could help with. There were some people in my life that ended up not what they initially seemed to be," my heart clenches at the vast understatement.

Brooks nods with empathetic eyes gleaming from the twinkle lights. He is waiting for me to go on, so I do. My walls shift down another inch.

"I had a bad break up and our friends ended up siding with him," I fumble with the fraction of the truth.

"I'm sorry, was it recent?" He asks, a little unsure of himself.

"Yes, no. I don't know," I sigh. "It was over for a long time before it was actually over. We just couldn't admit it. People change," I shrug, trying to keep the truth from falling out of my mouth, that this wasn't my first attempt at leaving Harrison, but it was just the first successful one.

"What made you stay?"

His question catches me off-guard; I am not ready to divulge more. My mind goes to the day I packed an overnight bag and slept at one of my uncle's hotel's downtown. One of my first attempts at escape.

We shared locations on our iPhones at the time, but in my duress, I forgot that small fact, and just put my phone on silent assuming he wouldn't notice I was gone for a while anyways. Harrison showed up at my hotel room, posing as room service when he tricked me into opening up the door without looking. He dragged me back uptown in his town car, berating me the entire drive-up 7th Ave about never leaving him again.

I told him I wasn't leaving, just taking a night for myself. He didn't believe me, but I don't blame him because I didn't believe myself either.

Brooks waited for my response while I replayed that chaotic scene in my head. "You know how it is, scared to be alone, or whatever." He nods along like he understands, but it is probably my distant voice that directs him to change topics.

"I know I keep asking you this, but how long are you staying in town? Or where do you head next?" My heart leaps knowing my real response would crush him, that I had no intention of staying more than a week at the most. But as I'm here with him on this clunky pontoon boat, I never want to leave this stinking town.

"I don't plan on leaving, at least not in the next two weeks," I say before even thinking.

He looks as surprised as I feel at the words.

"Really?" His lips start curling up. "What changed?"

Grappling at what I just admitted, I start digging my grave deeper. "I figured this was a good stop for now, maybe stay for a year and go to the next stop. I am... looking for an apartment now... know a place to rent?"

That lip curl turns into a full-on grin that reaches all the way to the crinkles next to his eyes. "Yes, in fact I do. I help manage Mrs. White's apartment that sits above the coffee shop. She's older and can't do the stairs anymore, so I go in and act as a landlord when there's a tenant, but it's currently vacant right now. It's nothing special but nice for the price, I'm not sure what price point you're looking at though."

Feeling excited about the prospect of an apartment then slammed with a bit of guilt that this man who has been so kind to me hardly even knows my financial standing, doesn't know what I could and couldn't afford. Hell, I hardly knew what was in my savings.

"I have some saved." I need to keep my circumstances under wraps for now. It's imperative for me to keep as much personal information to myself as I can manage, for as long as I can. While I don't think Harrison will come after me, I have no interest in sharing personal information to spread all over town in the event someone does come poking around. No need to make myself more identifiable than I already am.

"That's great, you should come stop by and see it tomorrow maybe? I can put in a good word to the landlord," he whispers the last part with a wink.

"Yes, please do," I play back.

The rest of the night was mixed with pasta, kisses, blankets, music, cuddles, conversation, and laughter. Lots of laughter. The fireworks were in the sky, but they were also on the boat. Every kiss ignited all the nerve endings on my skin, every pore opened up to bask in the ardor of his touch. Our bodies did most of the talking the latter half of the night.

I straddle his hips with my legs while the heat of his hands roam the arc of my hips. My shirt is hitched up at my waist, but I didn't care, no one was around to see anyways. His fingertips travel along the band of my panty line, sometimes dipping under my jeans near my ass before slowly sliding back up from that dangerous territory.

He makes trails of kisses down the column of my throat while both our hands drift farther under each other's shirts to find more undiscovered skin to touch. We slip into a fog of pleasure, drunk off each other's touch, unaware of our surroundings or the massive explosions ringing off above us.

Long, soft kisses along my collar bone turn into affectionate nuzzles into my neck while holding me practically diagonal across his lap. We sit in comfortable silence, rubbing gentle circles into our exposed parts of skin with our thumbs until I let my eyes drift close.

I almost thought I dreamt it when I woke up laying in Brooks' arms in the same tangled position we were before. We both must have drifted off for a while because my Apple Watch said it is 3 am.

I sit up groggily only moments before Brooks shoots up from our comfortable position to also check his watch, "Oh god, I'm sorry, Persephone, I didn't mean to keep you out this late, I must have fallen asleep." Brooks all but pushes me off him to pull the anchor quickly and get the boat back into the dock.

"Brooks, don't worry. We both fell asleep," I try to soothe his nerves while he anxiously readies the boat for our departure back to the land. My sex hazed mind wouldn't mind staying out here longer…

"I know, still. I don't even know what you're doing tomorrow, I'm sorry."

He still seems worried about my "today" and how my lack of sleep would affect the day's plans. I try to quell him with our normal dose of banter, "Seriously, Brooks, I have nowhere to be except seeing a random guy about an apartment tomorrow."

He drinks in my words, but they don't register until I arch both eyebrows up and start to let the wisp of a laugh poke through. He catches my joke and his face starts to soften. We break out into an exchange of nervous snorts before he pulls me in for a soft kiss and speaks into my mouth, "Make sure he doesn't try any funny business."

I mumble agreement when our lips meet, then we break our short, heated embrace to start picking up the boat. We make our way into the dock, and he insists we leave everything in the boat for him to deal with tomorrow.

The walk back feels faster than the walk there and I'm faced with a similar predicament as last night. I can't invite him up. Making out in the dark under a blanket, fully clothed, is one thing but going up to my hotel room is another.

How long can I seriously prolong having sex with this man? Our chemistry is off the charts, date 3 is common to invite a man up, and if you last until date 5, it's almost a guarantee. At the pace we're at, date 5 will be in three days... Not long enough for...

Brooks must have picked up on my apprehension and the gentleman in him made the decision for me. Stopping outside of Baxter's again, he gives me a long kiss goodbye and says against my lips, "I'll text you tomorrow morning about showing you the apartment."

I nod with my eyes still closed and my lips still tingling from our embrace. Before he moves to leave, I say into his chest, "I had a great time tonight Brooks, like a seriously amazing time, thank you."

With locked eyes and matching shy grins, he replies, "The pleasure was all mine, Persephone."

He strides back to press a chaste kiss to my cheek along with a gentle stroke to the other cheek with the backside of his fingers, turns, and walks towards downtown just like last night.

Chapter 8

Persephone

───────────

The next morning, I reached for my phone again hoping for a text from Brooks, which I did not receive even though it was 10am. He said he would text me. Maybe he was annoyed about not coming back up to my room after such a romantic date? Did I screw this up already somehow? Did he figure out I am the girl from the bar and decide I was a liar?

I hop into the shower and wash last night's lust off me. My brain can't stop going over every detail of the night, overanalyzing every kiss, touch, joke, and response as if some detail would rationalize the lack of contact. Nothing I could think of would prompt him to not text me the next morning. He was so direct the night before, but now this felt like a game. Did I misjudge him?

Even Harrison, in the beginning, would at least check the box. A good morning text before work to acknowledge me for the day. Maybe he would pepper in some midafternoon messages here and there, at least when we first started our courtship, maybe not towards the end.

Barely out of the shower with a towel wrapped around me, I hear a knock on the door that nearly scared me out of my skin. I check the peephole and see one of the house keepers, who is always in jeans and a muted pink Baxter's t-shirt. Opening the door enough to poke my head out, smile and say hello.

"Hello Ms. Kline. I have room service for you," she says sweetly, but smiles mischievously.

"Oh, I'm sorry, you must have the wrong room, I didn't order any room ser-." I start to close the door and she stops me mid-word.

"You didn't, but Mr. Dawson did, ma'am," she inclines her eyebrows to try to get me to open the door more and scoot the cart in. My jaw drops and I slowly open the door, finally remembering that "Dawson" is Brooks last name.

She wheels the cart in and shoots me a quick smile before slipping out of the room without another word.

Standing in front of the cart, which had a metal cover keeping the heat in for the food underneath, my mouth is still bowed with shock. I lift the lid to find a beautiful French toast plate nestled beside a side of quiche, bacon, maple syrup, fruit, and a small note, which I immediately snag to read. It was in actual handwriting, which looked more like a boyish scrawl than feminine script.

Persephone,

I'm sorry for such a late night, hope you slept in. Will you go out with me again tomorrow night for our 4th date? Check a box for your answer.

Yes

OR

Definitely yes

I couldn't help but laugh at the ridiculousness of the note. The man brought out the giggles in me, even from afar. In my time, I've met a lot of lawyers, but none like him. He can switch from professional to fun in the blink of an eye. He is sharp when he needs to be, intellectual in conversation, but wild and free in-between. He is a breath of fresh air for my battered, city polluted lungs.

Grabbing a maple syrup doused French toast and the quiche, I plop on my bed, snag my phone and take a quick selfie of the plates on my lap. I draft the text to Brooks thanking him for the breakfast and send it off, completely forgetting I'm in my freaking towel!

His response was quick as usual, like he was waiting for a message from me any minute.

Brooks: Good morning to you too. I didn't think we were on the level of sending saucy pictures yet.
Persephone: Oh please! It's just a little leg.
Brooks: I meant the French toast's sauce! Gosh, get your mind out of gutter!

Oh my god, I am so stupid.

Brooks: Just kidding. My mind was in the gutter, but I liked it nonetheless.
Persephone: Not sure maple syrup is a sauce.
Brooks: Is this like the debate of whether a hot dog is a sandwich?
Persephone: Feels like it could be.
Brooks: I plead the fifth.
Persephone: You don't feel up for a debate this morning?
Brooks: I'd rather tongue tussle when I see you today. Speaking of, when do you want to see this apartment? I talked to Mrs. White, and she was happy I found someone interested.
Persephone: Hmm…. What works for you? You're the one who has an office job, though you do text a lot for supposedly being the only town lawyer.
Brooks: Fridays are slow, no one's getting in trouble until later tonight after they drink. I can meet you at 2?
Persephone: Sounds good, do I just meet you outside the coffee shop?
Brooks: Yeah, that works.

We text a few less insignificant things up until I leave to walk downtown at 1pm. I have been mulling over applying to the coffee shop part time to give myself something to do. Money isn't a problem,

I have plenty to last me a while, in addition to whatever my dad left me.

My bank account did seem substantially lighter than I thought it would be. I hadn't looked in a few months, but it was nearly the same amount despite it being several paychecks later. While I didn't tie my accounts to Harrison, he did have access to my credit cards and main bank account.

I had one account I opened after my last failed attempt to leave Harrison. He had tracked me down by a credit card charge. That was how he found out I was in Montauk. I made sure to discreetly open a new account and syphon some money in every paycheck for padding.

I made my own money the last 10 years working, but my father had given me a nest egg after college that I put into the stock market and made a small bit of money with. While I was always careful with my spending, I was not frugal. Most of the money I spent was on hair appointments, clothes, and my rent, which halved itself once I moved into Harrison's three-bedroom apartment.

When I travelled, my dad paid for most of my trips, since they were mostly with him. When I shopped, it was out of necessity more than anything. I dyed my platinum hair dark brown partially because the upkeep on blonde hair is substantial cost wise and partially because I wasn't immune to that intrinsic female instinct of desirable change after the dissolution of a relationship. Partially to conceal my identity and start fresh.

When Pops died, I stopped going to my hair appointments, I stopped buying things in general, and I thought my bank account would at least increase with the lack of spend, but it only increased a few hundred dollars, which I found odd. I questioned Harrison about it once and he said it was just funeral expenses, this and that dinner, or went into a long diatribe about stocks underperforming. All of it sounded very legitimate at the time, but when I left, I made sure Aisley closed all my accounts, froze all my credit cards except my emergency one, and transferred all my funds to a private account only I had access to. She also cut off all our *shared* credit cards and switched my financial advisor, which was one of Harrison's friends from college.

Thinking back on it, Harrison was definitely stealing from me, but I was too depressed to care or notice. I have no idea how much he took, now so far gone it doesn't actually matter. My mind wandered while I started scrolling on my phone at old bank statements from months before.

There were charges from hotels, airlines, restaurants, and even jewelry stores that I never saw before. He must have had himself a field day when I stopped being a functioning human. The thought of his taking advantage of me when I was in that state made my stomach twist with regret. Money I'll never get back. In the end, I rationalized it as my payment to him for taking care of the funeral arrangements.

Stepping into the coffee shop to apply for this job made me laugh internally. I had been in charge of an HR department, technically an owner of a company, applying to make coffee at a small mom and pop coffee house, and I was nervous!

"Hi, what can I get you?" The nice young man behind the counter asked. His name tag read Michael.

"Hi, uhm, I actually wanted to apply for the part time position if it's still available."

"Oh! Yes, yes, it is! Hold on, let me get you the application!" He lights up, happy to help me, and scrambles to get a pen and the paper application. "Here, just fill this out and I will let Maggie know you're here. She will probably just interview you now if you don't have to run."

"Sure, I'll just be just over there," I jab my thumb in the direction of the booths, smile and walk away.

Scribbling down my work experience was awkward. VP of HR and Junior Associate were the only two positions I held from 18-29. I worked two summers at Pop's country club serving food, so I wrote that down too, but that was when I was 16-18 years old! This woman was going to laugh at me when she read this.

Maggie saunters over shortly after I fill in the application entirely and submit it to my new friend behind the counter. She smiles and introduces herself then sits down with me on the opposite side of the booth.

"I'm not sure how to say this Persephone, but I've never had a VP of HR apply for a job at my coffee shop," she looks at me concerned while I smile nervously. "There must be a reason you're not trying to find another job more suited for your qualifications. I can try to get you acquainted with a friend I know from the city ne-"

"I know it's odd, it's a long upsetting story that I'd rather not share, or have you share with anyone either. All I can say is that I'm not a fugitive of the law, I am not running away from being fired or something, and I'm really just looking for a fresh start in a new city where no one knows my name. I work hard, I show up on time, and learn quickly. I'm really only looking for a few hours here and there to meet some people and make a life here, but I plan to stay." It was a white lie. I wasn't planning on staying forever, but no one needed to know that right now.

"I understand if that's not the type of person you're looking for, or you don't want to take the risk on someone who is not going to give you the full truth of why they are here in this town," I laugh at the end of my diatribe, realizing how crazy I must sound. I search her face for any indication of sympathy.

Maggie pauses a moment and takes a deep breath.

"That was a lot to process. You clearly are capable and willing. The job itself isn't difficult, literally just requires a warm body, but we like to consider ourselves a family here. The ideal person is someone who can connect to the customers and team behind the counter. Whatever is happening with you, I can tell you need someone to throw you a bone right now. Gods be damned if I'm not the person to do it."

She pauses again, with pursed lips, looking on for my reaction, which at the moment is confused. It sounds like she is trying to let me down softly, but the end part alluded to maybe helping me out. I waited in a silent stalemate with her until she finally breaks, "That was me giving you the job. Assuming you pass a background check."

"Oh! Oh my god, sorry, thank you! Seriously, I won't let you down and I will pass a background check, I promise. Thank you so much." I get up to shake her hand, like I would with any client or business meeting, realizing instantly how silly I look in the real world doing it.

She stands regardless and shakes my hand warily. She's an older woman, mid 60's with salt and pepper hair. Her fine lines around the eyes doesn't detract from her looks but adds character to her sculpted face. The bright piercing gray eyes are intimidating, but I notice they softened over our conversation. I note her apparel, as well as the kid behind the counter. They're both in coffee-stained jeans, a coffee shop t-shirt with an apron, and sneakers. I'll have to make a clothing run for work clothes, no reason to stain nice jeans.

"Can you come on Monday around 2pm? We'll work out your schedule, how many hours, and get you trained."

I nod and confirm, "Of course, thank you again. See you Monday."

Perfectly on time for Brooks, I walk out of the coffee shop with new employment and a new lease on life. The job at the coffee house will give me something to do a few days a week and maybe give me some cover about how I afford living on my own to the people of the town.

It's 1:55pm when I see Brooks walking up the street with a big grin on his face. He's adorably cute when he's excited, like a puppy ready to play.

"Persephone," he smiles, leans in to kiss my cheek and lingers there a few moments longer than a friend would. I can't help but to blush and smile from the warm greeting.

"Hi," I say meekly.

"Ready to see this little gem?" He flashes a bright smile and leads the way to a door next to the coffee shop entrance. He unlocks the plain green door and we walk up a flight of old cricket-y stairs to a hallway. The current visual is not convincing me this place will be suitable, but Brooks is paying close attention to my facial expressions, so I keep my face neutral until further notice.

He makes quick work to open the apartment and pulls open the blinds to let the natural light in. There is an old southern charm to the place. The interior is entirely brick with exposed beams overhead. The room is large, open, with a small kitchen in the corner, a two-person table, and an old rug on the wood floor. The appliances are new, and everything is well kept. I turn into the bathroom, which is a good size, full tub and sink in good condition.

I reach for the next and final door, assuming it is the bedroom and find it to be a rather small closet.

Oh. It's a studio.

Brooks sees the look fall from my face and he shuffles his feet a bit before asking me if I like the place.

Straightening my face and taking a deep breath, I turn to respond, "It's adorable, a really nice spot." I'm not sure if I can live in this box, but I take another lap around contemplating how to handle what comes next.

"It's small, and it's $850 a month," he says apprehensively. I am not sure if $850 is good or bad for this area. The rent in Harrison and I's apartment was much more than that, most of which Harrison paid for, so it was truly apples to oranges.

"That's not bad for the location, right? Why has no one else taken it yet? Seems like a perfect little spot."

"Celia actually lived here for a long while, the waitress at the diner you met earlier this week. She moved back home a month or two ago to help out her Momma. To be honest, Mrs White raised the rent, and it's just a little more expensive than most folks are used to around here." He starts playing with the cabinets, avoiding eye contact with me as he unloads the truth of the matter. "But the location is worth it."

It doesn't bother me, money isn't the problem in this case, I've saved enough to get by for now. It's close to work and the weekly cleaning will be minimal. I have to keep most of my things in storage, another added expense.

This town and new life are filled with opportunities. I need to keep grabbing them as they come, so I say it before I could fully think it through any longer.

"I'll take it."

Brooks stops mid cabinet open and whips around, "You will?" He is confused. "I… didn't think you liked it very much."

"Well, you don't know me well enough to say that," I snip back defensively.

He frowns, "I didn't mean it like that, honestly. I just saw your face drop when you opened the closet thinking it would be the bedroom."

My defenses vanish with a crack of a smile at his astute and correct observation. "You're right, I did think the closet was going to be a bedroom," shaking my head and walking towards him. He looks up at me with apology in his eyes.

"I'm sorry if I offended you," he meets me halfway and locks an arm around my waist, then leans in for a tender kiss. His lips slant onto mine and we embrace for a few seconds before I tear my lips from his.

Shoving playfully at his chest, "This is highly unprofessional to kiss your new tenant."

"Not my new tenant, I don't own the place, just a fill-in-sometimes-for-an-old-lady landlord who can't get up the stairs," he snags me tighter to him and reconnects our lips for another kiss, this time with a bit of tongue, like he promised in the text earlier that day.

"Where do I sign, mister landlord?" I sneak in between kisses.

"I'll have my lawyer send you the lease," he laughs, and I capture it with my mouth as he plants my butt on the kitchen counter for a little midday make out sesh and heavy petting.

Walking outside after verbally agreeing to a new lease, I am ready to head back to the inn and start arranging my move, including buying new furniture to fit inside my tiny new apartment. Brooks grabs my hand, brings it to his mouth and kisses the back of it in an obvious show of affection.

"Did you bring my note with a box checked?"

I quirk a single eyebrow at him and give him a face, "You're a nut. Yes, I will absolutely go out with you tomorrow, but only if you tell me what to wear again." He fakes a sad face at me for not bringing the note but brightened back up once he heard my enthusiasm about seeing him tomorrow.

"I can do that. What are you going to do tonight?"

"Probably order some stuff for my new digs and maybe some Chinese take-out, if there is any around here. What about you?" I didn't know why he didn't ask me to hang out tonight as well, but I didn't want to bring it up unless he asked. Things were already progressing very quickly between us, and I didn't want him to burn out on me in a week.

"Finishing up on some cases this afternoon, maybe getting a workout after work. I... uh... ya. That's all," he shifts a bit on his feet and avoids my eyes. Was he hiding something?

"Oh, okay," I say wearily. "Well, I won't keep you, I have to get going anyways, bye!" I practically spun and ran away, releasing a breath I didn't know I was holding. God, I'm so awkward sometimes!

I stop to grab two bottles of wine on my way home, figuring it might be one of those nights, thinking about what my non-boyfriend/man friend was doing on a Friday when he clearly wasn't telling me the entire truth.

My cocktail of emotions made me spiral into a paradox of thoughts. While Brooks has given me no reason to distrust him, I can't ignore the yellow flags our interaction pinged inside me. I ignored my instincts once before, and it landed me in a toxic black hole of a relationship.

Am I ready to run that risk again?

Dating sucks.

Chapter 9

Persephone

———

F riday evening crawled by, minute by minute, ever since I got home from the market with two bottles of wine to sponsor the entertainment for my night. My mind was laser focused on Brooks and his potential plans, overanalyzing every moment from today to try and find a reason he was weird at the end. Was I reading this situation wrong?

Brooks had come on to me strong from the beginning, asking me personal questions, persistently taking me out, and sending me breakfast. Receiving gifts so early on is only sweet when you are equally or even more smitten with the person you are *receiving them from*. If you're not, it's creepy. An unfortunate reality and universal rule of the world of dating; *it's only weird if they don't like you.*

And I like him. I like him *a lot.*

I like his flashy lawyer smile, the way he asks inquisitive questions and waits for answers like they will solve all of the world's mysteries, and his general manners around town. I like this man who is truly kind and honest. He's loyal, funny, and sweet beyond measure. I *like* him, *despite having the residual marks from another man still peppered on me.* I like him despite my own emotional baggage telling me I don't deserve him if I keep lying to him.

I like him and now I'm scared because I hadn't heard from him since I left him at the apartment this afternoon. I'm sliding down the rabbit hole of irrational and obsessive fantasizing.

An entire bottle of wine down and four episodes of *The Vampire Diaries* later, I'm scrolling through my old Instagram account looking for anyone from my past to distract me. I had already blocked my ex and all his soulless pricks he calls friends, so there was no possibility of scrolling on something potentially upsetting. Not that they'd be posting anything lewd on their profiles, they only reserve that discomfort for face-to-face conversations.

I couldn't count how many times I would have to remove a hand that traveled way too far north on my back after a greeting hug. My mind couldn't comprehend what they might do to a female who wasn't dating their friend if they were so inappropriate with me.

The sexy and mysterious Salvatore brothers made my wine filled spiral a painful trip down self-blame lane. Do I attract men who excessively lie? Was it something I brought out in people? Was I destined to be with a man who had both a light and dark side? A ripper like Stefan? A morally grey man, depending on the year, like Damon?

The wine had gone a bit to my head as I scrolled through photos of girlfriends I hadn't talked to in months. I was still in hiding, no one knew my current location, so I was careful not to post or like anything. I was under the guise of a jolted fiancé, not a woman running away from a cheating ex. I preferred cyber stalking over obsessively overthinking about a guy I've known for a week.

I had already tried stalking Brooks on Instagram, but all his socials were super private, giving me virtually nothing to work with. The best picture I could find was his LinkedIn profile, where he looks as handsome as the day is long. Giving up my stalking, I toss the phone across the bed and focus back on the seductive smirk of Damon Salvatore.

I hear a buzz on the bed and my spine freezes, giddy excitement rockets through me to my ears. Scrambling to answer it, I unlock the screen to find the name I've been fantasizing for hours pop up.

Brooks: How's your night?

If he's texting me, he's probably not with someone else. It's only 9pm, but a first date that went poorly could have started and ended by now. I've had Tinder dates only last enough time for me to slug down a glass of Montepulciano. He could have been on a date that went lukewarm, too. He could have also just not wanted to see me. I'm not sure which answer I'd prefer at this given moment, but I push all deprecating thoughts away.

Fumbling for a response that doesn't make me seem as drunk as I currently am, I carefully type out a reply as whimsical and interesting as I can muster.

Persephone: Enjoying Georgia at night, what about you?

Technically it wasn't a lie, I was enjoying Georgia, it was at night, I was just inside, alone and ready to pop my second bottle of vino while watching TV in my hotel room. If he inferred I was out and about, that's on *him*. Assuming makes an ass of you and me.

Brooks: Just enjoying my rarely used television tonight.

Brooks: You ran out of the apartment pretty quickly earlier today. Everything ok?

Shit.

Persephone: Just forgot I had something to do, all good.

Brooks: Okay, just wanted to make sure. We still on for tomorrow?

Persephone: Of course

Persephone: Unless something came up on your end?

Although my text rang of perfect assuredness, my overactive mind is working out a few scenarios where Brooks either doesn't text me to confirm our plans for tomorrow or cancelled them. I was thrilled to be proved wrong but needed the double confirmation of the plan regardless.

Brooks: No, not at all… just wanted to check.

I pause again, uncertain what to say next, but not wanting to end the conversation just yet. My brain builds and deconstructs several texts until my phone buzzes in my hand and snaps my attention back to my screen.

Brooks: Did you do anything fun tonight?

Persephone: Define fun

Brooks: Tough question, I'll bite. The Webster Dictionary defines "fun" as enjoyment, amusement, or lighthearted pleasure. Does that help?

Persephone: Smartass.

Brooks: :-)

Persephone: Yes, I did something fun tonight.

My vagueness would annoy me if I was on the receiving end of it, but my inebriated side is not feeling guilty for my coyness. Flirting via text is a difficult art.

Brooks: You are sassy tonight, are you sure I didn't do anything wrong?

Persephone: *Shrug emoji* What about you?

Brooks: I should be sassy back and give you a similar answer, but I'll play nice. I got caught up on the administrative work I had been putting off and am now watching a movie.

He didn't have plans, or he is lying, but my gut leans towards the former. Since my earlier sketchiness was more likely due to misplaced jealousy of a fictional date concocted solely in my mind to help remove my heart from cloud 9, I decided to become more playful.

Persephone: Let me guess the movie. Give me a quote.

Brooks: You're gonna need a bigger boat.

Persephone: Too easy, Jaws.

Brooks: Where did you come from?

Persephone: Sorry?

Brooks: I just cannot imagine my luck in meeting a human like you that I enjoy more and more the more I talk with. How is that possible?

Persephone: Unsure, sounds like a problem.

Brooks: The best problem I've ever had.

I smile at that. I am an idiot for thinking anything less about him tonight, for assuming the worst.

Falling asleep that night practically smiling from ear to ear was a novelty for me. Even Harrison and I never had those moments of inundated honeymoon bliss where I'd forget the room around me and focus only on conversation. Brooks and I never dropped our cheeky banter while continuing to text for hours. At almost 1am, I joked how we probably should have made this a phone call, but instead of texting a reply that time, he rang my phone to laugh in my ear and told me to sleep tight.

Saturday afternoon rolled into the evening as I lounge around my room counting the flowers in the wallpaper trying to pass the time. It's almost two hours before my fourth date with Brooks and we had yet to "seal the deal". Another date filled with longing and abstinence was positively dreadful to consider but still excites me since it is with a man I have grown to adore in a week's time. I just wish I could physically *show him* how much I enjoyed him.

"Tell me about your wild teenage years, it must be safe to assume you were a handful for a single father," Brooks pokes at me curiously while we stroll along the boardwalk where his boat is docked.

His hand finds mine and never leaves it once we exit the boat to stretch our legs and I relished in the constant contact of his warm hands.

"I was raised by wolves," my tone is mocking, but the meaning of my words aren't entirely untrue. His eyebrows raise slightly and chokes back a laugh before realizing there is a hint of seriousness in my smirk.

"The 'cadre', I call them, my 'uncles'. Dad's group of friends would be over the house all the time, or he'd drag me to whatever bar or club they were dwelling in the back of that night. It was exciting being around them and that life," I admit with a shrug.

"You don't seem too thrilled about it now though, what happened?"

"I learned a lot about people being around them, how cruel humans can be, how even a good man can do bad things. I watched them all do bad things eventually, even my father." My eyes mist into thoughts of the past, seeing the cadre pick up women despite having girlfriends at home or make back alley deals with bad people. They *were* good men, *and are still* good men, but that didn't make what they did behind closed doors any better.

"How old were you when you started playing poker with them?" Brooks asks me inquisitively, almost non believing my tales of high stakes poker games are real.

"Remember the scene in Goodfellas where they are all at the restaurant sitting around talking like they're all holding court? That's them, minus the mafia part," my eyebrows inch up looking for a concerned reaction from him.

All I find is pure amusement and intrigue, so I continue on.

"They were raucous on their own and even more boisterous together, five of them in total. They had all gone on to own companies or restaurants, win town elections, marry, divorce, then trade in for younger wives, and give important speeches at functions. Uncle Rocco was the head, the oldest, the wealthiest, and the loudest. He had made his fortune as a hotelier but retired a few years ago to own racehorses. From what I heard; he is the one who gave my father the initial capital to start his own business many years ago."

While all the men are connected in different ways, some buddies from school or through friends and business deals, the lifelong clan I was born into accepted me as their own long ago.

"None of them are currently married or have kids of their own for a variety of reasons, but they all love me like I was theirs because I was *his*. My dad's."

I purse my lips thinking about that honor I'd carry forever; my uncles as stand in dad's. That's what they are. People who love me unconditionally, but they aren't *mine* really, they are there for when Dad can't be. And I love them all the same for even being that involved in my life.

We don't talk often, Uncle Marty will give me a call once and a while to check in on me, but they don't need to keep tabs on me.

They are perennial staples in my life, the only family I have left on this earth. I would move heaven and hell for them, as they would for me. We don't need to talk to each other every day for that to be known.

"My Dad started bringing me to their poker games when I was 10, right after my mom died and I didn't like to be home alone. They all taught me how to play cards, how to bet, how to laugh loudly, bluff bombastically, and unapologetically be myself in any crowd. My Dad taught me that too, by way of example by always being *him*self," I laugh to myself, fondly reminiscing quickly and then focusing back on Brooks. He is looking at me with his thoughtful eyes, carefully discerning where to place his next metaphorical foot to get closer to me.

But dating me is much like walking a minefield. One wrong step could send you flying in the opposite direction, twenty feet back to where you were before. I know he recognized my walls early on and considerately treaded lightly with his personal questions. It's why I was now considering offering a piece of me he hadn't asked for yet.

I had seen my faux uncles a few times these past months. We played in a handful of poker games immediately after my father's death, but I didn't consider those nights "social" outings. After my father's death, I became more of a wallflower during those nights, observing, laughing hollowly occasionally, but mostly just absorbing their good vibes while they told tales of my notorious father.

"He was the jester of the gang, always pulling a prank, saran wrapping cars or toilet papering an office after hours. He loved to laugh, he loved to watch people laugh, but loved to be the reason they laughed the most." I look up to Brooks who is astutely studying me, trying to read every facial expression I make, trying to empathize with a girl who has secrets she may never reveal willingly.

I went on, "My dad died last year." The lump in my throat forces me to swallow hard and Brooks captures my hand to press it to his mouth. He peppers kisses along my fingertips too, consoling me for the admission as much as the moment as well.

"I'm so sorry," he mumbles softly into my palm while our eyes stay locked on each other. I can see our connection like a stream of energy flowing from one heart to another. This secret opened the gate to our hearts.

My own stopped trying to protect itself and allowed my dad's memories to guide the conversation, almost like he was alive sitting with us.

"The laughter from my life died along with him, but his 'cadre' refused to dishonor him with silence. They kept laughing *because* he was gone. They laughed *for* him, in his stead. Maybe that is why I feel so connected to them all now that he passed, why I don't mind being around them when every other person makes me want to peel my skin off," I scoff to myself.

They don't pry either, just leave me to my own devices. Always a few cordial questions in the beginning of the night, "How ya doing my lady?", "How's the office?", "How's Harrison?"

Uncle Drew, the lawyer of the caste, would drive me home, give me a quick chaste kiss on the cheek and wish me well for the week. They didn't know how to handle a spiraling woman; it was half the reason they had all been divorced once or twice. They couldn't handle an emotional twister, my permanent presence was about all they had room for in their life and that was enough for me, too.

"Where did you go just now, Seph?" Brooks gently snaps me back to the conversation with a new nickname since my mind wandered aimlessly away at his question and never actually answered it.

Shaking my head while I quirked a brow at him, I ask "'Seph?'"

"I tried Persephone and you didn't respond," his chuckle was friendly and assuring, not because he thought me ignoring him was a laughing matter.

"Sorry, just thinking. My uncles are an interesting group of men." I kick a rock into the harbor, keeping my misty gaze away from Brooks' observant eyes.

"I feel like this is where I should say I'm sorry you didn't have a normal childhood like most people, but life experiences are what shape you. You wouldn't be you without them and I like you quite a lot the way you turned out, so I'm not sorry." He adds quickly, "though I wish you had what it is you desire in addition to the oddities."

His honesty levels me, a wayward thought in essence, but it is vastly more endearing than a halfhearted apology for my adolescence that was no one's fault, especially not his.

"But I am sorry you lost your dad, it's not easy losing a parent."

"Thank you," my heart sings while I look up at him through my eyelashes. Desperate to steer this topic away from me, I took the helm, "What was it like growing up here?"

He snorts a laugh, "As fun as you'd expect any southern small town. Everyone in everyone's business. Friends' daughters date their friends' sons, expecting them to get married."

"That sounds oddly specific," my nervous sarcasm slipped out as I battled back any hints of potential jealousy.

He waves a hand absently, "You'll find out eventually." He pauses and I jerk in a breath to hold, "Celia and I dated for a long while, she's my mom's best friend's daughter. We broke up in college, but our families are still thick as thieves."

He exhales as I do, strangely happy to hear it was just an old girlfriend and not anything worse. Not that I was one to talk, my baggage was not only clunkier, heavier, and much more shameful, but had a marriage proposal attached to it.

"Everyone has exes, Brooks. It's not a big deal." I wish I could use my own comforting words for myself.

"I know, this is just a strange case where I am still friendly with mine because I have to be, most likely until the day I die," he snuck a glance up at me to catch my reaction. "Not everyone can be Julia Roberts and pull a *Runaway Bride*," he chuckled, unknowing how close he was to the mark.

I force a smile back at him, knowing the joke was not pointed purposefully at me and the ex was not a true deterrent, just a minor inconvenience.

"Sounds like another sister," I joke to downplay the awkwardness that sprouts up from his admission.

His smile slides across his face, lighting up his eyes even in the dark. The man is drop dead gorgeous any time of day with his chiseled jawline, always dusted with a short 5 o'clock shadow. I like seeing him after work and after his perfectly quaffed hair breaks out of its nine to five gel bind to twist and turn whatever direction. His locks are free and wild, an odd reflection of a rather tame man.

We sit the rest of the night on his boat in the middle of the bay talking about everything under the sun while I snuggle into his side under a blanket. Words fail us at one point, when lust took over and steered the night into the direction I have been silently begging for since I met him.

My face pokes up at him while hooded lids stare back at me. Reaching to brush a stray grouping of hair away from my face, his knuckles slowly graze along my cheek.

"You're too beautiful, you know."

I preen under the moonlit compliment, inching my face closer and closer to his, trying not to lean into his touch too much. "I didn't, but it's nice to hear once and while regardless," I smirk up at him and he returns the grin.

I bite my lip while I admire his chiseled features, perfectly bronzed by a Georgian sun. His eyes dart to my mouth, and I slowly free my bottom lip from my teeth. Brooks sucks a quick breath in before he leans down so close, our noses are almost touching.

"I'm going to kiss you now, you know," his breath warms my nose, and I almost can't respond because my brain is short circuiting from sensation overload.

"I didn't, but it's nice to hear," I whisper back. His lips twitch with amusement before they softly press against mine.

Our lips explore each other, probing and slow at first. I feel his hand snake around my nape, and I let out a moan-like exhale from the erogenous contact on my neck. I haven't been touched like this in too long.

With my clear approval of his roaming hand, his other skirts under my shirt and up my back. The touch sends me into a frenzy, and I take over the kiss, turning the heat between us up a few notches.

Our bodies clearly just speak the same language, he grips me harder while I shove two hands through his messy dark mane, all the while begging for hotter open mouthed kisses.

Tongues finally find each other when our shirts start to slip off under the blanket, but our kisses don't stop, not even for a moment.

Like teenagers who couldn't control themselves, we let our baser instincts take over and passion rings free. I felt like I was having an outer body experience, like this moment wasn't mine, but someone else's I got to feel for myself. I forgot my own name, my past, forgot anything that wasn't Brooks' lips on mine, and slid deeper into the oblivion that was his touch.

Once we are both stripped bare, our lips both swollen and red, he slowly lowers me, so my back is on the blanketed deck floor and he towers over me. Never disconnecting from my skin, he keeps kissing every crevice of my neck, across my collarbone, while I try to stifle the moans escaping from me. I would do anything for this feeling to never end. Give anything, be anyone.

He could ask for my social security number and my mother's maiden name, and I would write it down and laminate it for him.

Still kissing down my neck and chest, I close my eyes and breathe him in, breathing in the scent of the water mixed with his natural boy musk. Like the ocean breeze mated with an oak tree. Strong and fierce, but also wild and free.

The blanket gives us a bit of shelter from the water's chilled wind and any late-night prying eyes. In the dark night of the bay, under poorly wrapped string lights, Brooks and I do what every ocean wave does to any boat that it crosses in its path. We crashed into each other.

Over and over and over.

We rocked that boat. All. Night. Long.

Chapter 10

Persephone

_____

L aying in a sea of tangled sheets and napkins from my earlier breakfast in bed, I feel my phone vibrate from under me.

There's only one person on God's green earth that has my number these days and coincidentally, it's the only person that makes my heart race.

Brooks: Hey there darling, how's your morning?

I sigh, phone clasped to my chest as I roll over into my pillows in "early stages of dating" bliss. You know that part where everything they do is just perfect? Where he could have told me he murdered someone for me and I'd smile and say "how romantic, he wants to protect me".

Yeah. That's where I am right now.

Persephone: As good as it gets, how's work today?

Brooks: Another day, another dollar.

I snort a rush of air from my nose as a shortened chuckle, picturing him shrugging while saying it in person. Another text comes in before I can respond.

Brooks: I know we just saw each other a day ago, but are you up for another date tonight?

The smile that slices across my face could cut a pear in half.

Persephone: I surely am, what do you have in mind?

Brooks: I happened across tickets to the hottest show in town, I'd rather not say exactly what, but I think you'll love it.

Heat finds my cheeks in adornment, the man could do no wrong, even when I fiercely hate surprises like this- where I can't gauge the activity for attire. Like he read my mind in that moment of pause, another text pops up on my screen.

Brooks: I can hear you thinking from here. Jeans are fine, I'll pick you up at 6:30. ;-)

The afternoon flies by without warning, and I find myself for once in my life, late and scrambling. I am a prepared person, one who plans my time accordingly, and does not typically procrastinate or lollygag, especially before a date.

I chalk the strange behavior up to nerves, for when was the last time I went on a date with a guy like Brooks? Not Harrison, that's for sure.

The two are practically opposite, despite their similar office attire. Brooks is jovial and cool, nothing rattled him or threw him where Harrison is a ball of fire, exploding randomly. Harrison is volatile, with his emotions rarely in check. The unpredictability of him was always alluring to me, as someone who is so insanely predictable.

Well, it was alluring until a few weeks ago when I left him, seemingly out of nowhere. I smirked at the thought of Harrison coming home, expecting the same broken mess as the day before only to find half the apartment empty, my draws cleaned, and no ability to contact me.

I might have paid to see the reaction if it didn't send a tingle of fear down my spine, coupled with a flash of frightening memories.

Forgoing any major effort to my hair, I pin it up into a messy bun quickly and grab my purse only a second before I hear the telling triple knock. I spin towards the door, practically leaping to open it with an unrestrained smile.

We already sealed the deal two nights ago on his boat, multiple times actually, so there is no reason to tone myself down. He still wants to be with me, still wants to text me and call me, and take me out on dates. I suppose it can change at any moment, but everything in me told me it won't. That this feeling inside me would only grow with every second I spent smiling back at him.

As if I was staring back at a mirror of happiness, Brooks' grin may supersede my own in excitement. Carrying a single sunflower, gingerly extending it out to me, Brooks gives me an appraising graze of my body and says, "You look perfect."

I ignore the flower for a moment to step into his space, slowly curling my hand over her shoulder to press a kiss to his mouth. Brooks didn't hesitate to deepen the kiss while wrapping his hands around my waist and sliding them up my back with a groan. I feel his smile in our kiss before he turns to peck my cheek and whisper in my ear.

"I could get used to greetings like this."

I purr my agreement and nuzzle my cheek into his face where he keeps giving me soft pecks along my jaw.

"As much as I want to continue this, we do have to get going…" Brooks mumbles when I catch his lip with my teeth.

I have never attacked a man like this before before picking me up from a date, but the two days we spent apart made me weak with need for him. I wanted nothing more than to rub my entire body along his for hours, to get as close as possible and never leave.

Pulling away, I fake pout, then step back from him to close my door. Brooks' gaze didn't leave my face for a moment when I worked the door's lock, nor did his smirk.

"Come on, cambion, or we'll miss… showtime," Brooks chuckles and entwines his hand through mine to lead me outside to his car.

We pull up to… what looks like a baseball stadium.

"I didn't think Georgia had a team…?" I muse, half to myself.

Brooks laughs and says, "The Savannah Bananas sell out almost every game, these tickets are practically worth their weight in gold."

My laugh chortles up, "Excuse me? Did you say Savannah Bananas?" I couldn't hide my amusement in the name or the fact their games were a hot commodity around these parts.

"Yes, the Bananas are widely regarded in these lands, here Miss Persephone. I've secured only the best for my girl," he winks and rocks himself out of the car to quickly open my door on the other side.

Frozen in shock by both his admission that I am "his girl" and the anomaly of a not even minor league baseball team garnering this much press, Brooks makes it to the other side in ample time to open the door for me.

Taking his outstretched hand, I find my other one to press against my mouth in awed shock. This beautiful and extremely polished man is really taking me to a podunk baseball game as a date.

I have never been more excited.

We find our seats on the third base line, almost directly behind the dugout. Fans are pouring in for the sold-out game, which were kids and adults alike. Brooks and I were not the only two lovers on a date, the stadium is filled with all types of fans from young to old.

There is a deep sense of community here. Not like the Bleacher Creatures of Yankee Stadium, who are drunken fans seeking the cheapest seats in the park to watch their favorite team, but more like a small collective of neighbors, enjoying a night of entertainment.

The pre-game activities were wrapping up, the crowd pumpers were doling out free shirts to wild fans cheering. Hell, there was a man in a full-blown banana costume jumping up and down for free swag.

It is like nothing I'd ever seen. I'm sure my face is as stunned as my eyes when I catch Brooks covering his mouth in silent laughter.

I whip towards him, "What? What's so funny?"

He only raises his eyebrows in guilt and turns towards the rowdy crowd to our right, "Just taking in the scene."

I give him a questioning glare, then say, "I can't believe this is where you took me tonight…"

Brooks sobers quickly, almost nervous, and speaks, "Do you really not want to stay? We can leave whenever you'd like. I just thought…"

Feeling horrible from my tone deafness, I cut him off, "NO! No, not at all. This is incredible. I just am dumbstruck right now at how… passionate the fans are. That's all, I swear." I try to smile at him to make him feel my sincerity, then press a quick kiss to his lips to emphasize it.

He grins back, "Okay, do you want a drink? I'll go grab some for us."

"Hmmm, I'd love a beer, I think," Brooks nods and gets up to squire us beverages. I greedily take in the fantastic view of his ass in slacks before he turns to go up the aisle and disappears.

I spend the next ten minutes taking in the scene, which includes fans with Bananas masks on, the team dancing their way to their positions, and music blaring for their aid.

Some players did front flips and handsprings, and choreographed dances on their way out. It is like going to a circus, not a baseball game.

Brooks made his way back with two beers in hand, a bucket of popcorn, some peanuts popping out from his pocket, twin hot dogs balanced on the beers, and a boyish grin smattered on his face from all the food.

The scene made me break into laughter before I shot up to help him carry the dogs at least the rest of the way down the row.

"Oh good, I didn't miss the first pitch," Brooks remarks while taking the first bite into his hotdog.

My stupid face's default setting was a lovesick smile with doe eyes. Everything from the moment he picked me up earlier tonight felt totally surreal. Like I was in a fake world, with a fake man, and on a fake date.

"You okay? You're looking at me weird," Brooks mumbles with a bit of hotdog still in his mouth.

Shaking my head to clear me of my haze, "Yes, I'm perfect, this is perfect." I grabbed his free hand and gave it a squeeze as we watched the first pitch start the antics of this peculiar baseball game.

By the 5th inning, we are four beers deep, hysterically laughing with the group of middle-aged men next to us, singing along to "Sweet Caroline" as the teams switches to the field.

The back of my head was blistering pain from how much I was laughing at Brooks' side comments, at the players who are there more for amusement than baseball, and indiscriminately, with the crowd of this game.

He is teetering the line of tipsy as he nuzzles into my ear to talk privately, whispering random anecdotes, "This is a ballpark, you know? Not a stadium. Doesn't have the same vibe, right?"

He pulls back to look for my agreement, and I try to hide my smile as I nod along with him.

Brooks is right though. The seats are wood benches, not plastic bucket seats like you'd find at Yankee Stadium. It was a small park, no seats even in the outfield. It honestly feels more like a D1 college field than anything. But there is something very special about this park, about this place.

I feel a sense of community while I am here, like I am part of something so big and so small at the same time. If I never saw Brooks again in my life after tonight, I'd still hold this moment in time near and dear to my heart, for I'd never experienced anything like it before.

I thought of my dad sitting in the seat next to me, he'd get a kick out of this. He'd love the dancing bananas, the constant beach balls popping up along the crowd, the giant shark blow up that made its way across the rows, and of course the jacked-up Banana mascot with Ray-Bans on.

"I seriously can't believe how fun this game is, and they're losing by like 10," I mutter to Brooks.

"Shh, don't say that too loud, the fans aren't here to watch them win, darling, just *entertain*," Brooks winks and looks back towards the field where the half inning was finally starting.

"If you could be a mascot, who would you be?" I ask out of nowhere, with Split the Banana in mind.

Brooks turns to me and huffs a laugh, "Well, that's a doozy… hmm. It would have to be someone super cool."

After a moment of silent contemplation, Brooks scares me when he jumps in front of me and exclaims, "Introducing the World's Strongest Banana! The King of Potassium! Please welcome, Split!" Then he points towards me to finish the shtick.

I flinch hard from the sudden movements, throwing my hands up to protect my face, but not as badly as if I were sober. I hope Brooks didn't notice or find my reaction too exaggerated. I quickly recover and hop into position, fake flexing my biceps, as if I was anywhere near as jacked as that damn banana. We both break out into hysterics at the pathetic parody attempt and fall into each other's sides, forgetting about the question asked.

Brooks and I stagger our way back to the car, cackling like children while reliving memories of the game. Like when the third baseman did the worm every time he ran on the field to his position, or the giant cup snake that the fans behind us were building. They stacked empty beer cups on top of one another until it formed a long snake that practically made it from the top of the section to the bottom before security politely asked them to "break up the snake into smaller snakes" for safety reasons. We contributed our beer cups to the cause, of course.

When we get into the car, we chat idly more about the game, and a little bit about Split, the very strong banana.

I repeat the question from before, "You didn't answer me, mister." I poke him hard in the shoulder and feign a hurt arm while he yelps.

"You're sure serious about your mascots, ma'am. Do I sense a fetish?" He volleys back.

My face flushed, embarrassed by my repeated question.

"Oh my god, no! You just… didn't answer it before!" I stutter.

Brooks laughs at my uncertainty. "I'm kidding."

"Oh…" I nibble my lip and wait in deafening silence for him to change the topic.

He grows intensely quiet while he pinches his lower lip in thought. I zoned him out, trying to think of anything else but my awkward blunder to cap off this very delightful night. I want to both stick my head in the sand forever or get into bed with him to forget this in other ways.

More deviant ways.

Brooks ends the silence though, and my growing sexual thoughts, like we are in the middle of a conversation. "My initial thought was like maybe Michigan's, he's a wolverine. That seems pretty cool, right?" Brooks flexes his hand in emphasis on the claws.

I try to giggle cutely, fully breaking myself out of my shell of ambivalence, "And why would you pick him?"

"Well, much easier to open Amazon packages and envelopes, don't you think? I am a man who opens many envelopes." Brooks took a quick moment off the road to glance at me, hoping to find a hint of amusement in me.

"You're nuts. That's not what I meant!" I laugh and nudg his shoulder, my hand buzzing from the contact.

We are getting closer to my place, closer to the end of one of the best dates I've ever been on in my life. I don't want it to end. My laughter dies, and I go deep into my own mind again, now to wonder if I should just invite him up and how that would play out.

Did he assume he is already invited up since we already slept together a few nights before?

Did he just want to get home and go to bed because he probably has work the next morning? Client meetings or calls, I'm sure. Maybe even court.

And if he does come up, what would we do? I lick my lips in anticipation, at the mere thought of repeating our night on the boat, on a bed. Clearly my body wants one thing, but is my mind ready to let him into my space as well?

Noticing my silence once again, Brooks continues on, "Benny the Bull could be cool too.He got to hang out with Michael Jordan."

"What?" I snort.

"Your mascot question. I think my vote is Benny. It would have been cool to play quarters with MJ before the game with his security dude."

My thoughts of indecision wash away from me because I am completely enamored by this beautiful, lovely, innocent man.

A man who never stops making me laugh, not cry like Harrison.

He is too good, too pure, too *everything*, to be *anything* like my ex.

At this moment, I know I can trust to invite Brooks up tonight into my home.

Moreover, I can trust to invite Brooks up into my heart.

Chapter 11

Persephone

———————

I t's been four months since I left NYC and nothing has been sweeter than my life in Georgia.

I still work part time at the coffee shop. I have a few friends at work, Michael and Shannon, who are 21-year-old baristas trying to get through college while working full time. Next month for Christmas I'm going to give them a little of my inheritance to help pay their college loans off and go backpacking through Europe after college. They are hardworking, good kids who just don't have the finances to go away to college. My dad had paid for mine, I felt like I am paying it forward by giving to them.

My hope is they can enjoy their last semester senior year and not have to work so much. My worry is they wouldn't be able to keep their mouths shut about it and tell the whole goddamn town. I'll have to scare them to make sure they don't let it out to anyone.

Aside from their work ethic, they make me laugh. After months of watching the world spin around me, I am finally part of the conversation again. I *wanted* to be part of the conversations going on around me again. Michael and Shannon reminded me of easier times with less responsibility and worry. Our friendships reflected that, too.

I was envious of their youth and addicted to their lack of awareness. Shannon is an attractive brunette with a short little bob cut that perfectly framed her face. She has thick rimmed glasses I have never seen her without paired with a cute ballcap, she is the epitome of a barista. My soul sung for her sarcasm and relentless torture of poor Michael, who is hopelessly in love with her.

He has never told me as much, but I watch him watch *her* longingly from across the counter, or when she isn't paying attention while restocking. Michael is cute in his own right, still awkward from his young age. He will fill out to be a heartthrob once his chest fills out. Mark my words, come 25 years old, Michael will get any woman he wants with his flirty smile and boyish good looks.

He has some work to do in the maturity department and needs to shake his nerves around the ladies, but I am confident he will grow into it eventually. The melodrama of young love kept my days interesting, watching the two of them orbit each other with different motives while I sprinkle hints of each other's attraction along the way.

One time, I left a flower from Brooks' house on top of Shannon's car to see how Michael would react, maybe giving him the push to finally ask her out. He huffed and puffed around the store for two days until he got the nerve to ask her who gave her the flower. When she admitted she didn't know *or care,* he finally let it go and chalked it up to a weird customer. He didn't ask her out though, to my displeasure.

I feel myself come back to life with every prank and giggle. Michael loves to roll up tiny paper towel balls and throw them at Shannon or leave them next to the register. It drives her nuts to find them, but I saw the small curl of her lip one time when she spotted one. The games were always in good fun, and it has nurtured my soul to see the innocence of young love blossoming while my own was as well.

Harrison has tried to contact me a few times via email, demanding I call him or write him back. The first few times were on the friendlier side, but the last few were demanding and mean. He keeps saying I took something that didn't belong to me, and he wanted it back. I have no idea what he means, nothing I took was worth much, mostly just antique furniture from my grandma that held no value except sentiment. I thought maybe the engagement ring, which I pawned immediately after coming to town, but he would have just asked for it back and not been so elusive about it.

I didn't feel bad pawning the ring. *He* was the one who cheated.

If work and removing myself from NYC has been therapeutic, my relationship with Brooks was soul mending. He has been the most incredible boyfriend who smothers me with affection, attention, love and everything in between. Our sex is magical, our conversations are intellectual, and our time together has been nothing short of perfection.

The room I rented ended up being better than I thought, too. I got a king size mattress in there with a cute chaise and a chair. Brooks and I didn't go there much anyways, I mostly stayed at his house, unless I was working the next day, then we'd stay at mine.

Our life was easy-breezy like that. We went wherever the wind took us. We made our relationship official about two weeks after we slept together for the first time. Brooks just blurted it out one day when I was making us dinner at my apartment. He said he couldn't hold it in any longer, that all he wanted to do since our first date was ask me to be exclusive with him.

It warmed my heart he liked me so much so early on, especially since the feeling was extremely mutual. We fell into an almost everyday habit of seeing each other that felt healthier than any relationship I had thus far.

Being with Brooks was as natural as breathing. Some nights he would work late, and I would just nestle in the crook of his shoulder and read a book. Xanax was usually the only thing that would calm me out of a panic attack, but Brooks gave me such a sense of peace that I never got to that level where panic would hit. I trusted him with my life and more importantly, my heart.

We went on dates to local food spots, even traveled hours or overnight to find a good spot to try out. I tried not to get too weird about going North, but even the mention of going to NYC to try out a good Italian dinner put my teeth on edge.

Brooks had noticed.

"Are we ever going to talk about your abhorrent aversion to your hometown? Or will that just be our pet elephant in the room for eternity?" He'd joke.

"I quite like elephants, Brooks, so don't tempt me," I'd tease back. It was never seriously discussed or pressed upon, but I knew it grated on him deep down. He knew I wasn't telling him everything about myself or my past, and the kind soul he is, never forced me to tell him more than I was willing to.

We didn't talk much about my time before coming to Dorian, Georgia, but the few things I did share were vague. I admitted my father dying was a catalyst for moving across the country, along with a 'series of unfortunate events' that I never went into detail on and avoided whenever he asked me about them. He never pressed or questioned my motivation for concealing the truth from him, he just asked that I try to tell him when I was ready.

The lie that weighed on me the most was my lie of omission about my current financial standing and my ex-engagement. Every time exes came up, he never directly asked me if I had been engaged before, so I never felt compelled to share that tidbit of information. It felt like if I opened that one wound, it would show the rest of my damage. He'd see the part of me I've been hiding from him all this time, the part where I deserved a little bit of the abuse Harrison doled out on me, the part where I was a failure of a partner and a fiancè.

To my immense pleasure, we never talked about money or the future either. Brooks lived his life 3-5 days at a time, hardly ever looking past 'next week', which made sense why he only just now told me about his sister's wedding that was to take place two weekends from now.

"Hey, I, uhm, need to ask you about something, Seph, but you can't get mad," Brooks said to my shoulder while twirling my still brown hair around his fingers and stroking the other hand down my arm. I never went back to blonde, never mentioned my old hair color to Brooks either.

I opened my eyes and turned towards him, "Uh oh, what now? Did you buy another chicken?"

Brooks had a soft spot for farm animals, even though he didn't know how to care for them in any regard. He just liked the idea of having chickens and pigs and goats. When he bought the first six chickens, I nearly fell out of my seat laughing. Then we spent the next four days constructing a chicken coup and reading about how to care for them so they wouldn't die. Always an adventure with Brooks and his big heart.

It was no wonder I kept all my secrets close to my chest. I couldn't risk losing him, I couldn't survive losing him.

Brooks slid his hands around my waist, with my chest to his back and his mouth to my ear.

"No, it's much more serious and I'm sorry I haven't asked you yet, I just wasn't sure how to, and I think you're going to say no, but I really don't want you to say no…" He rambles on quickly. "My sister is just demanding an answer as soon as possible…"

I twist around to face him, "Brooks, you're scaring me now. Just ask me. I won't be angry," that was a lie. I might very well be angry, but I would do my damn best not to be.

Brooks look down at our hands, now tangled together in between us, "I know you never want to go back… bu-"

It's been four months of me evading the same question and four months of Brooks being understanding of my aversion to talking about my past. Every now and again, when the conversation permits, he'll bring up New York casually, most time pertaining to his sister. Sometimes I don't even pretend to respond, others I clam up and tell him "I don't want to talk about that part of my life".

He usually shrugs it off, but the intelligent and perceptive man collects each of my responses to categorize and study them later. I can feel with each brush off his mounting desire to piece all my off handed comments to string a theory together to arraign me with.

I immediately knew where this was going so I cut him off at the pass. "No."

"Seph…"

"No. I'm not going back to New York, out of the question," I walk away from him and continue folding clothes that were left out on the chaise to keep myself from screaming at him. It is my cancelled wedding weekend, and I had no interest in flying into my hometown to possibly run into anyone, *especially* not this weekend.

"Sephy… It's, uh, for my sister's wedding," he mumbles.

I whip my head towards him and shoot daggers with my eyes. "Your what's what now?"

"Sister's wedding…"

"Repeat that for me. The whole thing."

"My sister's wedding," he said a bit more loudly while clearing his throat. "She's getting married in a town outside of NYC, in, like Westchester or something. I forget what she said, I can look up the town. It's not Manhattan though. I wouldn't have asked you if it were Manhattan," he looked at me earnestly with sad eyes, knowing how much it's killing me for him to even ask. He knew how I felt about going home, how it only housed painful memories for me. I've let him think those memories were solely of my father, not my old life.

Westchester was a better scenario than the city itself, it's the county that neighbors the Bronx. My main concern was flying into JFK or LaGuardia, but if it's in Westchester, I'll just fly into White Plains, which is a smaller airport about 20 miles outside of the city. I'd pay more for the ticket, but it would be worth every penny to avoid the possibility of running into anyone I knew. Lord knows with my luck I'd run into the gaggle of old girlfriends flying off for a weekend trip or co-workers en route on a business trip. Or worse, *him*.

While I stayed in minor touch with Aisley, very sparingly and without any details about my whereabouts, I didn't know if the rest of my co-workers had tried to contact me or not. I had never doled out my personal email address prior, and Aisley understood enough that I wasn't looking for people to reach out, despite their intentions. Aisley hadn't said as much either, she kept our conversations short and to the point, filling me in about my replacement and office politics occasionally. My reciprocation was only to ask questions, never provide answers or offer information about my life.

Any intel about me could lead back to *him*. And that wasn't something that was worth risking.

"Maybe. Depends on the town," I say quickly, making sure to not take too much time in between responses, even when my thoughts flutter into a million directions.

Brooks grabs his phone and taps the screen, looking at something on his internet browser. "It says here, New Rochelle? VIP is the venue. Looks like a regular banquet hall type thing. Black tie, not surprising for my sister," he reads off his phone from her wedding website.

My stomach rolls.

Ugh, New Rochelle is a popular wedding location. They have four wedding venues lined up that face the Long Island Sound with pretty water views. I had no interest in getting married there, but Harrison's mother was desperate for her son to be married at one of the venues. It was part of the status quo for his mother's upper echelon of friends.

"New Rochelle is near the Bronx. It's 20 minutes outside Manhattan," I explain lifelessly. "Brooks, I really don't feel comfortable going. You know I would love to go with you if it were any place else…"

"I know Seph, I do. It's just…" he sounds a little annoyed, "it's really hard to hear you say all this and have no idea why you have such an aversion to your hometown and home state. I'm flying blind here and I have been for *four months*," he rifles his frustration at me like a basketball to my gut. I wasn't expecting this level of animosity. It has clearly been building under the surface for some time now, unbeknownst to me.

I have the delusional thought that if I keep feeding him small snippets of my life, it will be enough to hold him off from demanding the answers to the bigger questions. The questions I had avoided with subtle indignation.

It's not fair for me to pick and choose what parts of my life I share with him. It's not fair I'm hiding so much, but I can't bring myself to admit to the truth. I'm too scared of the judgement.

People's parents die all the time, not everyone goes into a tailspin, 6-month depression where they cancel their wedding and detach from their friends and loved ones. But I did, and the embarrassment I felt about my circumstance, the position I had been in with Harrison was my own fault.

Brooks' dad died, too. He didn't lose his mind like I did. People's parents die every day, and they don't have a mental breakdown for months like I did.

We only talked about his father once.

We were laying on the bow of his boat, watching the stars flutter above us when he said, *"This was my dad's boat."*

I stiffened, unfamiliar with this form of empathy since my own father's passing. But Brooks, the damn bleeding heart, kept going. "I miss him a lot, we all do. No one likes to admit to it though, like if we don't mention dad, it won't hurt as much. But I miss him and I'm not afraid to tell you that."

I snorted and said under my breath, "I wish that was the case, I'd be entirely over it myself."

"I'm sorry, Persephone," I could tell he didn't want to push anymore than I'd given him tonight. Didn't want to rock the boat; physically or metaphorically. I hadn't exactly been forthcoming on other personal topics, like why I moved down here in the first place and he probably figured I'd be as timid about this as well.

He picked up on my apprehension to share and spewed his own feelings instead, "The months after he died... Hell, my friends took me out every weekend for two months to drown my sorrows, until eventually life became a little more normal. Whatever normal is after... that." He shrugged and his gaze drifted from the distant stars to the glassy film collecting over my eyes.

He was normal, his grief was normal. He mourned, and didn't shut out his friends like I did. Didn't crumble apart like I did. Didn't call off a wedding and ruin a relationship like I did.

We never spoke about it again after that night.

"I'm sorry Brooks, I can't talk about it," I shove the metaphorical ball back just as hard.

"Yeah, I know. You can never talk about it," he says mockingly. We've had this conversation before, but never so tumultuous or turbulent. He is genuinely mad for the first time in our budding romance.

I turn on my heel so fast to point a finger at him, "That's not fair, you have *no* idea what you're talking about."

"You're right, I don't and that's the problem," Brooks starts gathering his clothes to leave. A *dramatic exit* doesn't work on a woman like me. It takes several minutes of silence for him to get dressed and gather his things before he stands in front of me waiting for me to tell him to stay. I was not about to open up just because he has threatened to leave, but his eyes are begging me to tell him to stay.

"I think you should probably go now," I whisper while trying to hold back all my angry tears that are pressing up against the corners of my eyes. I could see the hope in his face fall to the floor along with a sock he dropped.

"I am," and without looking at me again or grabbing the sock, he leaves.

I reach for my bottle of pills on the counter to pop one in and relax. I am angry at him, but simultaneously feel so much guilt for making him anything less than happy. We've been in a perfect cocoon of bliss for months. Going on dates, having incredible sex, sneaking to each other's houses every night and waking up in each other's arms every morning.

It's like the happiness I've accrued here makes the previous 6 months before it feels more palatable. He's made my life more palatable. He's made everything more palatable, without an ounce of explanation from me why I am the way I am. Why I was so guarded, why I needed Xanax, why I flinched so hard at loud noises. He gave and gave without asking for a crumb of me in return.

His disappointment was directly tied to my inability to tell him the truth of my situation, a truth he's long deserved. And that's entirely on me.

We didn't talk for three whole days after that fight. We had never had a disagreement to this magnitude before, so neither of us knew how to handle each other in the days following. Harrison would continue to text me household things when they popped up, like if we had to get eggs or milk, and he'd be cordial until eventually flowers would show up at the office, or I'd send him a new tie. We never talked about anything further, someone just had to surrender first. It was usually me.

I wasn't sure how my fight with Brooks would pan out. We both were headstrong and stubborn, but Harrison and Brooks were not the same. Harrison wanted me to be involved in his antics, while Brooks just wanted to know a small piece of my past. He wasn't asking for more than a boyfriend should. He wasn't asking for very much at all, I just wasn't willing or in the position to give it.

Unfortunately, I held all the cards; I either go to NY for his sister's wedding, or I tell him why I can't go to NY for his sister's wedding, which he may or may not accept as a reason to not go. The latter seemed absolutely nonexistent as an option. Every time I went to form the words in my head, my body seized up and tears started pouring out of me. Panic wrapped around me without Brooks there to soothe me.

How could I ever tell him what truly happened? He'd never look at me the same again. He'd see me as weak, stuck behind a desk with no backbone, mourning the loss of a parent in an abnormally unhealthy way. He'd find out how much money I have and would judge me.

I couldn't tell him about Harrison. I need to figure out a way to get to this wedding and get the fuck home to Georgia without being seen.

Thinking back to dad's letter, I squeeze my eyes shut and exhale. He told me to take risks, not hide. I want to move on, want to set roots and start building a new life with the sweet, affectionate, thoughtful man I met here in Georgia. I want to stop fleeing from my problems.

I booked a flight from Savannah to White Plains, NY on Saturday morning, the day of the wedding, then the 11am flight home on Sunday. I'll be in and out of New York State within 24 hours. How bad could it be?

After printing the tickets in the back room of the coffee house, I strut my cute ass down to Brooks' office at the end of the block. Plopping into the office chair opposite Brooks' desk, he glances up and tries to hide the quirk of his lips that peaked on his face once he registeres me sitting there.

"What can I do for you Ms. Kline?" He tries to hide his excitement with annoyance, but I could tell he is thrilled to see me just as much as I am to see him. This silence and time apart are the most we had in four months of dating, and I could tell he was as miserable as me by the bags under his eyes. My eyes are swollen from crying. His are dark with circles.

Nervous butterflies flit through me. I am excited to give him the news that I am going because I know it would end this fight for now and he'd be happy again. We'd be back to normal, and I could melt back into his again in bed.

Pushing the plane ticket across the desk folded up, he raises a single brow in question and goes to grab the papers from under my hand. I stop and pull them back for a second, teasing, "This is me saying I'm sorry for how I reacted the other day," and he nodded in agreement. I slide it the rest of the way towards him.

Sitting back and watching him unfold the paper, his blank face went from zero to sixty with excitement. He lunges out of his seat and picks me up in his arms to squeeze and kiss me all over.

"Thank you, Persephone, thank you, thank you," Brooks keeps kissing me all over my face.

"I'll be missing all the pre-activities, but I'm sure you'll be able to come up with a cover for me. Do you forgive me?" I say with mock puppy dog eyes, knowing his reaction is forgiveness enough.

"Yes, all is forgiven." Brooks absently waves a sarcastic and theatrical hand before he envelopes me into a hug where my face tucked into his shoulder.

"God, Seph, it's been the worst three days without you. I didn't know how we were going to solve this one, but I was hours away from giving in and saying sorry so I could talk to you again," Brooks picks me up again and presses a hundred quick kisses to the top of my head while I fight a genuine smile.

I am kicking myself internally though too. I should have just waited him out. Damn it.

"I missed you, baby."

I mutter into his chest, "I missed you too."

PART 2

Brooks

Chapter 12

Brooks

———

Persephone's arrival has me anxious and giddy since I touched down on Thursday. I want the weekend to be enjoyable even though I am still feeling uncertain about our communication abilities after this past fight. While she eventually did see my side, I practically had to throw an ultimatum her way to garner it.

I'm not sure if that is a tribute to how tenacious and stubborn my girlfriend is, or an indication of how lacking of a lawyer I am that I couldn't win a simple argument. I try not to think about it too hard. She is here soon and all I want to do is have fun at our first wedding together as a couple.

She has yet to meet my mother, who spends half her year in Florida with her sisters, or my own sister, who hasn't come back to Georgia in months. Both women are important parts of my life, and I am thrilled for all three of them to converge, knowing they would all get along perfectly.

Blaire and I didn't get along much when we were younger, she was always a little jealous of my academic success, but with time and her own professional success in the business world, we found more common ground. She often calls me on the way home from big events or dinners, half to brag about who she was rubbing elbows with and half to check in on her very single and lonely brother.

Blaire's questions and actions always carry duality, or ulterior motive. She often asks how I am, who I'm dating, or what I've been up to, knowing my chatty self will openly share without thinking twice. But my small-town life, my small-town tales of bad dates with girls from high school makes her feel better about her own decisions.

While I should care, I don't. I love my sister despite her malice. I love her because even though every overly expensive Christmas present is smeared with flaunt, she's still thinking of me enough to buy a present she knows I would like.

I'm a glass half full kind of guy, and I don't mind seeing the best in people instead of the worst.

Persephone, on the other hand, is genuinely a good person. She over tips servers, holds every door, and does errands for her elderly landlord when she needs it. She asks inquisitive questions and makes people feel like they are being heard, not just spoken to. My girlfriend is one of a kind, and her coming to New York for me showed me how she could be willing to put my feelings first. It was something I had never had before in a relationship.

I have been hooked on her the second I saw her at the diner talking to Celia. She was like a beacon of light shining in the dark, beckoning my boats to land. I have never seen a woman so beautiful, which really said something since Celia was standing right next to her and was known as the town beauty.

Persephone's long mane and those striking green eyes were enough to reel me in, then when I saw her again at the coffee shop, I knew I had to make a move. Each time I saw her after that, I was scheming up a way to see her again and again, until it was implied we'd be together every weekend, then every night.

It might have been her beauty that attracted me, but it was her wit that kept me coming back for more. It was her sarcasm, taste in movies and music, and indisputable fire within her that kept me in a constant state of awe since that night at the steak house. She was as sharp as a tact, quick as hell, and has kept me on my toes every second since we met.

I found myself laughing out loud in my office thinking about things she has said on dates or in texting conversations. She enjoys long silences which make her witty outbursts all the more impactful. I thought I would die of rejection if she started pulling away or declining my dinner invitations. She never did, thankfully, and my heart has never sung so happily after each acquiesce for our dates.

Blinking out of my daydream of my girlfriend, I remember where I am. The rehearsal dinner is uneventful, something Seph didn't need to be at, I rationalize, though the thought of her there makes my heart squeeze. My family asked where she was, and I made up an excuse about how the flights were booked because I told her about the wedding too late. It was reasonable enough for me to forget. It also took the blame off her shoulders and onto mine. No one needed to know the truth, or even half the truth. I wanted them to have a blank canvas for a first impression, not her already in the hole trying to dig her way out.

No matter the reason for her absence, I wish she was here. It has only been two days and we Facetimed both nights, but I miss seeing her in person. Miss feeling the soft skin all over her, missed sleeping next to her and waking up to her face.

I glance down the table, regarding each of the bridal party members and their dates with cool indifference. They're not my type of people, too swanky and high hatted. They drink too much, talk too loud, and brag too often.

Graham, my sister's soon to be husband, is a nice guy as far as I can tell. He dotes on my sister, my mother seemed to love him, and the aunts swooned over him kissing their hands. He seemed to be less affectionate with his buddies around, but what guy isn't to some degree?

I can't put my finger on why I have a strange feeling swirling in my gut, but I can feel it there. Maybe it is nerves for my sister, excitement for Seph to land tomorrow morning, or my protective brother nature rearing its head.

My sister grabs me by the collar and yanks me down to hug her. She is drunk and happy, and I am happy for her to have found the kind of love I have with Persephone. The easy kind, where it flows out of you and into every aspect of your life, inseminating joy to everyone around you, where you exude glee. That's how Seph makes me feel, like I am a bird feeder of happiness for everyone to feed off of. I am glad to share the wealth.

I wrap brotherly arms around her waist, pat her back, and let her prance off to the next neck to hang on, her fiancé's groomsman, I think.

When the after-rehearsal-dinner-party moves to Blaire and Graham's room, I notice the drugs and liquor in their bathroom. The piles of coke are more than I have ever seen, but I chalk it up to being with an upper echelon of the NYC crowd that my sisters and Graham's friends seemed to be. The groomsmen and bridesmaids are shifting in and out of there gradually as I sit in a chair and take in the room. It wasn't like I haven't done drugs in my life or am even super opposed to it now since I am only 32 years old, but it does feel excessive to do on the night before your wedding.

It is a large suite with extravagant drapes and furnishings. It looks like there's just one master room, but multiple bathrooms and a large kitchen, dining area, and living room. People are bopping around, swaying to the music that's pouring out from a bluetooth speaker somewhere. Blaire is cackling in the corner, drinking a martini and somehow never spilling it from it's gravity defying glass.

The scene is not my comfort zone, so I text Seph instead.

Brooks: hey, I miss you.
Persephone: I miss you too. How is the dinner?
Brooks: We moved to the after party. It was nice, my mom loves Graham.

Everyone looooves Graham.

Persephone: Does Brooks loooove Graham too?
Brooks: He's a good guy. I have a weird feeling I can't shake, but I can't tell if it's because I'm anxious for you to get here already, or if

it's something about the wedding, or maybe I'm just nervous to walk Blaire down the aisle tomorrow.

Persephone: Whatever it is, your gut is usually right. Remember when you had a bad feeling about the milk when you smelled it? And it was actually expired?

She's making fun of me and I fucking love it.

Brooks: oooo you're a funny one tonight. When does your flight land tomorrow?

Persephone: 1:30pm, they changed the flight again. I should make it just in time. I'm going to just fly in full hair and make-up and bring my gown, get dressed at the venue.

Brooks: As long as you make it to the reception, no one will notice. There's gonna be like 250 people there.

Persephone: Thanks for the vote of confidence. LOL get to bed, sir, it's getting late and you have an important job to do tomorrow!

Brooks: Dance with my lady?

Persephone: Yes, that among other things…

Brooks: oooo, now we're talking! Pls bring that lacy black number for later.

Persephone: I'll see what I can do ;-)

Brooks: Goodnight baby.

Persephone: Night. <3

The day has been a blur from the second I woke up. I ran out for coffees when needed, I relayed Blaire and Graham's presents to each other. I played coordinator and shuttle, getting the old Nana's to the venue early, then from the front door to their seats.

By the time I got to shower, it was time to go to the venue. My phone has been on silent the whole day, so I didn't hear or feel the buzz of Seph's calls, but on the ride over, I saw the 10 missed ones and no text messages. It makes me nervous she isn't going to show up today and left an iron knotted ball in the pit of my stomach. How would I explain to all my family if she didn't show up?

I can't shake the feeling of dread and I got frustrated that I am now worrying about Seph instead of focusing on my sister on her special day. My mom must have read it all over my face because she pulled me aside and asked what was wrong.

"It's nothing, Mom. Seph just called me a bunch but didn't leave a message and now she's not answering," I reply while also trying to walk back into the bridal suite.

"Well shouldn't she be on a plane right now? Or getting off one by this time?" My Mom seems annoyed, which isn't surprising. My mother did a lot of wonderful things, but she was not overly understanding or compassionate.

She already isn't Persephone's biggest fan, but by no fault of Seph's.

"It's odd we haven't met her yet, don't you think?" Mom hedges.

"No, Mother. You haven't been in Georgia since she arrived. You know I don't like Florida in the summer," my tone is stern but patient. I know it irked her that I was dating someone other than her best friend's daughter, Celia.

"Does she still work at the coffee shop?" Her words drip with disgust over a service job, even though Celia was a waitress, too.

Celia's mom and her grew up in a town about an hour away and then moved to Dorian together to raise a family. Both our dads died within a few years of each other, so our moms bonded even more over their losses. Celia's mom goes to Florida every year for a week to visit my mom and her sisters while she's there. Then, they're thick as thieves when Mom is back in Georgia.

"Yes, mom. She works part time there." My replies are only out of obligation.

"She could at least work full time…" mom mumbles under her breath and suppresses an eyeroll. My mother is a difficult woman, but I love her just the same. She is my mother, the woman who raised me.

After a few calls going straight to voicemail, I resign to obsessively glancing at my phone screen, hoping that from one glance to the next, Seph will call back. As if I manifested it from the eather, a text pops up on my screen from Seph.

Persephone: Just landed. Sorry about the missed calls. I'll tell you when I get there. **Brooks:** Glad you landed safe. See you soon, gorgeous.

I am aggravated that she is late, aggravated that she chose a flight so close to the wedding time that made her late with a small delay, but so insanely relieved she is going to be here. There is a large irrational part of my worry that my gut feeling had to do with her not showing up. She's never not shown up for me, whether it was for dinner, a cup of coffee, or even the morning after an argument. She is reliable, so why am I distrusting her so maliciously?

I try to rationalize it and reason it had nothing to do with her since the bad feeling remained in place despite confirming her arrival in NY.

I take a deep breath and turn the corner to where the bridal party was hanging before walking down the aisle.

The buzz is chaotic with bridesmaids chirping, cameras flashing, my mother in tears of joy, and Blaire freaking out. I poke my head out the doors into the ceremony room, which is covered with botanical greens and colorful flowers. I want to see if Seph made it, but can't find her in the crowd of nearly three hundred people.

The music starts to play, and the groomsmen make their way out as Blaire gets out of sight for Graham to walk down the aisle. While the bridesmaids line up, I notice Blaire breathing heavier and heavier.

"Are you okay? You seem nervous."

"OF COURSE I'M FUCKING NERVOUS!" She bit back at me.

"Okay, well, he's the guy you love, so don't be?" It is my only brotherly advice at the moment, my head and heart are somewhere else. Somewhere potentially bailing on me from my own sister's wedding.

"Wise words of wisdom from the big brother, I'll take them to my grave," Blaire sputters under her breath, rolls her eyes, and hops gently in place to shake out her nerves, but not too much to mess up her hair.

I hear the clicking of heels behind me, and the angel voice that accompanies it is music to my ears.

"Brooks! I made it! Ah! Blaire! You look... incredible! So nice to finally meet you! I'm sorry I am so late..."

We are both out of breath, but for different reasons. She is panting because of her pace, clearly she ran from the front of the building all the way back here to where the ceremony is. I am out of breath because she is simply breath*taking*.

Long curls spiraled down her back, donning more makeup than her usual bare face, I can't imagine a prettier woman. With charcoal coating her eyelids and a pale lipstick painted on her perfectly plump lips, I can barely look away.

She looks... beautiful, magical... and oddly familiar.

I brush the strange sensation that I've seen this face before, and not just hers. I've seen hers nearly every day for months, but I mean this painted face. It looks like something I have seen before.

The shrieked mumbles from the women in front of me don't shake me out of my thoughts. Blaire's sudden movement does snap me out of my trance, blinking rapidly as I forget the unsettling thought of my girlfriend's face being overly familiar, yet not.

Blaire has since latched onto Persephone in a bear hug like she is her long lost friend, then starts dramatically sobbing crocodile tears.

"I'm so nervous! I don't know why! I think he is great, we have so much fun together, but we have only known each other for a year! This feels so crazy!" Blaire just starts rambling to Seph, and I am floored by the calm grace of Seph catching all Blaire's ranting with compassion and love. I have never seen this side of Seph, one where she is comforting and patient.

Persephone's default emotional state is "cold and distant", until you get to know her. Since this was their first meeting, it seems unlikely the pair would click like this so immediately.

Hell, it took me a little while to crack her shell.

"It's okay! It's okay. You said yes for a reason, trust your gut. You're just nervous because there's 250 people out there and your logical brain is telling you one thing, but your heart is telling you another. Yeah?" Seph nods, coaxing Blaire to loosen her death grip. She seems to have calmed the beast since the tears were clearing up and in perfect time since the wedding coordinator is flipping her lid, screaming at the door for us to hurry up.

Seph gives me a long lingering look with a quick peck on the cheek to wish me luck. She hangs back to wait for us to make our full descent down the aisle. I hand my sister off to the coke snorting, NYC man she loves and my duty is fulfilled. I can now kick back and relax the rest of the night since my task for the day has been officially completed. All I can think about is how long until I get to dance with my beautiful girlfriend.

With the ceremony over and the celebration moving easily to the patio next door for cocktail hour, I try to find my girlfriend amongst the crowd.

Westchester weddings are something to behold. I have never seen so much food in my entire life. There are five different types of pasta, a table of meats and cheeses spanning 14 feet long, a section where they cook steak and tuna on salt slabs to order, a mac and cheese station where someone mixes a fresh batch for you with any ingredient, a guy shucking oysters alongside a raw bar, a man cracking lobster claws open, chicken, meatballs, sausage, passed appetizers floating around. It is beyond my wildest dreams, and this is just the cocktail hour.

After not being able to find Seph on my first lap around, I grab us two vodka sodas at the bar. On my third lap, I finally find her chatting with my mother, politely agreeing to whatever asinine decor recommendations I overhear her mentioning for the small studio Seph lives in.

Seph lights up to see me with a drink in my hand for her and discards her empty cup for the new one. Seph and I aren't big drinkers, so I am surprised to find her with a finished drink before trying to find me, but I chalk it up to nerves. How many had she had already? Seph is a nervous person, I know she has had some problems with anxiety in the past and tries to stay away from daily medication but takes Xanax for situations she knows will bring on a panic attack. My concern with the second vodka soda is only if she already took a Xanax before the wedding.

Seph is touchy about two things, the root of her anxiety and her history in New York. I know in my heart that I may never know what occurred in the months leading up to her arrival in my hometown in Georgia, but every single day, I wish for her to just come sit on my lap and tell me the whole story. Whatever happened, scarred her beyond words and I can't fathom to guess at what caused that kind of damage.

Every now and again, I hear snippets about her father, but she is also very vague about details about him as well. There are significant pieces of information about my girl that I am missing, like her old job she left, the seriousness of her previous relationships, and her finances, but I adored her beyond words so none of that mattered. Yet. I decided very early on to look past it, to accept her for what she was now, not what she used to be.

She is honest about every other moment of her life, about her struggle with mental illness, not having friends growing up then having a lot of fake ones in her adulthood, traveling with her dad, and then working for him, though she didn't get into specifics about what kind of company it was or what she did. I assume it is a deli or restaurant and that's why she got the job at the coffee house. Whatever her father left her is what she was living off of for now, not the measly part time coffee shop salary. She has never disclosed the amount that was left to her, but she said it was substantial enough for "a while".

Watching her interact with my aunts, uncles, and cousins is like watching a gazelle run through an open field. She is a natural grazer, able to shift from conversation to conversation without slighting anyone or making a wrong move. I am having more fun watching her chat with my family than I am participating in any of the conversations. My Sephy is bewitching in action; I felt like I am seeing her in her natural habitat.

We have been out with my friends before, on double dates and parties where I saw her flex her innate ability to attract people with her light, but never in such a tense setting. Meeting your boyfriend's extended family can be vexing, tiresome, and stressful, yet she flutters from conversation to conversation as if it was as easy as breathing.

"Seph," I touch her arm to get her attention and she politely bows out of her chat with my uncle to come along with me. "I've barely said two words to you, I'm sorry, you seem to be enchanting the entire Dawson family. Do you need a break?"

She leans in with both her hands on my chest and presses a restrained kiss on my lips. "I'm fine, but it's me who needs to apologize. I missed the ceremony."

I laugh, remembering our earlier texting conversation, "What do you mean? I saw you before we walked out."

"I know, I waited for you guys to go down the aisle, then tried to open the door, but the damn coordinator must have locked them behind you! I'm sorry!" She puts her hand to my cheek and knits her brows, obviously she feels guilty.

"Don't say sorry, you saved the wedding by what you said to my sister. She was about to lose it until you walked in and calmed her down. I should be thanking you, not forgiving you," I sneak a quick messy kiss to the side of her neck and lick it until she wiggles me off. We are both a little tipsy and I am feeling frisky from not being near her the last few days.

Seph has sent me a few sexy pictures the night before as well as a tantalizing Facetime on Thursday night where we released our pleasures together, but nothing was better than the real thing.

"Brooks! Your family is here!" she cries, pretending to be scandalized, then nibbles on the outside of my ear. With the first skim of her teeth, I feel my pants grow a little tighter. God, she turns me on in every way.

I lean in to whisper into her ear, "I can't wait to get you back to the hotel, naked, later on. Did you wear that… thing?" I wiggle my eyebrows and she moans into my neck, biting at my skin again. I can feel her grin against my skin and the crotch of my tux starting to get tighter.

"You look absolutely stunning tonight, by the way. That dress looks incredible on you," I break away from her in an effort to stay decent in public.

She was a thin, lithe woman when I met her, with slight curves but a beautiful figure, nonetheless. She filled out these past months in all the right places. Looking back, I realize that she was an unhealthy weight, and her natural weight gain has been a direct correlation to her happiness in Georgia. She is still petite and hardly any excess fat on her, but it was like life had been blown back in her frail frame.

The swallows of her collarbones were a little less, the dip from her waist to her hip was larger, and her ribs no longer protruded. It has been like watching a caterpillar become a butterfly in front of my eyes. She evolved from her whatever former self she was clinging onto and became a stronger Persephone.

"Thank you, I think I spilled a little cocktail sauce on the bottom of it, but it should come out," she motions to the bottom hem of her deep red floor length gown. I can't spot any discoloration, but I play along with her.

"Was it expensive?"

She takes a sip of her drink and chokes at my question.

"A little, but don't worry. It will get good use," she fumbles. "On the floor." She winks and my chest tightens at the thought of her standing in my hotel room later with just her black lace teddy on. She will be a vision.

With cocktail hour winding down, we make our way through the ballroom to find our seats. My sister sat us at a far table because she knew I wouldn't care where we sat. Trying to see the bride and groom from where we are sitting is like trying to see home plate from the left field bleachers at Yankee Stadium.

Even though I walked Blaire down the aisle, I'm not truly part of the wedding party, so I stick with Persephone as they announce the entrances. We are in the back with a bad view, but cheering like lunatics at a football game, nonetheless, having our own fun behind the sea of people.

One thing I love about Seph is how fun she is when she drinks. It isn't often to catch her drunk off her ass, at least not in the few months I've known her, but there have been a few times where we drank a few glasses of wine too many. She is a radiant delight, spilling every brilliant and hilarious thought from her head or dancing on the kitchen counter while making brownies from a box, swearing she was an excellent baker.

She loved everyone, showered people with compliments, danced, sang, and laughed. Like a flower in full bloom and I am always mesmerized. I wonder if the alcohol makes her forget the anxiety she holds onto during the day, or if it was as simple as, she just forgets to care.

She is a beautiful soul and watching her flit through today's social interactions made me realize how madly in love with her I truly am. We haven't broached the subject of "I love you" yet because I feel like she is concealing a huge part of her, but today showed me I don't care what that part looks like, or if I ever see it because I can't live without the other parts of her, the parts I do know and adore.

We sat with our backs to my sister and brother-in-law, not caring about the world around us, and especially not the weird table of second cousins Blaire sat us with. We joke and laugh, enjoying dinner, then eventually get up for the night to mark our territory on the outskirts of the dance floor. We are in our own little world, which is fine by me since the only other people on the dance floor I really know are a few drunk aunts and Blaire's sorority sister bridesmaids.

Something told me that interacting with that gaggle of women for too long will get me a one-way ticket to the doghouse for the rest of the night.

'At Last,' by Etta James comes on and Persephone instinctually melts into my chest for the slow dance. I love the way her body curves into mine while we dance, how the top of her head nestles right under my chin so that when I glance down, she only has to tilt her head up for our lips to meet.

I bow my head down so my lips brush her ear and I whisper the words I've been thinking about all day, "I'm madly in love with you, Persephone Kline."

My face feels her smile by the shift of her skin on mine, she whispers back, "I'm madly in love with you too, Brooks Dawson."

Tilting her head up to meet mine, my mouth molds onto hers in the passionate embrace of love that is so natural to us. I am in love with this woman, she is in love with me, and we both finally admit it. Time stills in that moment because for the first time in my life, I am truly happy.

Not that I hadn't been blissfully ignorant of loneliness before, I was, but I didn't realize the hole Seph filled until she did it. I didn't think about our future, her past. We are just together at this moment, loving each other as we are.

My cousin Trip asks to cut in once we break apart from our kiss, and instead of savoring the moment, I do the polite thing and hand her off. Trip is here alone, so I feel guilty not letting him dance with my smokeshow of a girlfriend. I go to find my mother who is deeper on the dance floor with the aunts. A few songs later, another slow song starts, and I try to find Seph, but oddly find her in the arms of one of Graham's groomsmen, while some of his other friends stand around them.

She isn't dancing. It looks more like she is trying to courteously wriggle herself free of his firm hand in hers, but couldn't shake him off.

She looks uncomfortable and pale and that strange feeling I've had in my gut all weekend stirs again.

The groomsman looks annoyed, like he was speaking to her harshly while the others acted like bodyguards, shielding the conversation and preventing her from leaving. No longer able to watch from afar, I decide to break it up before it escalates any further. Maybe they knew each other from her time in New York?

What sick odds that would be.

"Mind if I steal my girl back?" I say through my clenched teeth, eyeing all the men around her to mark my territory as well. There is something wrong here, but I am the only one who seems to not know what it was.

"Of course, you may," the guy retorts, his eyes never leaving Persephone. She stares back at him too, practically spitting venom from her stare. I have never seen her so alive with anger, she is vibrating with it.

The men excuse themselves politely, but not before saying a few strange goodbyes to Seph and I pull her in close protectively. She is as stiff as a board, not nearly as loose and happy as when I left her only fifteen minutes ago.

"Why the fuck did you leave me for so long?" She snaps as soon as they are out of earshot.

Completely thrown off by her anger shifting towards me, I stagger back a little from the harshness in her tone. "I'm sorry, Seph, are you okay? Did they say something to you?"

She is flustered and disoriented, flipping between anger and confusion with a blink of an eye. "No, no. They didn't. I just thought it was weird he wanted to dance with me, I don't know him. His friends are assholes, too."

My heart sinks at her words because I can tell she is lying. She won't look past my chin, won't meet my eyes while she lies to my face. It is the same lie I've received for months when I ask her about NYC. She just told me she loved me, and now she can't even tell me the truth.

"I can tell you're lying, Seph. Just tell me how you know them, I won't be mad," I try to reassure her at this moment instead of getting annoyed. Opening up was more important to me than being right. She looks up at me and nods slowly.

"We... uh, have mutual friends. In New York," she mumbles while playing with the button on my jacket. I can tell she doesn't want to say more when the pools of tears collecting in her eyes threaten to spill over. She blinks them away while continuing to avoid elongated eye contact with me.

Can I really blame her? It's part of her past cracking wide open in a room full of strangers. My girl is breaking open in front of me, I can see how much this is hurting her, but I can't do anything. I don't know enough to even help soothe her with words, so I resort to rubbing comforting circles in the small of her back. Instead of being selfish and forcing the rest of the truth out of her, I help stuff it back in.

"Let's forget about it. We can talk about it when we're back in Georgia, Seph. I don't need to know anything more now, just that he bothers you and I'll keep him away from you. But we need to talk about this eventually. I can't go on with the big black hole of your past looming over us from behind." I press a few reassuring kisses onto the side of her head and hold her for a few seconds until the end of the song.

Deep down, I am pissed. Livid, hurt, and angry. But it is my sister's wedding. Causing a scene in the middle of a family affair will take away from Blaire's night and that is the last thing I would ever do to my sister.

"Let's grab another drink, okay?" Seph squeezes my hand in agreement, then again as we walk to assure me, she is okay.

"I still love you, nothing will change that," I whisper into her hair and she nods, squirming further into my side as we walk. My heart aches for her, for her fear of running into someone she knew coming to life after I begged her to come. My guilt weighs on me with every step we take in tandem, but I have to pack it away for now and lift the mood for both of us.

Laughter never finds her eyes for the rest of the night, but she dances with me and converses like normal. At one point, I worry maybe my mom has also said something to her because she wasn't thrilled after her conversation with her either.

Seph breaks off from the dance floor to go to the restroom, but after 20 minutes and no return, I go to search for her. Nowhere to be found, I make my way outside the front doors since it is the only place I haven't looked yet. I see her off towards the side, grabbing a bit of fresh air.

When I get a clearer visual of her, I notice one of Graham's groomsmen talking to her and she is mad. Livid, actually.

"Please, leave me alone. I don't want any issues; I promise I won't say anything. I don't even know what he's talking about either. Just leave me alone, Brooks doesn't know anything, I won't tell him," I can hear her whisper yelling.

"You fucked him over, you know that? No one will ever forgive you for leaving how you did, either. Fucking coward. I can't believe you thought you could show your face in New York again. It was pathetic to run. He's going to fucking kill you for what you took, you know," he spit back at her. My blood boils from the exchange, not sure what to be angrier about; how he is threatening her life or the fact she is clearly lying to me about something major, something she has permanently resigned to never tell me.

The groomsman, I later learned was named Doug, spotted me, turned the corner and gave Seph a searing look then nodded at me before he headed back inside. Seph still didn't see me, and I can see her body rack with a sob as her hands fly to her face. I watch her body convulse a few times before I move to react.

"Seph? Are you okay?" I whisper.

She startles at the sound of my voice and whips around, wiping a tear from her eye quickly.

"Brooks. Hi," she says curtly.

"What was that about?"

"Nothing. Just a misunderstanding," another lie.

"Didn't look like nothing, Seph. You're crying." And he was degrading you without you putting up a fight.

"I'm fine. It's fine. Seriously, just drop it," she goes to brush past me, and I catch her arm. She flinches and gasps like I have hit her. I drop her arm immediately when I see the look of panic on her face.

"I'm sorry, I'm sorry... Can you just talk to me for a second?" She spins towards me, several feet away now, and nods with her arms folded.

"Seph, what was that about?" I try to keep my tone light, but my words to the point.

"Did you know your mom said Celia is who you're going to marry. That I should just not bother flying back to Georgia, and just stay in New York?" She snorts with her reply. My face drops in shock.

Grappling with how to respond properly, I pinch the bridge of my nose, "Please tell me she did not say that to your face and you're just kidding." I know she was not.

"No, I overheard her say it in the bathroom to one of your aunts, who enthusiastically agreed. She's been sweet as pie to my face. I heard that about Southerners. Nice to your face, fake behind your back," she draws nonchalantly, like it doesn't affect her at all. Her face is emotionless for the first time, like a corpse of herself, and it scares me.

Reaching to caress her face, I mumble, "I'm so sorry Seph, Jesus, this wedding has turned into a war zone for you," I regret it as soon as I say it. This time, the laughter is humorless and the look in her eye is deadly.

"I'm glad you're finally seeing why I did not want to come in the first place. New York has nothing good left for me. I should have stayed in Georgia."

My eyes soften, feeling guilt, empathy, anger for her all in one. There are no words I can say to comfort her, but her desire to be back in Georgia is the only hope I can cling to right now.

Her tune changes again, and I notice the tears pricking at the corners of her eyes suddenly disappear. "I'm going to go. You can stay. You *should* stay. You *have* to stay. There's still an hour left of this wedding to enjoy, and the Venetian hour is still up. I'm sure the end of the night snacks will be good, too. Grab me something on your way out for a midnight snack." The ghost of a smile doesn't quite catch the flame on her mouth when she turns to see the car rolling up.

It all happens so quickly, the car, then her snagging her overnight bag that I didn't notice perched next to the door behind me. It takes me multiple moments to realize it was Uber that stopped next to us and Seph was climbing inside it.

It didn't hit me until the car was no longer in sight that she never asked for the name of the hotel, my room number, or the extra keycard.

Chapter 13

Brooks

———

A little drunk and a lot of heartbroken, I tried calling Persephone repeatedly the second she left, but she wouldn't pick up. My heart feels like someone is reaching inside me and squeezing it, then taking a mini chainsaw and repeatedly halving it in two. My shoulders ache, my jaw won't unclench, and I am scatterbrained on what to do. She left me with my heart in my hands, and my hands tied behind my back.

Where did she even go? To the airport? White Plains is too small of an airport to have a red eye home. She refused to fly into JFK or LaGuardia on the way here, but maybe if she is desperate she may have braved it? Newark Airport is drivable, but it's an hour away as well. That's a solid 200-dollar Uber fare or more for 10:30pm on a Saturday night.

I try to text her. Repeatedly.

Brooks: Sephy, where did you go? Let me come to you. I want to be there for you, please let me be. I love you.

It gets delivered. Silence. Not even the dancing dots.

Fuck.

Shoving my hands through my hair, I swirl around and curse under my breath.

"Tough night? Same," Graham's slippery smile lengthened as he jaunts down the steps and takes a drag of a freshly lit cigarette. "She leave you high and dry?"

I don't respond, but looking away from him in silence is answer enough.

"Don't worry, she does that. The good thing is she won't be back, though," he chuckles to himself and turns away, puffing. I wonder how he knows that about her and who their mutual friend is. It must be one of *his* friends or a coworker.

"How do you know her?"

"Through friends." Same answer as the one she gave earlier about his groomsman; it must be true then.

"She didn't seem to be happy about seeing any of your friends."

"I'd imagine not. She clearly didn't tell you why, so it doesn't sound like my business to share," he answers smoothly while inhaling another drag.

"Fair," I replied absently. It's *not* fair but I'm not going to get into it with the groom on his wedding night. I'm definitely not going to get into it with my *sister's* new husband on *their* wedding night.

"You should just forget about her, brother. She's not worth the trouble. Believe me on that,'" he flings his still lit cigarette into a bush and walks back inside.

Asshole.

I called her another 20 times before I went to bed at the hotel and thanked my lucky stars I booked an early flight home on Sunday. I will be home by 3pm and my first stop is Seph's apartment.

The last five calls went straight to voicemail the next morning, so she must have turned her phone off. The flight was excruciatingly long and the woman next to me asked me several times to stop shaking my leg so hard, but I couldn't help my nerves.

I just want to touch her again and talk this out. So much has unfolded in the past 24 hours, it is hard to shift through all my feelings as I drive to Dorian from Savannah. We just told each other we loved one another, and now this unknown monster from her past is rearing its head, threatening to break us up. I won't allow it, not for a second.

I'd spend the rest of our lives in the dark about her past if it made this weekend's nightmare go away forever.

But I couldn't help wondering about the words I had overheard. What was she hiding? What would she never tell me and what did she not want me to find out from Harrison's groomsman? Why was Doug so mean to her? The questions rattle through my brain all night and throughout my drive. I can't answer a single one.

Do I even know my girlfriend?

My mother is a different problem, one that we'd really only have to deal with for six months of the year. She was a much easier beast to tame, and a secondary issue I will solve once I get Persephone to answer my damn phone calls again.

I finally make it to my hometown, barrel down the street to get to her place. Luckily parking near her apartment is easy, so I bound up the stairs to her front door. I knock on her door for several minutes, but the silence that answers makes me feel just as stupid as calling her 20 times with no response. I don't even know if she is there or not. She doesn't have a car in her parking spot, not that she owns one to begin with, and the lights are off in her apartment, except one. The bathroom window.

"Seph, please, please talk to me," I yell into her door. "I can't handle this silence and you ignoring all my calls. I need to see you," with each word, I feel more and more desperate for her. How can she cut me out like this? I thought she loved me.

I went back every day, twice a day for a week. I went to the coffee shop for both shift changes on the days she normally worked, but she was never there. After a long week of space, silence, and no sleep, I decided that enough was enough. I have the key to her apartment, and I was going to use it.

Knocking again only led to more silence, so I announced, "I'm coming in," before I unlocked the bolt and the handle only to be stopped by the chain.

"Seph... seriously? You can't just talk this out with me? You can't stay locked up in this fucking room forever."

"Go away, Brooks. I clearly... don't want to... see you..." she is sobbing in between words, and I can't handle the pain in her voice. What happened to her? What happened at this fucking wedding that I'm so blatantly missing?

"Seph, you're killing me here," I all but cry into the crack of her door. "Let me be there for you. I know you're hurting; I'm hurting too because you won't let me in. I love you Persephone, you hear me? I fucking love you and you're killing me," I sound as desperate as I feel.

She is crying in the bathtub; I can hear the weeping and sharp inhales alongside splashes of water echoing in her apartment.

I sit outside her apartment door almost all-day Sunday, waiting for her to leave or for a noise to be made. She didn't turn on the TV, I didn't even see a light from the street when I left at 5pm.

Monday, I came back after work and decided to try to open the apartment again.

"Seph, you in there? I'm coming in," I announced loudly.

I unlock the bolt and knob and rejoice when the door finally opens without the chain, but reality slaps me hard in the face when I look around and see the entire room empty. Seven checks sit on the counter, signed and dated for each remaining month in her lease.

Devastation rolls over me and crashes inside like a car smashing into a wall. I feel like I'm getting atomized from inside of this studio apartment.

She fucking *left*. She left *me* without talking this out.

My breathing starts to pick up, my palms grow sweaty, and my chest is tight. Was this the panic she always talked about? How the walls feel like they're closing in and no one can save you?

I don't think I've cried since my dad died when I was nine, but in this moment, my eyes sting and my cheeks are suddenly wet. I sit where her bed used to be, where we have made love a million times, where we stayed awake one night when the air conditioner broke and shared all our hopes and dreams.

Her bed is gone, but the memories of the room remain. I want to bathe myself in them, in the lingering scent of her permeating the air around me. I want to let every molecule that reminds me of her surround me and hug me tight. No, I want my girlfriend, my best friend, my lover, my light. I want the silly girl who made bad coffee and burned box brownies. I want the woman who stole my heart.

But my Persephone left me. High and dry, just like Graham had oddly said she would.

Chapter 14

Brooks

———

Until Seph came along, and my life took a new meaning, my daily routine would have been fine. But since she came and went, the hole inside my days are too great to fill.

I prowl my office, almost running burn marks in the carpet from pacing so often these days and take off to the coffee house after finding no reprieve from the distraction of work.

All I can think about is her. How her mouth lines up perfectly with mine, her movie quotes and impressions, all the little food rules she lives by like when to order chicken. The way she gracefully leaps from conversation topic to topic, her smiles, her laughter.

I try not to think of her or obsessively text her phone. I might have thought she'd have blocked me by now, but the messages keep going through. So I keep sending them.

Two weeks post-wedding and one-week post-Seph taking off, I make my way into the coffee shop for the first time since she left. I couldn't go in before, it reminded me too much of her. I still didn't want to, but I had to feed my curiosity to ask Michael or Shannon if they had heard from her since she still wasn't answering my texts or calls.

"Hey Brooks, how are you?" Michael asks wearily.

"Not great. Have you heard from her?"

I called and asked them a hundred times already, but never in person. I felt the weight of their silence but seeing the color drain from their faces at the mention of her made my senses spike.

Michael shifts nervously and looks at Shannon, who starts busying herself with cleaning an already clean spot on the counter. They know something.

"You're terrible liars, guys. Tell me *something*. Please. Anything, just tell me she's okay…"

Shannon looks at Michael and clears her throat.

"Okay," she relents, "but you cannot tell anyone else. Our parents don't even know, she swore us to secrecy." I nod, waiting anxiously for even a breadcrumb from Seph's world.

"You swear it, Brooks Dawson, so help me God!"

"I swear, I swear!" I fight back, curious what information they hold.

"Well… before the wedding, she gave us… she gave us two checks. *Really* big checks," Shannon says and nervously waits for my reaction.

"Okay? Like how much? A few hundred dollars? A thousand dollars? And for what?" I shake my head, confused as to what this all means in relation to us or the secret of her whereabouts.

Michael clears his throat and he and Shannon exchange more nervous glances, like they were reconsidering telling me.

"Please," I beg again, softer this time.

"She said they were to pay off our student loans…" Michael responds.

"And then some," Shannon adds.

Confused, I press more, "What do you mean by, 'and then some?'"

"She gave us both a check for $100,000, said to pay off our loans, enjoy Senior Spring, go backpacking in Europe after graduation, then save the rest," Shannon says quietly.

I keep blinking at them, unsure if the information I heard was truly about my girlfriend. My girlfriend who worked part-time at a coffee shop. My girlfriend who never alluded to having any type of trust fund or massive stash of money. My girlfriend who lived modestly in a *studio* apartment with nothing flashy, not even a goddamn car.

Breathe, Brooks, just breathe.

"I don't understand," was all I could say. My mind was racing to find a conclusion that made sense. She said her dad left her money, but she never said how much. I assumed it was a sizable amount, but not enough to give away a quarter of a million dollars. I didn't even think the *total* in her bank account was even ten thousand dollars.

"She said she didn't want anyone to know any more than they already do, but that she wanted us to have a good life, that we work hard, and deserve it... she said not to share it, and be selfish and use it on life experiences, not partying or our parents."

"She's right. That's a lot of money, a life changing amount of money for you both." I am still processing, but I backed her wishes absentmindedly while I chewed on possibilities.

"We will. We still have to work here for now, but we're gonna be smart. She forced some of it into a trust or something. But that's all we know. She didn't tell us anything else."

I force a half smile, knowing that Seph is looking out for these two even in her absence makes me want her even more. I still don't know what secret she is hiding but hearing this one only makes me feel closer to her. It's one piece of a bigger puzzle. I am still missing so many pieces though, now more than ever.

Sephy, who are you? *Where* are you?

When I get back to my house, my mind is still turning over what Michael and Shannon told me about Seph and the money.

Where the hell did she get that money? Was it hers? Her dad's? Was that what Doug meant when he said she fucked *him* over? Did she steal it then give it away?

From what I know, Seph is frugal, she doesn't spend much and she doesn't make a lot either. She has one credit card and one bank card, both Chase Bank. She doesn't carry cash or own expensive furnishings from what I can tell. Her sheets are soft, they could have been a high thread count, but if that is the only thing I can think of, I am seriously grasping for straws.

Maybe she sold a bunch of stuff to give the money to Michael and Shannon? I'll check the pawn shop today on my way home. I noticed a few designer handbags here and there, but nothing more than the average girl with a nice boyfriend or father, or they could have been fake,too. Hell if I know.

Her father, another massive hole in Persephone's life story that I let stay hidden. I know a lot about him, his jokes, his stories, his friends even, but I don't know the name of his company or what kind of business it is. I respected her need for privacy, but in hindsight, was that my downfall? It is time to make some calls.

My first is to the Sheriff, Ray Valentine. He is an old high school buddy of mine and we worked in tandem most days between those he arrested and arraigned. I've never asked him for a personal favor, despite doing countless for him between taking some pro bono cases and going to the town's middle school to present to the kids about drug safety when he got tied up at the station.

He owed me.

"Ray."

"Brooks, what pleasure do I owe this occasion?" He crooned through the phone.

"I need a favor."

"Shoot."

"I need a background check done, a thorough one," I say.

"Okay, who's the lucky man?"

"Woman. Her name is Persephone Kline."

My next stop is to the local pawn shop to see if I can dig up anything she recently sold. Nothing she could have sold would equate to the 200 thousand she gave away, but I am desperate and reaching for anything to get my hands on.

"Hiya Brooks," the shop owner chirps as I walk in.

"Hey Paul, how are ya today?"

"Just swell, just swell. How can I help ya?"

"I have a question I'm not sure you can answer, but I'd be mighty grateful if you did, friend to friend," I sing. He isn't my friend, heck, I am 10 years his senior, but I gotta butter him up a bit for him to give me the details I need.

"I probably have an answer, my boy."

"Has… Persephone Kline come in here recently?" I look at him to gauge his reaction, to note any perceptible ticks. He might not tell me a real answer, but if I am lucky, his facial expression can tell me enough to confirm or deny it. "To sell something," I quickly added.

He pauses for a minute, unsure how to answer until he finally nods "Aye, the cute new brunette?" I nod back, despite his Neanderthalic description of the love of my life.

"What did she sell, if you don't mind?"

"Didn't she leave town not too long ago?" He answers back, ignoring my question.

"Yes, she did," I weigh telling him more, but I am worried he would try to protect her if he felt like I was angry or after her in any way. I bite my tongue and pray he offers more information on his own volition.

"She came by four months ago, sold a big ass engagement ring. Three carats. I turned it to another dealer somewhere north. Made a pretty penny on it," he conceded the information without any additional prodding.

The reality of the exchange leveles me. She was…. Engaged?

My ears zeroed out and began to ring while sleep deprivation finally started to settle into my eyes. I hadn't slept more than three hours a night since she left, and it made me overly emotional. Tears glassed over my eyes, and I thanked God above for the Ray Bans still on my face from the sunny day in November.

The silence creeped on a few more moments before Paul broke it.

"I'm guessing you didn't know she was engaged?"

I nod.

"She ripped it out of her pocket, slammed it on the table and asked for whatever I was willing to give her for it," he went on without me asking for more. "I had to take money out from the bank since I didn't carry that much in the safe. She waited, snagged her cash and zipped out of here. Gave her a shit deal and she knew it. Didn't care about the money she said, just wanted it gone," he shrugs and pretends to clean off the counter. He already gave me more information than I asked for, but I am grateful for every crumb.

"Thank you, Paul. Seriously," I could barely get the words out to show my appreciation because the visual he provided me was too much to bear.

She was engaged. She never told me she had been engaged, she never told me anything.

Did I even know this girl?

Chapter 15

Persephone

———————

It's been three weeks since the wedding. I've cried every single day, had a panic attack every other day, and almost picked up at least ten of Brooks' most recent calls this week, to beg for his forgiveness. He still texts me every night. He sends me funny memes or pictures of his lunch occasionally. Some days he gets angry and asks me why I am doing this to him, then he apologizes the next day or hours later. It's almost like I had a residency in his head and the texts were a stream of his consciousness.

Every day he begs me to come back to him, begs me to tell him what he can do to fix this. Every day I have to re-convince myself that we can't fix ourselves, can't fix the situation *I'm* in. Every day I have to fight the urge to text him back and tell him to come get me.

In a manic episode, I drove 38 hours across the country in Michael's family's Honda Civic, which in return, I gave him 50 thousand dollars to buy a new SUV or something. I needed a car that no one would trace back to me. I made it all the way here without being followed, but Brooks might try a little harder than Harrison to find me.

I begged Michael for the switch, and explained that it was *life or death*, then swore him to secrecy again. He complied once I handed over the wad of cash I got months ago for my engagement ring.

I had been threatened at the wedding, threatened for my life. Harrison is still after whatever he thinks I took, and from the unwelcomed conversations I had at the wedding, he will stop at nothing to get it back. The confirmation of that came with my dance with Doug and talking with the other groomsmen. Who would have thought all my fears would be confirmed and I'd run into the one group of people I wish I'd never seen again in my life?

Most of my old belongings are still in storage somewhere, but with my location blown, I couldn't risk Harrison tracing anything. I had to message Aisley to switch my stuff's location, to which she immediately responded and dealt with. My belongings aren't much, but they were all I had from my former life. My life where I had a dad and a fun group of friends. I'd send her a Christmas postcard or something from Montana along with some designer shoes as a thank you. The girl has been a damn lifesaver this year. Literally.

When I left New York the first time, I didn't want to be found, not because I was scared for my life, per say, but because I just didn't want someone trying to drag me back. When I left this time, I was scared that someone was going to kill me to get to whatever they thought I had. Doug had told me as much outside the venue.

"He's not fucking around, Persephone. He will hunt you down and gut you for what you took," he seethed through his teeth at me.

"Doug, I. Don't. Have. Anything. What don't you idiots understand?" I stalked across the pavement, slamming my heels down for dramatic effect.

"This isn't just a stupid sweatshirt you took, it's… so much more. You can't run forever, especially now that we know the company you keep. The brother-in-law? How cute. Wonder what he'd think about all this." Doug flicked his hand towards the front door, motioning to the people inside.

"HE WON'T KNOW!" I yelled. Doug laughed and pulled a few more drags from his cigarette while I stared at him wildly protective of Brooks. "Please, leave me alone. I don't want any issues. I don't even know what he's talking about. Just leave me alone, Brooks doesn't know anything, I won't tell him either."

"You fucked him over, you know that? I can't believe you thought you could show your face in New York again," Doug chuckled to himself, "it was pathetic to run, anyways."

It has been three weeks since I left Brooks at the wedding, when I made my first serious mistake. I had been drinking that night to drown my sorrows and I thought I was answering a call from Brooks' since he was one of the short list of people that had my number, but it was actually Michael.

Sitting cross legged on my tiny kitchen's floor, leaning against the cabinets, I started crying while I thought about nights spent making midnight snacks in the kitchen. A kitchen that belonged to a very handsome and wonderful man.

My mind went to one time when Brooks had me against the fridge, where he flipped up the big t-shirt I was wearing to bed and slid into me from behind while he planted never-ending kisses against the back of my neck. I could still feel the heat of his breath on me, the feel of him rocking inside me, and his hands sliding across every inch of me.

Without him I was so empty, so hollow, so sad.

I remember a time where just hearing the upbeat tick of his voice on the other end of the phone would elicit a spike of happiness in me. Lost in my own misery, I beg a lord I don't believe in to give me a crumb of him.

Stupidly thinking the Lord himself is answering my pathetic prayer, mid sob, I pick up when my phone ringer goes off, "H-He-Hello?"

"Oh my God! Persephone? Is that you?"

I sniffled, "Yes, of course. Are you okay?"

"Shouldn't I be asking you? You're the one crying and running, you weirdo."

Oh. Not Brooks. Only one person calls me a weirdo, it's Michael.

"I'm not running anymore!" I drop my free hand to the floor in defeat, "I'm living in some dumb town called Baker. In Montana! I can't cook, I can't sleep, I can't find a good place to get take out," I cry and then immediately slap my hand over my mouth and gasp.

Fuck! I just disclosed my location!

"Fuck, Michael, please don't tell anyone! I just got settled here, got an apartment today. I really don't want to have to m-move again…" I slur drunkenly.

"I won't! But why are you so worried? Scared Brooks is going to track you down?"

"No, Brooks is the first person I'd want to track me down," I confess softly. I'm only shutting him out because I'd only complicate his life, not make it easier. I want him to find meso badly, but I want his all-around happiness even more and I've convinced myself that I just can't be, if he's with me.

"I'm running from something else, someone else. They are… dangerous so if someone comes poking around, you have to lie for me. I'm serious Michael, you're the only person who knows, so if I die, it'll be your fault!" I exaggerate the claim, hoping he takes the threat on my life seriously enough to not tell anyone. I don't *think* I'm *truly* in danger for my life, but what Michael doesn't know, definitely won't hurt him in this case.

"Okay, okay! Won't tell nobody… just keep your hollering down," Michael tries to make light of this, despite my clearly rattled state.

I huff, holding back all my tears.

"Seph?"

"Yeah?"

"Call him back, will ya? He's going crazy over here, worried sick. He comes in every day asking if we heard from you. Most days we don't have to lie," he complains.

"Okay, I will," I whisper, unsure if I will be able to keep this particular promise.

"Good. Even if you don't want to come back, I think he just needs to hear that you're okay."

My heart clenches at the thought of Brooks in pain because of me. I know he is. I heard him crying my name at the door the night I sobbed in the bathtub. It broke my heart every time he knocked, I knew I had to leave, or I would eventually let him inside.

I would never tell him what had happened the night of the wedding or why I left town. We'd be in the same spot as we were now, except we'd be screaming at each other and probably saying things we didn't mean that we'd have to apologize for later. I skipped the dramatics and just went to the inevitable ending, the part where I left and never came back.

"Got it, I'll catch you later, Michael," I say and hang up.

I begin rubbing my temples, thinking about the mental state I am in after talking to Michael. I want to run and cry and scream. I miss Dorian. I miss the coffee shop, I miss Michael and Shannon. I miss Brooks. I miss Brooks *more than anything.*

I can't call him, but I think I can manage a text.

Persephone: Don't worry too much about me, I'm okay.

Unsurprisingly, a text came back instantly. I imagine he has been waiting by the phone the same way I wait by mine to watch his name and picture light up my screen every night he calls. Seeing his name pop up on my phone makes me feel closer to him because it is the only 20 seconds in his day I know exactly what he was doing and what he looks like doing it.

Brooks: Where are you? Can I call? I just need to hear your voice. Please.

Persephone: No. It's not a good time.

Persephone: I'm sorry.

Brooks: Where are you? When can you talk?

I couldn't respond anymore.

Brooks: Seph?

I can't keep responding, the guilt is eating at me. How can he still love me after what I did? I left him at his sister's wedding, ignored him for a week, then left town and haven't picked up a single call since. This string of texts is my first contact with him since the wedding.

It broke my heart every day to ignore his calls, but I can't find it in me to block his number. Sometimes I'll get multiple texts in a row when he's had a drink or two. I can tell because those usually come on the weekends after 12am.

The text that broke me the most tonight was the one he sent before I fell asleep.

Brooks: Sephy, please come back to me. I'm begging you to just talk to me.

Par for the course for me, I don't respond.

It's him that eventually changes though. All of a sudden, after weeks of daily communications, of memes and pictures, of quick check-ins, or angry rants, *his texts just stop.*

Chapter 16

Brooks

———

W here did this Mustang come from? I sure as shit hope he didn't waste part of his school money on this yellow piece of crap.

On my way to work, I stormed into the coffee shop to ask Michael about the car parked outside of the coffee shop. I immediately assumed the worst, that he used the money Seph gave them both for a hotrod, but before I can even finish my question, he gets nervous and blurts, "She asked for my car. My family car."

What?" I stop dead.

"She asked to trade. $50,000 for the Honda Civic, no questions asked. I said yes."

"You're kidding," I whisper to myself, disbelieving. "She could have bought two used Honda's for 50k," I growled. I wasn't above mentally kicking the shit out of a 22-year-old kid for answers.

"I know where she is," he whimpers.

I freeze. My attention is all his now. Straightening out, I watch him carefully and wait for more to be said, but only silence and the countertop fills the air between us.

I blink at him. "Where is she?" The rasp in my voice is thick with emotion.

Michael fumbles around with some cleaning products, pretending to scrub at a random spot, glancing up quickly to respond to me.

"She asked me not to say."

"Do you think I give a shit? Tell me where she is," I am not fucking around today. After our text exchange went so badly yesterday, I threw my phone at the wall so hard it shattered the screen so I couldn't text her today at all, at least not till my 7pm appointment when I got a new iPhone.

"She accidentally told me and then cried. I think she was drunk. She said no one can know or they'll find her or something. She said her safety depends on me keeping quiet. Is she in trouble?" Michael's eyebrows drew together concerned for his older friend's health, and I was forced to remain calm while losing my ever-loving mind internally.

Was this connected to the threats from the wedding?

Is this why she ran? Was it nothing to do with me? Possibilities I have never considered before swirled around my head and made me dizzy.

"I need to find her, Michael. If it's this serious, she needs help. I would never let anything happen to her, you know that," I plead.

Michael puts down his cloth and spray bottle to look solemnly at me, "She… she did say that you're the first person she'd want to track her down…" He pauses to think about his next sentence, lips twitching as he finds the next words to say. My heart swells at the mention of me.

"She said my name?" I breathe harshly.

"No. I asked her if she was running from… you," he looks nervous admitting to it.

"Oh," I blink hard again, registering the indictment lodged against me.

"That's when she said you're the first person she'd want to find her. That's the only reason I'm telling you," Michael snaps at me, frustrated by the questioning.

My eyes didn't leave him when I slowly asked, "Where is she, Michael?"

Michael sighs, "She's in Montana. Baker, Montana."

I suck in a breath. "Montana? She drove there all by herself?" I'm talking to myself, putting the pieces together in my head. She drove that far to get away, but from who?

"Yup. All by herself in that shitty Honda Civic. I called a little bit ago. When she slipped about her location, she sounded tired, near hysterical and pleaded with me not to tell anyone because she didn't want to move after she just got an apartment," Michael is clearly weary telling me all this, but I could kiss him on the mouth right now for all the extra details.

"When did she leave?"

"A few days ago. I told you, she came in and begged me for my car. Shoved $50,000 at me and practically ran out of here crying."

Piecing together the details is difficult. Picturing her crying and running made my heart break all over again. *What are you running from, my darling girl?*

Walking back out to my car after interrogating Michael, I'm zoned out, completely running on autopilot while a million thoughts run through my mind. All about how I can get these to her, the time off work, the flights, the possible complications of trying to find her.

My phone buzzes and I instinctually answer it without looking.

"Dawson."

"Hello brother! I am back and beautifully tanned, thanks for asking."

"Blaire. How was the honeymoon?" I couldn't care less but going through the motions was what I am used to these past few weeks with Persephone gone. Asking the right questions, doing the same fake laughs and jokes in the right moments were key to tricking people into thinking you were perfectly fine. It is a skill I was either mastering or the people around me felt too bad for me to mention.

"Amazing! We ate so many delicious dinners, walked the towns, and got a couple's massages. It was…" Her voice trails off in my head, not wanting to listen to the amazing time my sister had with the man that clearly knew more than I did about my girlfriend disappearing on me. I am happy Blaire is happy, but I can't tune into listening to it, so I shift my thoughts to how I am going to cancel the rest of my meetings this week and get to Montana.

Blaire concludes after about 10 minutes of talking straight without interruption, to which I finally reply, "That's awesome, Blaire. Sounds like an incredible trip. Can't wait to see the pictures."

"It was, and the pictures are to die for. I'm so sad about going back to work. I just want to have babies and be a housewife already," she gushes.

"Well, you're halfway there, Blairey," I say, half focused on the conversion, half focused on getting back to my house to pack a bag.

"So, how's Persephone? I heard the uncles loved her, Mom not so much, but that's to be expected," she crows nonchalantly.

"Seph is… uh." I can't get words out to even lie about her. I don't know what to say.

Blaire cuts me off anyways, blabbing away, "Mom is delusional, Celia wasn't the girl for you when you dated her in high school, she for sure isn't the girl for you now. Plus, she's a waitress. Talk about slumming it, Brooks. You'd think Mom would think like that too."

Heat rises up in me, offended for Persephone since she is a food service worker too, "Servers are hardworking people, it's not her occupation that dissuades me from dating her. It's her personality."

"Well, aren't you the prickly pear today?" Blaire fakes shock at the harshness in my tone. "What's eating you Brooky-baby? Troubles with the lady?"

"Things are… fine." I don't want to talk about it.

"Sounds like they're not," she prods.

"They are," I snapped back.

"So why did Graham tell me she left you at the wedding?"

Fuck. I didn't think he saw that part too. "She wasn't feeling well."

"She never went to the hotel, stop lying. What's going on?"

"It's fine Blaire, just stop," I huff. Frustrated and confused, I am losing the last bit of my patience with my sister.

"Did you break up, was it messy? Come on, Brooks, give me the juicy deets. Sounded like it was dramatic, at least how Graham told it," she whines and I am ready to snap.

"She left! Okay? She left and hasn't come back!"

Silence fills the air on the phone. Blaire doesn't realize how she is poking the bear. I hear inaudible whispers on the other end, and I ask Blaire who she is with.

"Mona. She's asking me for my coffee order," Blaire pauses, "So, do you know where she went?" She asks more softly now, with compassion.

"No. Yes. I don't know," I grab my head, still processing all the new information and only surviving off two hours of sleep. I'm practically delusional, unsure if my thoughts are in my head or spewing out of my mouth. "She went to a tiny town in Montana. Baker? Why would she go there?" I say half to myself, then I realize those words that were pouring out of my mouth were meant to only stay in my brain.

Fuck, I shouldn't have told my sister if Persephone was scared by Graham's friends… fuck, fuck, fuck. My sister got me all out of sorts, I can't think straight right now.

"Blaire, you can't tell anyone where she is, not even Graham, especially not Graham," I pause, trying to gently persuade her to hear my reasoning. "She is running from someone in her past I think, and Graham is connected to them somehow. They have… mutual friends or something."

I stop what I'm doing to wait for her response. Blaire and I used to rat each other out when we kids to our mom, but we hadn't tattled like that since middle school. We covered for each other in high school when we had been out drinking or sneaking out. But would that adolescent truce transfer into her new matrimony?

"Doesn't surprise me, some of Graham's friends are pricks. I won't mention it to Graham though, just in case. It sounds like you should be on the next flight to Montana. What's the plan from there?"

I'm relieved she agrees, but still am worried she might tell her new husband despite her promise to her brother. "I'm not sure, ask around, I guess. What else can I do?" I exhale and slide my freehand over my scruffy, multiple-day-no-shave face.

Blaire is unreasonably quiet, but the lack of questions is a welcomed lull in our conversation. Finally, I break the silence and wrap up the call.

"I gotta go, Blaire. I'll text you when I know more. Please don't tell Graham. I don't know how serious this is yet."

Her pause worries me, but eventually she says, "Of course. I hope everything works out. Good luck, brother."

"Thanks. Love you."

"Love you."

Ending the call makes me worried for Seph. I had been so lost in my own head; I didn't even realize the words that were forming in my mind were actually spilling out of my stupid mouth.

Did I just endanger her? How could I live with myself if something happened, and I was the one who ratted her location out? All I knew for certain was whoever was after Seph was connected to Graham and his friends.

Grappling with regret and fear, I call my assistant quickly to push all my meetings to next week. I run the rest of the way home and grab a poorly packed weekender bag to then head to the airport without a ticket purchased. A few quick Googles later, I find the closest airport is Bowman Regional in North Dakota and the next flight out of Savannah is at 5pm. On the ride to the airport, I call the airline and book myself a damn seat.

Fuck, Seph. I'm coming.

Chapter 17

Brooks

Eighteen hours and one layover later, I touched down in North Dakota for the first time in my life. Weaving through people and securing a car, the hour drive to Montana has me on more pins and needles than the flight. Worry and anxiety has eaten me from the inside out, and I am now just a shell of a man who hasn't slept in days, passing through an extremely flat state.

I did some research on the town during my layover. It's another tiny, small town which didn't make a ton of sense for someone who is trying to stay hidden. If it were me, I'd stick to a bigger city, but I assume she is trying to recreate the small-town life she had in Dorian. I hope she hasn't found a lawyer boyfriend yet though, going to jail for murder wasn't on my agenda this week.

Driving through the small town, I notice shops and businesses, but nothing of note pertaining to her. Everything is spread out, even the cars barely park next to each other. My eyes catch on a coffee shop, and I immediately pull over, thinking that is as good of a place to start as any. Plus, I could always use a cup of coffee.

Walking into the shop has my nerves on edge, but with a quick glance, I spot no brunette vixen, just a few older couples and a middle-aged man behind the counter.

"Hey there, welcome. What can I get for you today, sir?"

There's no time for elongated pleasantries. "I was wondering if you've seen this woman," I hold my phone out and show a beautiful headshot of my Persephone, smiling after chomping into a burger at a place in downtown Savannah.

Finding the picture I would show to everyone was a painful process. I thumbed through hundreds of candid shots I had taken of her over the past four months. Ones of her sleeping on my chest, her tangled up in my sheets, and even blurry outtakes all brought me back to those very specific moments in time. I must have watched the live versions of the pictures a good hundred times. They were moments when I was happy, when *we* were happy.

Would I ever feel that overwhelming sense of euphoria when I turn over in the morning to find a woman heaven sent sleeping next to me? An angel from above to grant all my childhood wishes of a hot girlfriend, my adult prayers of a sensible woman, and every dream I've ever had of a loving *wife*. She is it for me. The end all be all, the one, the once in a lifetime love, and I somehow fucked it up.

She has been lying to me, omitted major truths about her past but it still isn't enough for me to move on from her. For me to forget her and shake this horrible feeling that she is in danger.

In the five months I had known her, she had ensnared my heart in more ways than one.

It was the hours of genuine laughter under the sun, the late-night pillow talks where we'd share our dreams and feelings. It was long discussions about the movie we watched that night or singing along to 70's classic rock in the car. It was the breakfast dates at diners in neighboring towns, the thoughtfully packed lunches that always featured a note with her sweet words, or making dinner together in my kitchen that occasionally turned into making love on the floor.

I know now that she lied about her past. Lied about being someone's fiancé, lied about being wealthier than she put off, lied about the groomsman's words to her. But I also know she told the truth about *who* she was.

She couldn't fake all those moments I fell in love with her.

My investigative mind wants to uncover her secrets, but a bigger part of me wants to figure out how I can break down the superficial parts she had lied about.

I want all of her, or nothing at all.

With each passing moment, I worry we might never have the chance to have the conversation I've been planning in my head for the last 18 hours, the one where I ask her a question and she actually answers it. The conversation I hope will deconstruct the walls she built around me, closing me out.

"I'm sorry, I haven't," I blink in rapid succession as I fall out of my daydream. The kid looks sad for me, clearing wishing he can help. "It's a small town though, I'm sure someone has," he says optimistically. I nodded, thanked him for his time, and walked out to the street.

Two hours later, a few random purchases to appease shop owners, no one, random pedestrians or other, has seen Persephone and I have almost given up hope of finding her.

Sitting in my rental car, I look into the street, wishing that every woman that walks by is the one I am looking for. I am in a daze until a familiar face strikes me.

It's Graham, or what looks exactly like Graham. He's not in his normal suit and tie, he is rocking jeans and black sweatshirt with sunglasses, but even dressed down, he stands out.

He walks out of the town's gun shop with a small bag, but I can't make out what he has in the bag, but he is carrying it carefully.

Fucking Blaire.

Wanting to believe this is a figment of my extremely overtired imagination, I text my sister to confirm Graham's whereabouts. For all I know, he is sitting right next to her and I just created a mirage in my head of my worst fear. I don't want to rock the boat with Blaire yet, I didn't want to spring any alarms or worry her unnecessarily. For all I know, it could be a big misunderstanding. Graham is my family now and I need to give him the benefit of the doubt.

Brooks: Hey. Is Graham with you?

Blaire: No, he had a last-minute business trip. Said he'll be home tomorrow. Why?

Brooks: No reason, I wanted to pick his brain about something.
Blaire: *thumbs up emoji*

Fuck.

Unable to shake the feeling that Graham is somehow in the middle of all this, I follow my brother-in-law around town in my car until he ends up at a nearby hotel and seems to settle in for the night. Relieved my stalking duties are done for now, I get a room at the same hotel and settle in for the night.

Sitting at the desk in my room, I shove both hands through my hair, contemplating my next move. If she is in danger and I can't find her, she needs to know. She will be pissed how everything got out, but she needs to know. I struggle with my decision but end up texting her so I know she receives the message.

Pulling up her text string that my iCloud backup thankfully saved for me, I realize I haven't texted her in almost two days, exactly since I broke my phone. It has been a stressful 36 hours; finding out she is gone then where she went, and then the whole day I spent in the air trying to get here to find her.

Brooks: I need to talk to you. Don't be mad. Graham is in Montana trying to find you. I am too. Call me.

I haven't said it in a while, so I threw in softer follow up text.

Brooks: I love you.

Ten minutes later, I am lying on the bed staring at the ceiling, and I hear my phone buzz on the counter like a fire alarm. I shoot up and pick it up without looking.

"Hello?" My voice is trembling with anticipation, waiting to hear from that sweet sound for the first time in weeks.

"Brooks?" The voice is quiet and cracked. I hear watery sniffles and deep inhales on the other end and my spine instantly straightens at the sound.

"Seph? Is that you?" My hand flips my phone to check the caller ID and confirm it's Persephone who's calling me. It feels like a dream. Or a nightmare. I'm not sure which, yet.

"How does he know where I am?" I expect her to sound angrier, but the tone coming through is terror. It fills my veins with ice, but then I'm instantly relieved when I realize she's not upset that *I* know where she is. I am reluctant to tell her how that information chain snaked because without my boneheaded mistake, Graham would have never known. I don't want to start the first conversation we've had in weeks off with her being pissed at me. Though, I'm not sure how I'll navigate around that later.

She starts again without a response from me, "You need to leave, Brooks. You need to leave and stay as far away from me as possible. It's not *safe*." She is crying into the phone, begging me to leave instead of the bubbling anger I was expecting, and it throws me off guard.

What would make my fiery, sassy girl this scared? Better yet, who?

"I'm not leaving without you, Seph. Where are you? I'll come to you; we can leave together. We don't have to go back to Georgia," I pause to wait for her reply for what feels like several minutes but is only maybe 5 seconds of time.

"No... You need to stay away from me and my shit, Brooks. I know this all seems crazy, but I'm doing it to protect you, you can't be with me, there can't be a 'us' anymore" she cries harder into the phone, and I feel helpless on the other line. There are no words of comfort or advice to give. 'There can't be an us' spins in my hollow heart and slices through me, I don't understand why. Why can't she be with me?

"I can't help you if you don't tell me what's going on. How is Graham related to all this? Why does he want to find you? Is it about that groomsman, Doug?" It has been weeks of pain on my end, I need to start asking the questions that matter and stop thinking about our relationship, or lack thereof.

"They think I have something of their friend's… But I don't. I don't! I'm sorry Brooks. Please let me deal with this on my own. I don't want you involved in this," she's still sniffling and teary, but her voice is stern with reason. Everything inside me wants to listen to her and turn around to go home, but I can't find it in me to put one foot in front of the other.

"Seph, I can help you if you need it, just tell me what to do," I beg.

She laughs and the sound lacks all humor. I ignore it and push on. "Why do you need to do this on your own? Why won't you let me help you?"

"I don't need you to get tangled into this, it's not fair to you." Her voice is distant and cold, completely forced.

"I'm not going anywhere."

"Goodbye, Brooks," she whispers.

"Persephone," she hangs up before I finish the last syllable of her name.

Defeated, heartbroken, and beyond worried, I wake up from my very short night's sleep, and make my way back to my car which is in perfect view of Graham's hotel room. True rest has evaded me since my sad lady has vacated the spot in my bed next to me. I can't sleep through the night knowing it's devoid of her.

Graham's car isn't there, and a pain of fear plays in my gut. I wait, semi-frantically, forcing myself to think maybe he went to grab some food. But 10 am rolls around and the cleaning ladies park in front of his door to either start turning the room over or tidy up. I walk past the room to get a glimpse of whether his stuff is still in there or not.

It wasn't.

They are stripping the room to turn it over; he must have checked out already.

My mind jumps to Seph and her safety, I shoot her a text.

Brooks: Morning. Are you okay?

I didn't hear back for several minutes. Not hearing back *at all* is more common for me, so it's surprising when I see the alert come in that she responded.

Persephone: 318 Fairway Acres Road

An address is all she sent which struck me as odd, but my heart skips at the thought of this being an invitation over. Not wanting to get my hopes up, I grip the wheel with white knuckles the entire ride over, repeating the same words in my head, "It's not a big deal. It's just her address." But it's more than I've gotten in weeks, and I am desperate for a crumb.

Stepping out of the car, the snow crunches under my feet. Snow that seems to cover the flat land for miles sweeps out as far as the eye can see. Seph's cabin is the only building for at least a few acres which scares me in more ways than one. She is alone out here.

Walking to the small cabin's door, the nerves hit me again. Knocking then waiting feels like a trip around the sun. I hear her unlatch all the locks, my heart races with anticipation.

The wood door squeaks open and I catch the first glimpse of her face in three weeks. It's almost like looking in a mirror. She is gaunt, she has lost a lot of weight, back to a similar weight as when she arrived in Dorian almost five months ago. Her olive skin now has deep purple circles under her eyes that match my own, but she also donnes red blotches, puffy eyelids, and a rubbed raw nose and upper lip. Her eyes look haunted and scared.

A meek shadow of a smile crosses her lips as she holds the door open for me to step inside. Immediately after closing it behind me, she locks the door with four different locks. Two look freshly self-installed. My heart warms at the idiotic train of thought my desperate mind takes; she feels safe enough to be locked up **with** me.

Seeing her so broken down and panicked makes me cringe, and my heart drops to see the pills scattered around the table. They are the only indication a person lives here. Nothing is unpacked from her single suitcase that sits fully packed next to the door, ready for a quick getaway.

Unsure what to do next, I turned to her for a clue. Once our eyes connected, it was like two waves colliding out at sea. It takes several moments for me to realize she is hugging me for me to hug her back. Having her in my arms after weeks of imaging it feels like someone is over filling my cup, and the water is splashing all around onto the table. I can't get enough of her smell, her touch, her body pressed into mine. My arms wrap around her so tightly, my face buries into her neck then her hair, and I forget where I am.

"God, Persephone. I missed you so much," I mumble into the crook of her neck, taking long deep breaths to capture more of her scent. As if I ever forgot it.

She doesn't reply but I feel her body jerking in response and then I notice a wet spot on my shoulder. Seph is sobbing into me violently. I hold the back of her head in my hand and use the other to rub her back while I whisper empty assurances in her ear.

"It's okay. I'm here. I'm here. I'm not going to leave you. It's going to be okay Seph, I promise."

Some words seem to calm her, others seem to make it worse, so I stick to rubbing and telling her how much I love and miss her. She breaks us apart and looks up at me through swollen, glassy eyes to press a chaste kiss onto my lips.

I recoil from the contact, unsure of what to make of it. She just ignored me for weeks, then cried into my chest and was now kissing me. Be still my heart, the whiplash feels so good.

"I'm sorry, I shouldn't have done that," she shakes out of our embrace and covers her face in embarrassment.

Kicking myself for my reaction, I try to explain, "No, no. I wanted that, I want you to do it again and again. I just... I was surprised, that's all."

"I don't want to talk about this yet. I..."

The anger and confusion from months of lies unravelling are on the back burner right now, but there are several questions I need answered and her lack of transparency is painful to hear after that kiss.

Although her immediate safety is my number one concern, I can't live forever without answers. For now, in this moment, where I am finally standing next to her, breathing her in, all my aggravation and mistrust falls by the wayside.

"Seph, it's okay, I just want to make sure you're okay," I grab her hands and assure her.

"I need to ask you for a favor," she says warily, barely even meeting my eyes.

"Anything, Seph. Anything you need," I sound desperate, but I don't care.

"Stay here for a little? I need your company right n-"

I cut her off before she can finish, "Of course I'll stay. Of course, Seph." I bring her hands up to my mouth and kiss her fingertips.

She nods, slipping her hands out of mine gently, then makes her way into her bedroom to get into her unmade bed. She makes a subtle head nod to join her and I all but rip off my jacket and shoes to jump in alongside her.

We spent the rest of the day watching movies from different sides of her mattress, playing a few hands of cards, and eventually ordering a quick bite to eat from a local Chinese restaurant. It felt like old times back in Georgia, minus the stimulating conversation. It *felt* like we were back together, even just for a few hours, and even though we were completely silent.

Glancing at the clock, I notice it is 10pm and both our eyes are getting heavy. While I want to press my luck and try to stay, my gut tells me that I shouldn't try too hard too fast. I get up and start putting my sneakers back on to head out when she interrupts me.

"Will you stay with me tonight?" She glances at the space next to her on the bed, "We can talk in the morning… I promise." Her eyes are pleading unnecessarily. Wild horses couldn't drag me away from her tonight once she asked me to stay.

My mind swirls with so many different emotions and thoughts. She wants me to *stay* tonight. How could I get back into bed with the woman who offered me no explanation for breaking my heart into a million pieces? She is scared and alone, I need to be here for her, and I need to hear the explanation I am too scared to demand today.

"I won't be able to not touch you if I crawl into that bed with you, Seph. I can take the couch."

Her eyes lower along with her head, then look back up at me through her lashes, "Please come to bed with me, Brooks. One last night, then never again if you don't want to."

The plea in her voice is enough to melt my resolve, but the words level me beyond recognition.

"Okay," my strained voice croaks out in compliance.

I strip down to my boxers and white undershirt, then slip into the small double bed where she is already waiting for me to spoon her from behind. Our bodies sync together like puzzle pieces, my front to her back, and our legs naturally tangle together like they have so for so many months before. It's like we never left each other's embrace.

My face nuzzles into the back of her neck while my arms curl around her sides, pulling her closer to my chest. We both sigh loudly at the intimate skin to skin contact but stay quiet otherwise. There is nothing more to say that our bodies aren't already communicating. I can feel the prickle on her skin and I'm certain she can feel my heart thundering in my chest.

Her butt shifts against mine purposefully and she grabs my hand to move it over her breast. My fingers freeze at the contact with her breasts but I allow her to guide my hand to wherever she wants.

She moves our joined hands to her stomach, then lower, and I stall again, unsure what game she is playing. Turning her face around to me, our heads laid on the same pillow, noses almost touching at the tips.

Slowly studying my face in the dark, she makes a slight but concentrated move again for my lips, and this time I slide my hand across her cheek to guide her. Our mouths brush softly at first, as if dipping a toe in a cold pool, then fervently and all at once. Tongues collide and our innocent moment of exploring old territory turns very quickly into frantic groping and clothes being forcibly removed. Like a switch has been turned on, we go from zero to sixty.

It is not the nightcap I predicted when I went over this morning, but it's one I fantasized about for weeks in my day dreams. I'll take it for now, since tomorrow is likely to be my living nightmare.

Chapter 18

Brooks

———

The morning sunlight wakes me before I feel her stir. She turns towards me on her own pillow, but her hand opens on my bare chest and rubs absently to feel its surroundings. She looks like an angel in the sunlight, come down to rip me from this Earthly plane and take me away to Heaven.

Despite her promise last night to end my multiple weeks long desire to know exactly what's been going on with her, I beg God to not wake her up so I could enjoy this moment a little while longer. Did I even want to know now if it would change everything? I would rather live ignorantly blissful with her by my side than in the know and without her. Last night reminded me how good life could be with her and this morning, I face losing it all again.

Reaching out to stroke her cheek, her eyes flutter open as the sunshine cascades on her face. Even after all the tears from yesterday puffing up her eyelids, she is still the most beautiful woman I'd ever laid eyes on. The hair, the eyes, her soft feminine nose, the full lips, slightly rosy cheek bones, the perfect teeth, moreover, the heart of pure gold.

Thinking about her good nature and all the little things I've picked up since she left like the overzealous tips, the expensive studio apartment but low wage job. My brain is slowly piecing together how many unanswered questions surround Persephone still. It's not just her dodgy background, but the money she gave to Shannon and Michael, the gap in my knowledge of her work history, the vagueness around her family other than her late father, the engagement she never mentioned, and the insane aversion to New York City.

The months of wondering if she would ever tell me, the months of convincing myself it didn't matter, the weeks of being in the dark. Now that it is at my fingertips, did I even want to know anymore?

"Brooks," she strokes my cheek to break me out of my daze. The lingering feeling of her touch is dulled by the scruff that has turned into an unintentional short beard.

"Sephy," I look back adoringly at her, forgetting my internal struggle the second she purred my name.

"I have to tell you what's going on, and it's going to change everything between us." She keeps stroking my hair lovingly, while tears start silently rolling down her face. "Some of this, I should have told you sooner, but I didn't want to embarrass you. I didn't want you to think any less of me. I've spent this year trying to deal with things on my own, trying to be strong"

I nod for her to continue on, unsure how much I actually wanted to hear the truth now that the time has come. My wounded heart takes note of her referring to me in past tense when talking about her future.

"Some, I didn't know all the details myself. It wasn't fair to you for me to work through that with you."

"I would have tried to help you through whatever it was, Seph, you know that," I squeeze my hand on the back of her neck to reinforce my point.

"I know, baby. I know," she looks down and takes a deep breath, "You ready?" She laughs. I nod, definitely not ready.

"My brain went through how to tell you this a million times, and every time I said it differently. But here it goes... " she takes a big breath in and lets it out. "My father died. I became depressed, my relationship took a turn for the worse and I fled from New York City because my fiancé was," I watched her throat bob with a harsh swallow. "He was physically abusive... towards the end. He was cheating on me too, but that was just the straw that broke the camel's back." She shakes then dips her head in what seemed like embarrassment while my heart cracks open for her.

I stare at her blankly, unblinking, devastated hearing the word 'fiancé' even though I have already uncovered that particular secret, then immediately become distraught hearing the word 'abusive' alongside it.

"That's just the basics, there's a lot more to it, Brooks," she added when my silent response became unbearable. She sobs once into her hands, "I'm so sorry, I didn't know. I didn't know."

Next came confusion. Sorry? For what?

Instinctively, I pull her into my chest to comfort her, pressing kisses into the crown on her hair. I coo soft whispers of comfort, lost in a sea of whimpers and tears.

As if regaining a hint of reality, she pushes off me, rejecting my comfort in exchange for enduring the pain on her own. Her eyes don't meet mine, they drift off into old memories when she begins to talk again.

"I met Harrison at a party. He was my father's stockbroker. We started dating almost two years ago this month. Remember the dates, Brooks. They're important." She spares a glance before staring off into my chest again.

"Our romance was quick and exciting. Our lifestyles were parallel in a lot of ways; lots of late nights out with friends, lavish dinners at clubs and expensive restaurants, and luxurious vacations. Most of my dating experience was formal events or late nights at the club, sometimes going on dating apps, and then the random older men my dad wanted me to 'give a shot'. He was a hot ticket, my father, and all he ever wanted was for me to be taken care of. When Harrison swooped in, Pops was thrilled to see someone like him in my life.

Once Harrison asked for my hand in marriage last year, my dad showed him the ropes behind the scenes, showed him classified information, thinking his future son in law would take over my portion of the ownership and I could be whatever I wanted to be.

My dad loved Harrison. He was sharp, brilliant, and engaging. Loved hearing my dad talk shop about the business and loved looking over the inner workings of the company. Loved the idea of taking it over one day. Maybe that's what he loved most in our relationship."

"Then he's not smart at all, or at least has no sensibility of valuable things," my voice is low and grumbly, defensive of my Sephy even in the past.

"You know my father died. It was a few weeks after the proposal." She pauses to gather herself, tearing her eyes out of focus to meet mine. I can tell this is a difficult portion of the story for her, she is wringing her hands together incessantly working through a way to continue on.

"I'm so sorry for your loss, Persephone. I wish I had the pleasure of meeting him."

"Me too," she says sadly and continues softly.

"My depression slid over me slowly, then all at once. I wasn't a great partner or friend, there is no pride in how I acted during this time, and I actually commend Harrison for sticking it out with me. He organized everything, the funeral and wake, the memorials. I didn't lift a finger, not that I could have if I tried. My father was my best friend, without him, I was lost.

I was physically there, but never mentally. Always on autopilot. I made it through events such as Harrison's 'miserable date' for only so long before he stopped asking me to come along. My friends stopped inviting me to come out and only asked Harrison, leaving the decision to him to include me or not. It wasn't intentionally cruel, but they weren't used to being decent humans to begin with.

I don't know when it started or how it got so bad. When he started putting his hands on me, it was subtle and usually after a night of heavy drinking. A push here or there, a vase getting chucked across the room, or punching a wall near my head. Eventually it became slamming me against walls by my neck, split lips, cracked ribs, and bruises on my arms."

My veins heat up at the thought of a man hurting her, of her not being able to defend herself, and of me not being able to defend her either, even from the past. I want to murder this guy for touching her like that and I don't even know him from a hole in the wall.

Sensing my anger, she winces and swallows hard. I can tell her confession isn't over and the worst has yet to come.

"I'm so sorry you had to go through that, Seph. Tell me what to do, tell me how to help," I plead with her. I move to grab her hands and she pulls them away, but I leave my empty hands on her lap, desperate for any type of contact.

"Doug was reminding me of my previous life at the wedding," she says quietly, and I mutter a swear in response, pulling back my rejected hands.

"Where does Graham come into this?" I cut in, worried that my sister's new husband is friends with a man like this.

Her eyes darken and look guilty.

"I'm not sure exactly," it's a truth, but not the whole truth and it makes me uneasy.

"My father's estate requires a prenup if I were to get married. It was probably an old rule he never updated since meeting Harrison. I either got the entire estate along with the company but my future husband would have to sign a prenup or I'd lose it all to my father's company. I chose my father's estate," she stares into my eyes, looking for my reaction.

Estate? Does she mean her inheritance?

"It sounded like he loved you very much and just wanted to protect you. I don't understand the problem," I search her eyes for the answer.

Persephone places a gentle hand on my jaw and softens her eyes as if she's about to deliver a death blow and she's easing me into her knife.

"I inherited 250 million dollars, Brooks. Along with 51% of my dad's hedge fund, which is worth another 50 million," she dropped her hand and dipped her head in what looked like embarrassment again.

Blinking, I breathe out a shaky, "What?"

She stares back at me with a broken expression. I want nothing more than to lift her spirits, the shock completely eclipsing me, so I try to slide in a joke to test the waters.

"And you had me paying for every date the first few months?" I hide my grin, hoping she will find some amusement in my joke.

She shoots up out of bed, whips the covers off and starts pacing as her voice rises to a light yell. I sit up, realizing it backfired, and I watch her walk back and forth, pacing.

"You're not taking this fucking seriously. I'm filthy fucking rich and my fiancé got pissed when he realized he wasn't going to see a dime of it, so he beat the shit out of me. But my sad, pathetic self didn't leave until I found out he cheated on me. How terribly weak of me, don't you think?" She searches my face for disgust, but only finds my empathy. I wish I could take every ounce of her pain away at this moment, drain it like the cyst it is.

Without a verbal response from me, she goes on, "I fucking left with nowhere to go, and I came to Dorian as a stop on a long road to nowhere. My heart found yours the first day I was there and here we are, Brooks. Here we fucking are. I never wanted to go back to New York City because the first time I left Harrison, he tracked me down. He tracked me down and coaxed me back to our apartment, then *hurt* me. I just wanted to get away for a weekend…" She says absently, as if the nightmare of the memory pulls on her conscious mind.

"No one knew where I was or even what direction I headed towards this time. I left and never looked back! Going back scared the fuck out of me! Going to that wedding scared the hell out of me, and for good reason."

The bombshell explodes and my stomach twists. Forcing her to go to New York was asking her to potentially blow her cover. I unknowingly forced a battered woman out of hiding to go to a stupid wedding. Regret over asking her to go to the wedding now quadruples in my mind. As if I don't regret the event itself every moment of my waking life since she drove off that night. No wonder she fought me so hard to not come.

My hands snag hers to pull her in between my legs while she stands, and I sit on the bed we shared last night. "I'm so sorry for asking you to go to that wedding. I didn't know, but I don't see how anything you've told me changes anything between us, Sephy. I love you for you, not your money. Your past doesn't change anything for me and I'm so sorry you think it would have."

She settles a bit, and I see her shoulders slump. "That's not the part I meant."

"There's more?" My stomach drops.

"When I went to the wedding, I had never seen your sister and Graham. She looked familiar when I saw her before she walked down the aisle, but everything clicked together when I saw Graham's bridal party, then Graham himself."

She pauses and I fill the gap, "Sephy, tell me how you know Graham." Fear swells inside my chest. Fear that Graham is a much greater player in this strange puzzle than I want to admit.

Seph takes her hands back, brings them to her face and the tears start to fall again, rolling down her face like a dam breaking on a river. Bracing myself for impact, her words slam into me, "'Graham' is my ex fiancé, Harrison."

The room swirls and all the walls crash in on my brain, not understanding how this could ever come to be. My heart pounds out of my chest as all the pieces start snapping together in my head. Harrison, the man who brutalized my now girlfriend, or maybe exgirlfriend, overlapped his relationship with my sister, and is now married to her?

"How is that possible?" I breathe out.

"That's what I'm still trying to work out. We were engaged this time last year; our engagement didn't end until 6 months ago when I left. I don't know when Blaire got engaged, or when they started dating," she starts rambling, almost talking to herself and not me. "But the weekend they got married was the same weekend we were supposed to get married, same venue actually, too. He literally must have just swapped out the bride…"

I zone out her sarcastic defense to tabulate timetables swimming in my brain.

"They started dating last Thanksgiving. She said it was too new for him to come to the holiday gatherings," I grumble out, lifelessly. I am still trying to work out dates and times in my head, but the information overload is rocking my senses.

"Got engaged in June I think, right after you came to town. I don't know the dates," shaking my head, I try to get the thought of Graham and Seph out of my mind.

His parting words make a lot more sense now, "she's good at leaving." He knew first-hand, just like me. She left him, too. Twice.

"What did he say to you at the wedding?" My voice came out harsher than I meant, but the dam holding back my emotions is slowly breaking at the seams.

Seph shakes her head, "He said I took something from him, something he wants back, needs back. I don't know what. Everything I took was my own. He refused to tell me what it was, he kept asking where I ran off to, and that he'd hunt me down later to retrieve what was his," she pauses. "I never thought it was the ring, I pawned that already anyways. Everything else is in storage, which I moved after blowing my cover at the wedding."

A flicker of happiness runs through me at her free omission of one of the lies I found along the way. She isn't hiding anything anymore, at least nothing I knew of.

"How much was the ring?" My question was out of pure curiosity.

"I got $50,000 from the pawn shop. If he wanted that amount of money, he would have just asked for it. It has to be worth more," she brushes me off with a wave of her hand, like that amount of money was chump change.

"How much more?" The numbers were bigger than I can imagine. I make a very comfortable living, more than most people in the area will ever make in their lifetime, but the wealth being tossed around in this conversation is beyond my comprehension.

"At least a million, maybe two or three," she rasps under her breath, locking eyes with mine.

My eyebrows arch in surprise. "Are you saying he has something worth over a million dollars sitting in one of your drawers and you have no idea what it is?"

"Yes."

"Did you look for it yet?"

"No."

"Right, okay. So now what? You're just going to wait like a sitting duck til he finds you? What was your plan, Sephy?" I'm aggravated at her impending danger and taking it out on her lack of plan when I don't mean to.

"The plan was no one knowing where I was, especially not you because of exactly what happened. I couldn't risk someone slipping and telling Blaire, who would tell Harrison," she sounds exasperated.

"Graham. Harrison. How did my sister marry a man without actually knowing his name?"

"His middle name is Graham," she whispers.

My brain and mouth pause for a second to digest the truths of the scenario for the tenth time since hearing it all. My initial reaction was sadness for Seph, then sympathy, but now anger started bubbling up inside me.

"How did you not tell me my sister was married to a wife beater? Were you ever going to fucking tell me?" I let it out, figuring we were laying it all on the table now anyways.

Her tears turned back on, almost like clockwork, but this time it didn't twist every nerve on my body. I am mad, and rightfully so.

"I wasn't going to tell you, no. In my heart of hearts, I still think Harrison could be a good man, he seemed like a good man to her, I just brought out the worst in him. My depression brought out the worst in *us*."

The truth quells my fury more than expected, *she still thought this was her fault,* that she deserved to be hit. My insides couldn't help but to feel for her, my angel blamed herself for the wrongs done to her. She didn't realize how worthy she is of love, even during her darkest days. No one deserved what she endured and definitely not an incredible woman like her.

"I can forgive you for not telling me everything up until the wedding, but I'm having a hard time with you leaving town, leaving me behind without telling me my sister was married to an abusive man, Seph. I'm having a really difficult time wrapping my head around that part."

She bows her head and says, "I know. I wouldn't forgive me either."

Her candidness calms my heat, she always soothes my flames, which is probably why I am having a hard time accepting that she created this fire.

"I'll never be able to apologize enough for deceiving you all this time."

"We'll figure out your repayment when we get back to Georgia," I say half joking, but entirely serious as well. The pause without agreement left me nervous.

"Brooks… I'm not going back to Georgia, at least not until I figure out what he wants… even then, I don't know what I'm going to do next."

Her asserting she won't be moving back with me hurts more than anything else has in this conversation. All this pain, for what? For her to not even come back home with me?

"Well, he's gone for now. I saw his hotel room get cleaned out. He told Blaire he was coming home tomorrow. Let's go to Georgia and figure out your next move together."

She doesn't look like she is listening, she is far in thought, then her gaze turns to me to laser into my skin.

"He stole thousands of dollars from me, Brooks. I had my accountant look into all the charges from the last two years compared to past ones. He started skimming off the top of all my accounts. I think once the prenup got brought up, that's when things really got bad because he knew it was all for nothing and I wasn't worth the effort without the money. He didn't think we were going to *have* a prenup. I didn't either. I didn't think my assets were enough to have such a thing. Like I said, we uncovered he made it a stipulation within his estate that I do so for any man I marry if it was post-death. That came out after a month or two after Pop's passing and my lawyer asked me if he needed to draw up a prenup soon or not."

My laugh is out of awkwardness more than anything, "I stand by my original statement. Odd stipulation but sweet in a way."

She mirrors my laugh with a snort of air, "My father was a zany man. My uncles couldn't stop laughing about his will when I told them, saying it was dad's way to posthumously protect me from any man silly enough to marry me."

I'd be silly enough to marry her.

"Harrison wanted the company, a seat at the table at least. When my dad died, the board didn't care about his relationship with my dad, they told me to make a decision to either come back or sell, no option for Harrison."

"What are you trying to say, Seph?" I say, not liking where this is headed.

"He's not going to just stop looking for me. I was his piggy bank and whatever I accidentally took from him, he's going to reclaim."

I bring up the only question I keep coming back to but have been scared to even think, "Do you think my sister was in on this?"

"No, I really don't. She had to know he was in a relationship with someone, though. I realized after the wedding that I had seen your sister before, at my apartment. He told me she was someone's assistant dropping something off," her eyes skate away from mine.

I nod, agreeing my sister wouldn't be so callous, but it will be worth asking her about later on.

"Why didn't you just tell me once we got back to Georgia? Why did you push me away when all I wanted to do was help? You didn't just break my heart, you shattered it." I am angry, rightfully so, and it is slowly seeping out of me. "Not talking to you every single day was like being deprived of sweet tea on a hot day. You conditioned me to need your love, then you withdrew it from me. I was left with a crippling addiction and no fix."

"I'm so sorry, Brooks, I was scared that if I saw you, if we talked, you'd get the whole truth out of me. I was on the edge, ready to explode at any moment. I didn't want you to have to deal with my drama. I knew I could never be with you and your family ever again knowing I'd have to see him on holidays or special events. My mind wasn't thinking about us or you, I went back into survival mode. He's your brother-in-law…"

She is right. How would we even begin to explain this to Blaire? Would she even believe her? Knowing my sister, she would need proof, concrete evidence.

Unless, of course, it is already happening to her. The thought is fleeting but hangs around the back of my mind.

"I'd never ask you to come to another family event ever again, Seph," I assure her with the only words I can think of. "Hell, I don't even want him at family events. I don't want *him* anywhere near my sister."

"Your mother hates me, too," she says flatly.

"She's not even around most of the year," I counter, dismissing the thought entirely.

"Sounds like a great girlfriend, one who is never around during the holidays or family parties, used to fuck but currently hates your brother-in-law, avoids your mother because she hates her, and has a ton of emotional baggage from her past. You deserve better, Brooks. You're the most incredible man I know. You deserve drama free and simple."

The "used to fuck" part stung. This whole situation hasn't left me much time to think and digest the details, like how Graham has seen Persephone naked, been inside of her like I have, seen her moan and squirm when she comes. How he had probably been adorned with her soft kisses and pillow talk whispers. He had her in every way I had, and then some. He once had her heart, too, or she wouldn't have agreed to marry him.

It didn't matter, none of it did. I just want her. I like my life with her, I like who I am with her. Uninhibited, lighter, and free. I like what she brought out in me and what I brought out in her. Laughter, stimulating conversations, critical thinking. She forces me to think about more than just the facts, to read between the lines. Not to mention she lights up every nerve in my body with desire and need. The insane amount of money she has doesn't matter, my mother's deranged ideas for my love life doesn't matter, my sister's husband being her ex, or him being an abusive partner, doesn't matter.

"I deserve to have everything I want?"

"Yes, you do, and then some."

"Then I want you," I say desperately. "Give me you."

"Not what I meant," she rolls her eyes and falls back on the bed. I climb on top of her and start pressing open mouth kisses to the skin under her ear, all the way to her collar bone. Her breath hitches with approval, but then squirms away when my hand skirts the hem of her shirt.

"Let's take a break from this conversation. We should get food and regroup, unless you have stuff to cook here?"

"Nothing here, the only place that delivers was the Chinese we had last night," she states.

"Okay, I'll run out and grab something for us then. There's a diner down the street I believe. What do you want?" I start to stand and pull my phone out to take a look at the menu pinned to the corkboard in the bedroom.

She watches me as I thumb through pages, "You don't have to do this, Brooks. I will keep on moving now that my cover is blown here. Harrison might not be here now, but he'll come back until he finds me. He'll find out you're helping me, and it will just complicate everything for you. He's still your brother-in-law. I don't want to create problems with you and your sister. Cut your losses here."

My thumb stops scrolling and I contemplate how the scenarios could play out while looking at her pretty face, so riddled with exhaustion and defeat. "I'm not letting you leave me again so easily. What do you want for food? Bacon, egg and cheese sandwich?"

She nods and I place our orders along with a quick kiss before I leave out the front door. "I'll be back in fifteen minutes."

Pulling back in, the sense of dread fills my chest when I see the door wide open and footprints in the snow.

"Persephone? Seph...." I call out in the tiny one-bedroom cabin. Her bag is still here, the car is in the yard, and the fire is still lit. "Persephone?"

This isn't right, something bad had to have happened.

Nausea swirls in my stomach as I look around. I notice one of the kitchen table chairs flipped on its side and a set of boot prints at the back door with a few drops of blood nestled beside them. I drop the bag of food and sprinted outside, following the prints and random spatterings of blood every few feet.

"Seph?! Seph!" I scream, but there's nothing in sight for miles out ahead of me. My mind is running a hundred miles a minute while formulating a plan to find her. It doesn't look like the footprints lead anywhere, nor are there tire tracks. Did they go back inside? I didn't check the bedroom…

Running back in, I grab the poker to the fireplace and slowly creep through the hallway of the cabin again, this time opening all the closet doors. When I reach the end of the hall, I notice the bedroom door is closed. When I left just to get food, it was open.

Behind the door, there are muffled yelps and screams, I heard Persephone calling out, "Get off me! Get off me! I can't breathe, Harrison!" Then a slapping noise and a loud sob. I kicked open the door after I felt the doorknob was locked, and found Graham and Seph rolling around fighting for a gun.

"Brooks!!"

Graham now has Persephone pinned to the ground, his hips above hers, legs on either side of hers, and both his hands holding her wrists to the floor. Seph's face was bloodied, her lip looked cut open and there was a gash above her eyebrow. Graham had some red scratches across his face and some tattered clothes, but in much better shape than Seph.

"It looks worse than it is, brother," Graham laughs breathlessly looking up at my seething self.

"What exactly do you think this looks like?" I questioned while trying to push him off her. He staggered to his feet and Step slided herself against the bed. The three of us are just in a triangle looking at each other, waiting for someone to do something.

"Probably looked like I was trying to seduce your girl. I promise you, I was not," he sounded disgusted at the thought.

"I believe she was your girl first, wasn't she?" I couldn't help the jealous undertone in my voice.

Seph jerked at me and spitted a bit of blood, and Graham chuckled with malice gleaming in his eyes like a madman.

"Exactly, see my angel? He gets it." He gestured to Seph while practically licking her face full of blood. He turned to me, "We're working something out right now. Be a dear and shut the door."

"You know I can't do that, Graham."

He shrugged, "Didn't hurt to ask."

I lunged to punch Graham in the cheek, my fist connected, and he fell onto the bed and she dove to avoid him and also to grab the gun across the room that I hadn't remembered its location until now. It had to be the same gun I saw him buy a day earlier.

The rest happens so fast, I didn't know exactly how it all shook out moment by moment until the end.

Graham got up, and swung back at my head, knocking me good in the jaw. We wrestled, smashing each other into walls and back against the door frame. He took my head and slammed it into the wall, disorienting me momentarily.

Seph screams and pushes him, "Don't touch him!" He backhands her before she lands a blow on him.

I reach for her, forgetting Graham is willing to hurt me to get to her. He grabs the desk chair and blind-sides me by smashing the metal chair over my head as hard as he can, knocking me down while Seph scrambles to get up with the gun shaking in her hand. Through hazy eyes, I see Graham hit her in the face again with an open palm, then both of them wrestling for the gun in her hand.

The last thing I remember seeing distinctly is Graham tackling her onto the bed. My vision starts to blur after that and becomes red from the blood, but I hear Seph fighting for her life. She is screaming and crying while I hear the thumps and subsequent yelps from her mouth. I can't move, can barely see straight, but I slip the phone out of my pocket to try and call 911. It connects, I can hear the operator even with the phone in my lap. With all my strength, I grab the phone to bring it up to my mouth and whisper the address three times into the microphone at the bottom.

My eyes slide shut, and the phone drops from my hand. I can still hear Graham around the corner, but they are completely out of sight now, even if I could open my eyes. "Where... the... fuck... is... the...

furniture…" I can hear the slaps between each word, begging for the location of her storage locker.

"What are you looking for? I only have the furniture, Harrison! The drawers are all empty!"

THWACK.

"How much do you need? I'll pay you! I'll pay you!" It sounds like he let up to hear her speak but didn't like what she's saying and wailed on her again. I can hear every thud. "Harrison! Stop! Please, stop!" Her sobs burn through me, even though I am barely conscious enough to stay awake. I flop forwards to try to crawl towards her.

"You ungrateful bitch!" He screams.

Seph and Graham wrestle a bit more from what I can hear, it is all out of my sightline. It wasn't until I heard a loud bang go off and then a subsequent thud on the floor that my heart truly dropped into my empty stomach.

"Sephy?" I could barely get her name off my lips, thinking the worst. "Sephy!" I yelled as loud as I could muster before my voice cracked.

It took several moments of wrestling with panic before she came staggering around the corner, dripping with blood and starting to hyperventilate. Her eyes bulged and I watched her drop the gun from her right hand and began her descent to the floor, knees first, hip, then side, only a few feet in front of me.

My adrenaline kicked in at the sight of her, and it helped clear my head enough to see she's having a hard time breathing while crumpled on the floor. Crawling over to her, I clamp onto her hand, and we lock eyes as we both laid broken on the floor.

"It's okay, Seph. You're okay, we're okay, breathe, breathe," I shakily stroke her matted hair with my other hand as she nods and grips at her chest. Outstretched on her side with our heads almost touching, and her eyes are battling to stay open.

The panic was rising up over her, threatening to pull her under. Her body is shaking and quivering unnaturally, and all I can do is try to tug her body closer while rubbing her shoulder and cooing comforting words to her while I fight my own consciousness.

Police came a few minutes later to find our bodies puddled together in the middle of the bedroom floor, with blood everywhere.

I spend an hour going through the details with the local police and Harrison/Graham get rushed out on a stretcher, with a bullet wound through his chest.

Medics help Seph with her panic attack then sit her in the kitchen. Wrapped in a blanket, I watch Seph stare into nothing while "listening" to the police talk to her about next steps.

She is zoned out, vacant as a ghost while she robotically answers questions. A woman who normally uses her whole body to tell a story, including every muscle in her face, this Persephone in front of me is stoic and sedentary. She makes no attempts to defend herself, but made sure to mention this scuffle has nothing to do with me.

I attempt to interrupt her a few times, but I can tell the officers are growing impatient with my interruptions, so I shut my trap and painfully watch on as the woman I love broke into silent pieces in front of me.

Chapter 19

Brooks

———

I t's been five days and a mild concussion later since Harrison found us in Montana and all the omitted truths unraveled in front of me. Seph and I aren't sure how to deal with the next steps of our relationship or what that looks like if/when she gets back to Georgia, so we just didn't go home.

The first few days are a haze of take out, long naps in each other's arms, nursing each other's injuries, and complete avoidance of the problems. Neither of us wants to pop the bubble we are in. We don't want to deal with the eventual fall out of my family, nor did we want to rock the boat our relationship sat tremulously on.

We would have to talk to my sister, which I wasn't sure what lies Harrison already told her about being shot, almost killed, and arrested in Montana, but I'm not ready to ask Blaire that either. Another conversation I want to avoid for as long as possible.

My mother is another problem we have yet to face. The predicament is delicate and I want to shield Seph from any possible backlash from both of the other women in my life, who will naturally band together. I was angry when I heard it initially from a brother's perspective, that my sister's husband had hurt his ex. Hearing your husband had another fiancè, who he was abusing while dating you on the side, would be a much more difficult pill to swallow. Harrison will undoubtedly try to salvage his marriage and lie through his teeth, but I'm not sure if it will be at the expense of Seph, if he will gaslight her or try to discredit her to build reasonable doubt for himself.

We sat in a hotel room near the airport in North Dakota eating room service on opposite queen beds and watching a movie on TV.

"Adam Sandler's best movie was *Happy Gilmore*, I think," she comments absentmindedly with eyes ablaze from the TV light. I nod, thinking only of the days ahead of us, the conversations I never want to have but will be forced to endure, not the quality of movies by a 90s comedy actor.

She snorts and laughs at another classic line, enamored by the bathroom sink humor. Clearly, she is able to compartmentalize. Normally, I'd be right there with her, chuckling into a soda can and snuggled up on her side, but the week's events won't allow for my mind to focus on anything else.

"We have to go back, Seph, you know that, right? I have to go back," I say softly.

She turns to me slowly, eyes slowly rising from her food to stare into my chest. She sets her take-out container down on the pillow in front of her that's acting as a table while she adjusts herself to sit cross legged in the center of the bed.

"Can't we just go somewhere else? Start over fresh?" She says hopeful, but apprehensively.

While I'd love nothing more than to spend my days worshiping her in every way, I don't want to leave Dorian. It's where I grew up and where I want to stay for the rest of my life. No woman is ever going to change my mind on that, as enticing as her offer is. If I were to ever leave my small sleepy town, it would be for her, with her, but I can't do it under these circumstances. Not until I know things will get better between us, and we talk to my sister.

"No, we can't," my words are gruff and unnaturally cold.

"I know," she finally looks me in the eyes.

I unclench my jaw to lighten up, "There's a flight out tomorrow at 11am, do you think you'll be ready to go tomorrow? I don't want to put pressure on you. I just-"

"You just want to get back and deal with this mess, I get it, Brooks. Seriously. You have clients and work and a family to answer to. I might have none of that, but I understand," the undertone stems more from loneliness than anger. She's feeling alone which is why she's fine floating away into the wind instead of facing the issues back in Georgia as a couple. Going home with me to handle a shitstorm doesn't sound appealing to me either, so I can't imagine she's any more thrilled than I am.

"I'm not going to let anyone hurt you again, Sephy. Not my mom or my sister, or her husband. We'll deal with this, they will believe you and us. You're not the villain in this, you're the victim," I try to reassure her, but I can hardly even believe my own words. I don't know how my sister will react, she's not level headed on a good day, neither is my mother.

She scrubs her makeup-less face with her hands and groans, "We can go home tomorrow. It's fine, I'm fine, we're fine." She flicks her hand to shoo me, "I don't want to talk about this anymore until we have to again. Please, just let sleeping dogs lay for now."

Seph picks up the remote, flips through the channels before settling on an HGTV show about tiny homes. We are on two different beds in the same room, but we might as well have been in two different states. She has no interest in continuing the conversation we've been avoiding, but we need to have it.

"We need to talk about what I'm going to tell Blaire."

"I told you, I'm not doing this now," she doesn't even blink and keeps her gaze on the TV.

Her lack of empathy for me and my situation is concerning. It didn't reflect the woman I knew, never mind fell in love with. But my heart tells me to not judge her too harshly yet, since my gut told me there was a lot more to this story than I currently knew.

"Well, I am and despite what you think, we do need to do this now. If you think Blaire or my mother won't be knocking on my door the second we walk into town, you are out of your God-loving mind," I spit, trying to conceal my anger as best I can by keeping my tone even-keeled.

"Fine!" She turns the TV off and spins around to me with eyes glazed over with tears. We've been burying our problems with sex and food instead of dealing with them and it's finally come to an infected white-head.

"I think I should just tell Blaire what you told me, timelines and all. I have a feeling she already knew someone was in the picture when she started dating him, since she lied about where he was last year for the holidays." I eye her carefully when I talk through the last portion, not wanting to upset her more. She doesn't flinch and I move on, "Blaire is not going to want to believe it and I'm sure Harrison or Graham, whoever he is, will deny the abuse portion of the story." I wait for her to comment more, maybe provide some evidence or add to the plan.

"And I'm not exactly a credible source right now, I know," she mumbles with an expectant eye roll.

I hate admitting she is right, but she is. Though her lies of omission are only known by me, talk among the town will eventually spread. Blaire will tell mom, mom will tell Celia's mom, and so forth. There isn't an easy way to hide why a multimillionaire heiress is working part-time at a coffee shop. Living in an apartment below her means... I remember Harrison or Graham told Blaire he was engaged before, which is one step of truth above what I got from Persephone.

We both know what the visual looks like because even I am having a hard time believing this version of the tale is the entire truth. My gut is still pulling at me, hinting that she is hiding something else from me, that there is still more being withheld.

"Okay. If she doesn't believe me then, I don't know what to tell her. I found... Something incriminating. Like I said, he was unfaithful, so I packed my shit and left. I'm not sure what else to say here. I didn't take anything that wasn't mine. I don't need anything; I have enough money to last a lifetime." She is defensive and short, not trying to convince me of anything. Like she doesn't care who believed her or not.

It is the first time I've heard her brag about her own wealth, and it feels insanely unnatural out of her mouth.

We sit in silence for a few moments before I say, "You don't have to talk to Blaire, Seph. I can do that on my own. This is my bumpy road to fix, not yours. This is my family. I'd never ask you to relive the whole account to a stranger either, even if that stranger is my sister. I'm just asking that you be with me through smoothing it out."

Her brows scrunch together, and her lips press into a straight line to think about my words. She nods and twists a hair behind her ear in a show of absent-minded concern over the plan. I still haven't fully convinced myself we will be able to work this out in the long run, but I am operating as if we would. I promise myself to try until it doesn't work anymore, until I don't want it to work anymore, at least.

"My mother, I will play by ear, depending on how much Blaire decides to tell her. She needs to know the truth, but I'd rather have Blaire explain it than me. I don't want to seem like I'm trying to break up happy newlyweds." I get up and start packing some things into my bag and setting out my clothes for our departure tomorrow.

Her eyes follow me, and she softly asks, "What will we do if Blaire doesn't believe you? Or doesn't want to, despite the police report?"

My face drops at the thought. She's right, there is the very real possibility my sister will refuse to believe her husband not only abused Seph, but then also went after her, chasing her across the country to find something in her grandmother's antique furniture. I turn to her and drop my clothes back down. "I don't know, Sephy. I really don't know."

Chapter 20

Brooks

———

Touching down in Savannah has us both on edge. I can tell by the way Persephone avoids any and all contact with me until we crossed the threshold of my house. She made sure to keep her distance exiting the plane, didn't even so much as brush shoulders with me or let me touch the small of her back; she practically sprinted away when I tried. My hand instinctively tried to hold hers in the car, only to get denied when she crossed both her arms and leaned into the window, so her side was facing me.

The ice out was hard to swallow but I understood her lack of deference. My brother-in-law is not only her ex-fiancé and old co-worker, he has also stalked her across the country, threatening her safety, yet again, for an unknown mysterious item she is unknowingly in possession of.

Silence echoed between us the whole ride home; we don't bother putting on the radio to fill the void. We accept the familiar silence and our mutual nerves feed into it. My brain went to the worst-case scenario of Blaire screaming and crying, demanding to talk to Persephone, which I will not allow, at least until she calmed down.

I envision a hysterical Blaire, letting her emotions run rampant on me, then refusing to speak to me for months, or ever, if I keep dating Seph. My worst-case scenario is Blaire giving me an ultimatum, anything less than that, I think I can handle. Not that I won't side with Persephone, but it will kill my mother to do so.

Time stands still from the moment we step into my house, like I have entered the Twilight Zone or different dimension. This can't be real. This can't be what my small-town life has gotten tangled into.

Seph runs upstairs and gently closes what I assume is the bathroom door. The house is eerily quiet as I slide my bag off my shoulder and creep through the house. My sister is somewhere inside since her car is parking in my spot. I take a deep breath and walk past the living room and into the kitchen, where I see her in the dining room with a cup of coffee and a box of tissues.

"Blairey," I say affectionately with a sympathetic tone. At the end of the day, at the end of this extremely fucked up story, she is still my sister. She looks up with those big brown eyes that are ringed with bright red irritation. It looks like she's been crying for days, but her face isn't wet at the moment. Before slowly sipping her coffee, she jerks her head for me to have a seat.

My heart slams into my rib cage with every beat, with all my anxiety from the past five days accumulating into this singular interaction.

"What did he tell you happened?" I ask, mostly out of curiosity, but knowing where her knowledge level was currently at will help guide this conversation, too.

"He told me everything, Brooks. He's my *husband*," her pointed words drip with disdain. The inflection on the word 'husband' is purposefully made, to draw the line of who is part of this family and who isn't. I don't take the bait.

"Please, tell me what happened then," my eyes soften, and I wait for her to enlighten me to whatever lies my new *brother* has told her.

"He said… he said you'd need help finding her. He was in the area for business and went to help." The first major lie set my stomach in knots. I already knew by the tune of my sister that she isn't going to believe a word I say otherwise to contradict Graham.

"He said Persephone has a problem, a drinking problem and a lot of mental health issues. He said she was high and violent and the three of you tried to subdue her for her own good. She pulled out a gun and shot him during the struggle. Graham said she knocked you out then shot him to get away."

I press my fingers into my temples and rub, squinting my eyes closed and running my hands over my face, trying to figure out what to say next.

"Blaire, do you know who Persephone is to Graham? Did he tell you that?"

She looks at me blankly, "She was his ex," now looking more guilty, she continues, "he was seeing her when we started dating in the fall. He said she was suicidal, that he couldn't just drop her. I didn't recognize her at the wedding because I always thought she was blonde. I have only met her once before." She looks confused but I listen to my sister tell Graham's lies like they are the truth while I numbly sit through all the explanations.

"She must have dyed it," I say flatly, avoiding the millionth new fact I don't know about the woman I love. It is irrelevant and stupid but stings just the same. "They were supposed to get married the same weekend as you, at the same venue, Blairey. She left him in May, right before he proposed to you."

"Yeah, I know. We would have never gotten a wedding that quickly at that venue otherwise. He loves me, I know he loves me. He didn't *want* to marry her. He always had, even when he was with her." She is agitated by the simplest of truths and I start to get nervous.

Treading lightly, I say, "They got engaged in January, did you know that?"

"Yes, of course I kept tabs on my boyfriend's second relationship he was handcuffed to." Blaire avoids eye contact and looks to the right, a telling sign of a lie.

"Why would you knowingly be a side piece?" I ask, genuinely confused.

She stutters before answering, "We were a lot more casual than I let on earlier in us dating." Her admittance seems like the first genuine sentence she has uttered thus far.

I read between the lines, "So you didn't know about her until you were more attached…?" I guess at the latter.

She shrugs, looking guilty and ashamed, but brushed it off as quickly as it came. "Once he explained the scenario, that he couldn't leave her because she was too depressed, I understood." I glower a disgusted look and she reaches to whack me in the arm, "Don't look at me like that! Don't you dare judge me! I heard a lot of their fights, either from the hall or from speakerphone. She was... inconsolable and shut off." Blaire's glance up at me has a moment of empathy but turns cold immediately after.

"Her dad died," I start before she cuts me off.

"That's very sad, but I don't see why that matters in this situation, Brooks. Our father died too; I don't go around shooting people because of it!" Heat bubbles over and she slams her fist onto the table, shaking her coffee and spilling a splash. "She shot my fucking husband! She's gone off the deep end!"

"Graham wanted to be a partner at her father's hedge fund. When her father died, so did the possibility of him naturally obtaining that through marriage." I pause, waiting to see how she reacts. So far, expressionless. "Her father's estate came with specific stipulations, a prenup was required. Graham felt..." I pick my words carefully, "*entitled* to his promised partnership, but Seph felt obligated to her father's requests, if she didn't, she'd still have the company, but she'd lose her liquid inheritance."

Blaire shakes her head, "Okay, I still don't see where the shooting of my fucking husband comes into play, Brooks. Get to the fucking point. He said he just needed to marry her for the money, then he'd divorce her, and we'd be set for life."

I am stunned by her admission. Was she part of this from the beginning? Did she know all along that he was using her for her money?

"Blaire, please tell me you didn't condone this..."

"She. Shot. My. Fucking. Husband."

"A lot happened between January and May. Graham lost a lot of control over her and took it out in ways that *hurt* Persephone," I edge, unsure if she will lash out once the implication lands.

"Hurt her how? Did he shoot her like she shot him?" Blaire rolls her eyes and crosses her arms.

There is no other way to say it, I can't dance around it any longer. "Hurt her physically. Badly. For weeks, until she left him and came down to Georgia."

Blaire laughs. Actually, she cackles. A humorless cackle. "You expect me to believe this bullshit, Brooks? She shot my husband, and you want me to believe this sob story about my Graham physically abusing her? He's never so much as laid a damn hand on me or anyone I know," she bit out. "Her, on the other hand…"

"Blaire, you cannot be serious right now," I say, exacerbated.

"Brooks! You are so blinded by love. She is mentally unstable. I've heard her sobbing for hours. I've seen the filth she let herself dwindle to. She's still *unwell*. Didn't you see all her pills? Graham said they were just strung all over the apartment in Montana. She was clearly having an episode." Blaire's words are like fiberglass on my skin, pricking so deep I won't be able to wash it off me for days. She isn't wrong, the pills *were* everywhere. She *was* acting strange, asking me to stay the night after weeks of silence.

"Graham has been open and honest about his second relationship; he's never once lied to me. Can you say the same about your darling, Persephone?" Blaire's words are condescending, and she knew it from the nasty grin plastered on her face.

This is veering closer and closer to my worst-case scenario.

"That's not what happened in Montana, so that is a lie" I rebutted.

"Of course not, I'm sure she has a perfectly crafted tale for that too that makes her the victim and Graham the villain." Blaire's eyes are wild now with anger, "Come on, let's hear it." She urges me on with a mocking wave of her hand.

"He was hunting her, trying to track her down, Blaire. He snuck into her apartment when I left for *fifteen minutes*. He was stalking her, waiting. I slipped up and told you where she was. It's my fault. You hear me?" I beg her to blame me. "I found her first, but Graham slipped in when I was out grabbing lunch for us. I walked in on them fighting."

"So, you didn't see how it all started? And you just took her word for it that he attacked her?" she asks incredulously. Not thinking about that detail, I cursed myself for allowing any holes in this story, knowing Blaire will continue to rip them wide open with her natural doubt.

"He was on top of her, she was bleeding and Har- Graham attacked me, we fought, he smashed a chair over my head…"

"You have a concussion, Brooks. I think you're the one who's confused. Sounds like you picked your side and he felt cornered," she leans back in the dining table chair, staring holes into me, ready to defend her husband at every turn.

Desperate to conclude my version of events, I keep going, "Seph and him fought more and I heard him wailing on her, he said she had something of his, Blaire. He was determined to find it, and then I heard the gunshot. It was self-defense…" I look into her eyes, imploring her to see reason, but am only met with stark defiance.

"So, you didn't even see what happened? You didn't see her shoot him?"

"Well, no… I…"

"So now I'm supposed to take your word over his? At least he was *there*. Sounds like you are as helpful as the chair he smashed over your head." She has no intention of hearing any other side. I sigh, frustrated with myself for giving her the ammunition to tear my account of the story to shreds. Her doubt slips through some of my cracks, and I can feel myself re-evaluating the events of that day for myself. Am I the one remembering things wrong?

"Yes, Blaire. You are. I'm not lying, Seph is not lying. Harrison is lying!" I let my anger get the better of me and raise my voice.

"Who the fuck is Harrison?" She laughs, but there is no humor in it.

"Your goddamn husband, Blaire. You don't even know his real fucking name! His name is Harrison. Graham is his middle name."

"For fucks sake, a lot of people go by their middle name, that's not ridiculous, Brooks," still, defending him.

"So why did Seph go by his first?"

"Because I was his mistress, it kept things more interesting. I like the name Graham better anyways," she huffs, satisfied with her own answer.

I balance my elbows on the table and press my palms flat together, bringing my steepled fingers to my mouth, shaking my head, contemplating what to say next. This isn't going as planned.

"Look, Graham is a kind, generous, and successful man, he's not going to press charges, that's not why I'm upset right now. I know you didn't do anything wrong, except pick the wrong side to defend," she starts before I bite back.

Seething, I say, "Not press charges? You do realize the police arrested him, right? At no point was Persephone the "attacker". *He* came after *her*!" I raise my voice again. I thought I was in the Twilight Zone before, but now I'm entirely sure I am. How did Harrison twist this story so well in his favor with my sister?

"Like I said, no charges are being pressed on either side, not even from Seph. So you can't tell me who's wrong in this since the law says no one. However, I have to tell you, you need to stop seeing her," Blaire says sternly.

I didn't know Seph isn't going to press charges. She hadn't mentioned that detail in the last 24 hours we spent together. It stings. She must have taken the call from the detective privately.

"I'm not going to stop seeing her, Blaire. Not in a fucking million years. Not unless she tells me she doesn't want me anymore, and even then, that might not be enough."

My worst case just happened. And despite my resolute sounding declaration to stand behind my woman, I am scorched by another secret. For just a moment, it makes me question my own resolve when it comes to a future with Seph.

"Family first, Brooks. I'll give you some time to nurse your concussion and think about it. I'll be at Mom's until tomorrow night, taking a redeye home. I'm not going to tell you what to do, Brooks, but this is family. Graham is your family too. You're choosing a woman you hardly know, who has a history of lying and mental illness, and believing her instead of us," she lays into me.

With a final huff, she shoots back and the squeak of her chair on the hardwood jerks my attention to her.

"Think about it all, Brooks. Why would Graham go chase after a woman he was cheating on? She has issues, a lot of them. She's clearly not stable. She stole from *him*, and now he wants his shit back."

"Do you know what it is she supposedly stole?" I hedge, hoping maybe Blaire knows more than Seph and I.

"He said it was a computer or files or something. Stockbroker stuff." She passes by and strokes my cheek, "Her story doesn't make sense. She left you. How much does she really love you? Graham doesn't care about her anymore for a reason and neither should you."

With the final death blow, she walks out, leaving me reeling.

My sister is a fucking bitch.

Working all the words over in my head, I just need to be next to Persephone to sort some of this out. It's not that I don't believe her, I just need more details in certain parts. I need to be 100% sure and right now I'm only 98%.

When I get to the bedroom, I notice her lying in bed next to a pill bottle and my heart freezes in my chest. Slowly, I make my way over, trying to watch for the rise and fall of her body, but don't see a clear movement, if at all. Her face looks sunken in and pale. I touch her cheek and she's cold, which startles me.

"Seph?" I put my finger under her nose to feel for her breath.

My stomach returns to my body when I feel the faint blow of her breathing. Unfurling her fingers, I grab the pill bottle and read the prescription. It's for Alprazolam, brand name Xanax. It is her anxiety medication.

I place the bottle on the nightstand and notice the window open. I am so heated from my argument with Blaire, I didn't notice the temperature in the room is astronomically low. I close the window and draw a blanket over Seph. I get undressed for a shower and head to the bathroom. Tomorrow will be a long day back at the office and I need about 10 hours of sleep to get through half of it.

Sliding into bed with Seph, I settle myself across her chest, in the space in between her breasts, as she stays comatose on her back. I think about all the things Persephone hasn't told me, all the holes in her story that Blaire poked through, until darkness finds me and swallows me whole.

Chapter 21

Brooks

———

Waking up is a bitch but going to work after getting your ass kicked less than a week ago is not fun either. I left Seph still passed out in my bed this morning. She hummed in her sleep when I kissed her forehead goodbye but didn't stir. I wanted to talk to her before I left but thought better than to disrupt her. She needed to rest. She had a long few days, too.

She also didn't need to work for the rest of her life. Another surprise lie of omission I found out this weekend. My girl was a multi-millionaire.

It's a regular day of angry clients, contracts, and catching up on new court dates. Luckily, my assistant and paralegal are able to deal with most of the postponements without issue and push back anything that wasn't time urgent. I have a pile of work on my desk and a pounding headache by 2pm, but I press on, needing to distract myself from thinking about the conversation I will have to have with Seph later.

We have to talk about what happened again and I will have to ask her why she thinks he was chasing her. What he thinks she has, maybe ask her if it's computer stuff like Blaire mentioned. Then I'd have to try to convince her to show me the furniture to help her look through it. She wasn't going to want to talk, I knew it already. She is a master at shutting me out, at fixing the door perfectly ajar to make me feel like I am seeing everything from my view, when the whole half of the room is still hidden from me.

At the stroke of 6:01pm, I fling my last case file across my desk and pack up. I am not staying here a minute longer. Cognitive dissonance fills me, excited to see Seph, but equally wanting to avoid her, avoid this situation. I need to do this, though, to collect the facts, pick a side and stick to it. *Pick her side* and stick to it. Isn't that what you do for the person you love?

What I really need to do is believe her without evidence, but my logical brain just can't. I need all the facts laid out for me.

The lights are off in the house, even the top bedroom windows, and the bathroom. I am expecting to at least see the glow of the TV, but maybe she is in the kitchen, which is nestled in the back of the house.

The door is unlocked, which wasn't like Seph to keep open.

Walking through the dark house I call out for her, "Seph! I'm home." I lean into the front rooms, then up the staircase I call her again, "Sephy? You there?"

Did she leave again? My chest strained tight and my spine went cold at the possibility.

The tight feeling in my lungs unwound when I spot her phone and laptop on the center island in the kitchen, along with her purse. She must have gone somewhere today and just came back. Next to her things is a post-it note with just a single heart and cursive styled 'M'.

My mom came by? Fuck.

A sinking feeling starts wrapping around my stomach and I run out to the living room, take the stairs two at a time to search for Persephone on the second floor. She isn't in the house. I ran back into the kitchen to try and find other clue. I rip open the fridge in a panicked state and spot my mother's classic 'get better soon' chicken casserole. The sight of it makes me nervous. Why did she stop by today? Was Blaire with her? She is supposed to be home by now. What had Blaire told her?

Wiping my hand down my face to think, I go out to the back porch to check outside. Georgia this time of year is fairly warm, usually only dipping to freezing overnight, but it is still brisk. My backyard is clear, but then I realize the sliding door was cracked open, not locked like it usually was.

Did she leave out the backdoor?

Unable to determine her direction, that's if she left, I buck up and call my mom.

She answers on the second ring, "Hi sweetheart."

"Hi, Mom. How are you this evening?"

"Just fine, just fine. Did you get my casserole?" She asks sweetly.

"I did, Momma, thank you for bringing it over," I pause, unsure if I should ask, but needing to know. "Did you see Seph here today by chance?"

She clears her throat, and I can feel her straighten on the other line, "I did."

I wait for more, but it doesn't come, "How… did she seem?"

"She wasn't thrilled to see me or your sister to be honest. Your sister decided to stay longer. You should really sever that tie soon though, honey, she's not stable enough for a man like you." My mother has the Southern gift of making even the meanest things sound like a lullaby with her thick accent.

"Blaire came here too?" I couldn't imagine the interaction without breaking into a sweat.

"Blaire deserved to face her husband's attacker. We suggested Persephone should leave instead of forcing you into an impossible situation." My mom's confession almost slips by me since her warm voice doesn't falter.

"You did, what?"

"Now don't get testy. I know you wouldn't leave the damn woman on your own, even if your sister threatened you. We just made the decision easier and suggested she make the choice for you," her angry Southern mother voice is only a hair nastier than her sweet Southern mother voice. It could throw any man through a loop.

"Mom, what did you do?" I whisper in disbelief. "She left all her things here. Did she leave when you were here?"

"Oh, Brooks, don't go all pathetic and chase after that basket case. She ran towards the dead end, said she needed some air, like a wild animal. I didn't see her after that. We put the casserole in the fridge and left."

I don't respond. Gold digger? That is so far from the truth it is almost laughable. My mouth is fully open as I glance at the sliding door again. Has she been outside all this time?

"Mom, when did you leave?" My voice is strained at the thought.

"Around 3, did you eat yet, honey? Just pop it in the oven at-"

I hang up on her before she can finish and run upstairs to search the bedrooms in a desperate attempt to find some type of clue that will lead me back to her. The floor is entirely dark, all three bedrooms empty, not a single item moved from when I left this morning, except our bed is now made.

I call out again into each of the rooms and flick on both lights quickly to check the bathrooms.

Eerie silence is all that calls back to me.

I find myself searching the first floor again, then a quick glance into the basement, then eventually in the middle of my backyard, knowing she is not outside, but refusing to go back into the empty house.

She isn't here.

"Persephone," my strained voice breathes out into the night. The panic inside me is rising, ready to boil over into a full mental breakdown. I just got her back; how can I lose her again? How could she leave me again?

I make my way back inside, haunted by the empty house I find myself in when I hear a thump from upstairs.

"Seph!" I call out again before sprinting to the second floor, searching for the source of the noise. My eyes are frantically scanning the bedroom for a sign of her but find nothing out of place.

From the bathroom, I hear another thunk coupled with the sound of water sloshing in the tub. I skid into the master bathroom and rip back the curtain to find an incoherent, naked Persephone in a tub full of pink water.

She moans in what seems like pain, shifting slightly in the water, but staying submerged.

"Sephy?" As I get closer, my heart drops into my stomach.

She looks fine, pale, but fine. Her breathing is slow but steady. "Sephy, wake up for me," I cradle her limp head in my hands while stroking the stray wet strands of hair flopping against her face. "Persephone, please wake up for me," I beg, biting back a strange feeling in the back of my throat.

Her skin is cold, the bath water, too. I gently place her head back down on the rim of the tub and take my suit jacket off to roll up the sleeves of my button-down shirt. I snag the plug to drain the water. She moans and stirs again, feeling the water slipping off her slowly. Her brows twitch in confusion, and she shifts her head to the side, facing away from me, still not awake completely.

When the water drains completely, I scan her body quickly, looking for any sign of injury, but thankfully find none. The pink must have been a bath bomb, not blood, like I falsely assumed. I pick her up bride style and carry her to our bed, placing her down on the comforter, despite being soaking wet.

I run to grab a towel and as many blankets as I can from the hall closet.

"Seph, you're okay. You can't hear me, but you're okay." I kiss her hand and press her palm to my face to fake comfort by contact.

I must have fallen asleep sitting on the floor with her hand in my own and my head laying next to her hip. She stirs and wakes me with her movement.

"Brooks? What… what happened?" She is struggling to sit up and open her eyes.

"Seph, God, you're okay!" I jutt to my feet so I could wrap my hands around her face and kiss her forehead. She shakes her head to assure me.

"I'm fine. I'm fine, I… I don't really remember much," she looks lost, like she is trying to find her memories swirling out in front of her face.

"My mom came with my sister. Do you remember that?" I look at her and wait for her answer. My eyes are ready to capture then analyze every flicker of emotion that crosses her face.

"Yeah… yeah. I remember that now, they came. I'm sorry, it was not a great encounter to be honest," she confesses nervously.

"My mom and Blaire have a delusional version of the truth," my hand pushes her hair back behind her ear and out of her face. I sit half on the bed next to her hip, my hands still resting on her casually.

"I went to leave…" Her sad eyes pull me in, unsure of my reaction. "I went to leave but realized I don't need to keep leaving you. I don't want to keep leaving you." The faintest smile graces her face, and she goes on, "Then I think I took a bath to calm down, but I had a panic attack and forgot I had already taken a Xanax an hour or two before. It just made me sleepy, I passed out…" She looks up to me guiltily, like she did something wrong by having a condition that she can't control.

"Seph," I pet her head. "Please don't take baths with the curtain closed in the dark, it was hard to find you in the dark," my joke doesn't crack a smile on her face, but I force one on my own anyways to help lighten the mood.

"We need to talk, Brooks," she shifts to sit up and the sudden knife in my side forces my hands to move off her. "I can't let you alienate yourself from your family. They're right. Family is more important than anything…"

"No, Persephone. Stop, please. Just stop."

"Is Blaire going to leave, Harrison?"

"No… I don't know. It didn't seem like it," I say, eyes searching her face, confused why that matters.

"What do you think is going to happen, Brooks? What's our future look like? My in-laws with my ex-fiancé? Are you out of your mind?" She looks at me disbelievingly, still disheveled from her double dose.

I can't think. I balk. What *is* our future?

"It has to be figured out eventually," she says evenly.

"Thanksgiving isn't for another 11 months at least," I crack another joke and surprisingly this one lands a ghost of a smirk. I take it as a win. I stampede on, "Most families don't like each other anyways."

I get another smirk out of that one, too.

"We're not breaking up because my sister and her husband I've only met twice."

"What about your mom?"

"She'll get over it," and Seph's brow arches in question. "Eventually…"

She rolls her eyes and says, "Okay, yeah, you're right."

I roll partially on her to land an agreeable kiss on her, and she humd in approval. "Let's go take a shower and eat dinner in bed while watching reruns of Parks and Rec," my head tilts down over her to press my lips onto hers for a soft, but firm affirmation of my feelings. "Come on," I whisper into her mouth.

She follows me off the bed and grabs my hand to lead us to the shower.

We spent the rest of the night stroking each other's hair, giving and taking soft kisses, and naked snuggles in bed. It was like the heavy layer of snow over our love finally melted for the season. Like we slipped back in time before she left at the wedding. We talked about funny memories and stories about our childhood, anything and everything under the sun except the events of the last month.

"Did you know I'm a natural blonde?" She says grinning.

"I did not," I lie, having found that small tidbit from Blaire. "Brown suits you well. I'd love to see it one day, though."

"Nope." She teases me and presses a kiss onto my lips.

I grumble and nuzzle into her hair, "Why not? I want to see what you would look like as a sexy blonde."

"I dyed it once I got to Georgia, no reason to look backwards in life! Isn't that what you've been preaching, right?" She giggles while poking fun at me and our past, like it is nothing.

"I was a blonde too, you know, they said blondes have more fun and I needed to see for myself," my joke lands harder than hers. My heart swells at seeing her face light up. I reach around to grab my phone and call up a photo from Facebook of my 10th grade school picture, featuring perfectly gelled and bleached tips.

"Stop, you're going to make me pee myself," she grabs my wrist to shove the phone away once she gets a glimpse of the photo.

"Frosted tips were very stylish at the time," I argue back playfully.

"You look like you belong in a boy band," she is in tears now, wiping the escaping ones from her cheeks.

"Your legs are intertwined with mine; you're going to pee *on* me in my own bed?" She doesn't stop laughing, and I can't help but watch her face brighten as her smile deepens. I love seeing her happy again. After all we've been through, it is so good to see she can still laugh like this. Nothing brings me more joy than to see the woman I fell in love with finally smile with me again.

Call me a fool in love but falling back into our banter makes me forget the lies of omission. It makes me forget and not want to remember.

Ignorance is bliss, right?

Chapter 22

Brooks

————

Seph fell asleep tonight with *her* spooning *me* for once, and it made me giddy inside feeling her tiny arms wrap around my waist. *So giddy*, I couldn't fall asleep.

I lay awake thinking about our future, turning over possibilities and plans, vacations we should take, the number of kids we will have, how she'll redecorate the living room, and everything in between. Or the horrible possibility it will never progress past what we are now, which is nothing. Exes.

I think back over our conversation from the night. She told me she was a natural blonde and only recently dyed her hair darker. Blaire had said she knew her as a blonde too and her brown hair made her almost unrecognizable.

The thought of her blonde hair piqued my interest, and I couldn't picture my dark-haired beauty with champagne colored hair. She would be beautiful either way, that I am sure, but my curiosity wraps around me too tightly at 4 am. I feel myself reaching for her iPhone to look through her pictures, assuming I'd easily find one from her blonde days.

I know she got a new phone before her move, but the icloud usually saves everything. Thankfully, all her information had been transferred over, so photos from previous years are there. I know because she had shown me a video, she took of her dad flipping a golf cart with his friends. It was a hilarious group of very white collar, 60+ year old men acting like 17-year-old's, something you'd see reposted on the Barstool Sports Instagram. I said that she should send it to them, but she shrugged and told me she didn't use social media anymore.

Her not on social media was something I already knew. She told me she deleted it shortly after moving here, that she had to stop logging on to Instagram or it would eat her alive.

I tried finding her online despite her confession, but her online footprint was washed from every site that ever had her face on it. I couldn't even find her father's obituary online. Looking back with all that I know now, I'm sure she paid good money to be completely wiped from the internet.

Reminiscently, I slowly thumb through photos of us from the past six months. Happy, blissful, and intimate moments from our relationship force a goofy smile on my face. Flipping past the first one with us, it jumps to a lot of scenic pictures from her travels to Georgia, and I go back to scrolling through the thumbnails to skip all the very pretty pictures of the road. After a few scrolls, I find a thumbnail of what looks like a blonde hair mirror pic and click to make it larger.

My eyes focus on the woman I held in my hand, and my fingers go ice cold. It's a mirror photo, alright. She *did have* blonde hair, and she *does* look vaguely familiar. She also featured a slew of fresh purple bruises down her arm. I swipe to the previous picture, and it's a close up of her ribs, another massive black and blue wrapping along her side.

Swipe. A close up of her face with a busted lip, tears still wet on her face.

Swipe. Another selfie with a red mark on her cheek, running mascara on her face, and dried blood around her nose.

Swipe. A video... I freeze, unblinking, scared to press play. I take a deep breath and tap the screen, clicking down the volume instantly. It looks like a Blair Witch Project outtake. Seph is running through a dark house or apartment with a terrified look flashing on screen occasionally, and she drops her phone as she slams the bathroom door and locks herself inside.

BAM, BAM, BAM. The knocks in the video startle me, and Graham's voice billows through the speaker on the lowest setting.

"Get your fucking ass out here, Persephone. I swear to fucking God!"

BAM BAM BAM.

On the very edge of the screen, you can see half of Seph crying and wiping the tears from her face, curled up in what looks like shower tiles, rocking back and forth to herself, terrified of the man pounding at the door. I can hear her faintly whispering to herself, "Jesus Christ, Jesus fucking Christ," in between the loud hammering of his fists. Can faintly see her eye wince with each bang.

"You can't hide in there forever, Seph. This isn't normal! You're not acting normal! You need to get a fucking grip on your pathetic fucking life. Coming home to your sad, drunk ass just doesn't fucking do it for me anymore!" He's slurring his words, clearly intoxicated.

She yells back, "At least I'm home! Where were you tonight, Harrison? Where were you last night or the night before?" She sobs harder.

BAM BAM BAM.

"You're a fucking bitch! You hear me? A fucking lush, with a bitch of a mouth! Fuck!"

BAM. The camera fumbles and the view jumps to the wall tile and the shower door, like she dropped the phone. A loud screech shoots out of the speakers just before the video goes black. Then the video ends completely.

I stare at the paused screen for a few more seconds after the video ended, shuddering to think how she escaped the bathroom that night.

I hesitantly swipe to the next picture. It's an image of half of her face and neck with red marks sprinkled all over it in the pattern of a hand.

Swipe. A picture of her wrist, bruises swirled all the way around, up to the middle of her forearm.

Another video. Knowing what the other one held, I hesitated to watch. Can I handle watching more?

She lived through it, I can at least watch it. I click play.

A close up of her face, she cries into the phone whispering, "Get it together." A sob cuts through her, and she breathes deep a few times before composing herself to continue. "Oh God, Oh God, Jesus, fuck…," she is talking to herself.

BAM BAM BAM.

The camera jerks and she starts actively crying again.

"Persephone! You want to fuck with me? Fuck with my money? I swear to God, I will kill you! You hear me? Cry to your fucking self because no one else will listen! No friends, no family, you have no one but me!"

BAM!

The phone drops to the bottom of the shower, but in the right corner you can see Seph holding her face, shoulders shaking and sobbing.

"Get the fuck out of the bathroom!"

BAM! BAM! BAM!

"Fuck you, Harrison!" She screams with a shaky voice.

"I will fucking kick this door in!"

"No, no, no, no," she whispers, still hysterical, still rocking back and forth, poking in and out of the camera shot that was still facing the ceiling.

A few loud thumps clatter, different from the bangs from before. After several moments of silence, a large crash and Seph's scream rang out. Her phone still lays flat on the shower floor, but now she is out of sight completely. The camera only captured the sound and the ceiling.

"You're paying to fix that, you made me fucking do that. Get the fuck out of the shower. Do you hear me? Get. The. Fuck. OUT. Of. The. Shower!"

Silence.

I can hear Seph breathing when I see what looks like Harrison's arm reaching across the shower. Seph starts screaming "No!" In a quick flash, Harrison's hand grips Seph's blonde hair and drags her out, the phone untouched and capturing a split second of the scene from below.

Her screams trail off as he drags her farther and farther out of the bathroom to where I assume was further into the apartment. The chaotic sounds became distant and barely audible. I go to shuffle through to see how long the video is, but a blood curdling scream rattles through the phone speakers and stops me. I can tell it was distant from the phone, but it's still loud enough to pierce my heart.

My hand clasps over my mouth in horror. Every muscle in my body freezes. My lungs stop expanding, and I hold my breath for what feels like ten minutes. What the fuck did he do to her?

There is a long period of silence, then a door slam. I can make out crying in the distance, then it slowly increases in volume and proximity until Seph picks up the phone.

Her nose is busted, her eyes are swollen, and she is coughing and wheezing. The video cuts out on a still of half her face looking over the camera from above. I pause on the partial thumbnail of my bloodied woman, traumatized beyond words. How did she stay that long? My hand doesn't move from my mouth for several minutes, and I have to unlock the phone again because the screen goes to black while I process everything I have seen.

Swipe. Bruise. Swipe. Welt. Swipe. Blood.

I scroll past at least 20 pictures of different bruises, cuts, scrapes all over her body for the entire duration she mentioned briefly, about 6 weeks. I can't believe how much she downplayed the abuse. I never envisioned it to be this bad.

To see her bleed like she got into the octagon to fight is more than I can take. I feel like shaking her awake to scream at her for not showing me these earlier and then hold her tight so no one could ever hurt her again. My emotions are all over the place, unsure where they will land next. Sad, mad, upset, devastated, relieved. I ping pong between them all.

It's one thing to see the bruises on her body and the blood on her face. It's another thing entirely to see the videos, to see she has no other pictures in her phone except those from that particular span of time, as if the entirety of her life was absent except for him and his fury.

Yes, my curiosity got the better of me, and I looked through her phone when I should have just gone to sleep, hoping to find an innocent picture of her blonde hair. Instead, I found well documented abuse doled out by my sister's new husband.

I have already invaded Seph's privacy, so doubling down on the deceit hardly registered as an issue. I fire the videos and pictures off in a text to myself, then delete them from our message thread to cover my tracks. I need to take a second look at them when I have more time. I need to show my mother and my sister.

I click out of the message app and drop the phone to my forehead for a second before it buzzes. It's a notification from Facebook messenger.

She told me she doesn't have Facebook or any social media, for that matter.

Was it hurt or anger that I am feeling? Betrayal? How many lies was this girl going to spin me? My muscles tense as I thumb the icon to bring me to the message. I fear the worst, that it is another man in her life, that I'm not the only guy involved in this sordid tale.

It was from a person named Aisley.

Hi Persephone,

I hope you're okay. You didn't sound great when you called the other day. I moved everything back to Georgia for you from Montana plus all the extra luggage. The last of it should be there tomorrow afternoon. Here's the address:

15 Colonial Drive, Dorian, GA

I overnighted the key to Brooks' office, and I wasn't sure if you kept your old PO box or not and I assume you're staying with him now.

Take care,
Aisley

I stare at the message, unsure if I should be relieved it isn't from another lover, or sad she still isn't as forthcoming as I want her to be. I think she is planning on staying. If she is, why not move her stuff into *my house*? I clearly have the room, half the bedrooms here are practically empty and have been since I bought the place.

It's an old Victorian that I planned on gently restoring over time but never got around to doing much to it but painted a few walls, so it was just old and antique looking inside. Harrison had said something about the furniture though. There is something in that damn storage that either Seph truly didn't know she took or took willingly.

Either way, I am going to find out tomorrow.

Back to my insomniac ways, I barely got a wink of sleep last night. My thoughts drifted from my conversation with Blaire to the videos I uncovered, the storage locker, and empty Facebook page Seph kept alive to communicate with Aisley. I read through their previous conversations, and it seems like she is her old personal assistant.

I wonder why Seph didn't text her? Why is this so secretive via Facebook?

Other questions flutter into my mind too. Why not show me the videos or even a single picture when I mention Blaire possibly not believing her? She knows there is reasonable doubt, she knows Blaire might not trust her side of the story, and yet she lets her pocket royal straight sleep. She has the corroboration of her story on her phone. A single picture will be evidence enough, and a few frames of video could possibly put him behind bars, if she wants as much.

But all she wants is peace, and I can't even give her that. Our lives are much too strangely entangled now. If nothing else, I need to get to the bottom of this not only for my sister but also for the woman I love.

Chapter 23

Brooks

———

Waking up and leaving Persephone to go to work while she is still sleeping this morning is the hardest thing I've done since I met her. I stare at her for at least an hour before actually getting up, taking note of the harsh under eye circles that have formed this past month, the hollowness of her cheeks, how her eyelids are still so puffy, how they change the shape of her eye, and how the new gash on her forehead Harrison gave her from their showdown in Montana doesn't change anything about her beauty.

She was in pieces before we left Montana, and my mother and sister came to deliver the finishing blow. It almost worked too, she could have drowned. They weren't trying to kill her, only scare her off. But those types of accidents happen all the time, people fall asleep and drown in bathtubs. The thought burns a hole through me, to think my family could have been the catalyst for her death, no matter if Seph actually shot Harrison on purpose or not.

Harrison/Graham came to use her for his own gain, my sister came to scare her away, and my mom came to make her leave me again. She is right, despite me trying to ignore the details, and my family doesn't want anything to do with her. What is our future if we couldn't even have a simple Christmas dinner together?

Do I need to have a Christmas dinner with anyone? It's amazing how people who see you less than a dozen times a year can influence who you spend the other 353 days with. Yes, my family is my blood, and I will always love them, but where do they get off trying to tell me how to live my life and who to live it with when I barely see them to begin with?

Blaire never comes back to Georgia, and mom is gone most of the year. It's a shame Seph doesn't have family left because we could just always stick with her parents, but that isn't an option. She has no one left and it makes me sad for her, for us.

I make a pit stop on my way to work to see my mother and sister. Opening the door, I am hit with the familiar scent of scones, coffee, and high-pitched female chatter drifting from the kitchen. My sister and mother are perched on the center island bar stools while sipping on steaming mugs. With my entrance, both women welcome me with open arms.

"Brooks, sweetie, so nice for you to stop by. Let me get you a scone and a cup," my mother croons and starts fussing over a set up for me.

"No need, Mother. I'm just here to provide evidence that you both seem to need in order to believe an abused woman," I take my phone out of my back pocket and cue up the pictures I sent myself last night of Seph's myriad of bruises.

Blaire scoffs, "Pictures can be edited."

"Can videos?" I turn to her and fight back curling my lip.

"Some women are better actresses than others," she says flippantly.

My mother is weary but holds out a hand to see the phone. I hand it over and tell her to scroll. Her expression doesn't change, it remains cold and stoic as she flips through every picture. When she comes to the video, she pauses and purses her lips, as if contemplating not watching it, then eventually presses play. I can't help but wince when I hear Persephone's cries, knowing exactly what part of the video correlates to each sound.

I had already rewatched the videos again this morning in the bathroom, to make sure what I saw last night was real and not just a bad dream.

It's Harrison's voice, clear as day, but Blaire snorts through her nose every time his voice is heard in the background.

Mom winces a few times, offers a few rapid blinks, but stays otherwise emotionless. Then as the video concludes, she purses her lips to contemplate but doesn't look anywhere except the paused screen. Finally taking her stare off the phone, she looks to Blaire and affectionately says, "You can't fake this…"

Blaire rolls her eyes, slams her mug on the table to emphasize her point, "She's a known liar. She still *stole* from Graham. This doesn't change anything, *anything!*" The chair screeches across the wood and my sister stomps out of the room until I hear a door slam. It's the second time I've seen this particular Blaire performance in two days, and I've had enough of her theatrics.

"She's being dramatic and inexorable. She's ridiculous…"

"Everything is off screen; you don't even *see* him!" Blaire screams behind the closed door that hugs the kitchen hall.

My mother's eyes deepen with sympathy for her feuding children, maybe even a fraction of concern for her daughter and her abusive husband, but it fades away as quickly as it came.

"This all might be true, Brooks, and we might have been wrong to doubt her, or she's lying to you too. Either way, she's still got a lot of baggage. It still will upset your sister to be with her, and there's still the issue of stolen items. I haven't heard much evidence exonerating her from that charge. Harrison is married into this family right now, it would be wrong to side against him when the truth is clearly not black and white." She pats my cheek, hands me back my phone, and leaves me standing in shock in the kitchen.

How are these people my family?

I know a dead end when I see one, so I decide to let this play out a little longer, let the emotions die down, and plan to revisit the topic later one. They'll always be in my life, so I need to find a way for us four to co-exist, assuming Seph continues to be a staple in my heart.

Luckily, Seph never got my mail, so when I make a quick stop home from my mother's, I find the key meant for her in an envelope made out to Persephone Kline. I decide that I'll re-seal it and hand it over to her tomorrow, but today, I need to unravel more truth.

The storage locker is the only one in Dorian, but I need my car to get there. I quietly hop in, thanking myself for remembering to bring my car keys with me this morning.

I am familiar with the storage facility here, so I make quick work through rows and rows of outside hallways and garage fronts. I stop in front of the number on the key, 64. It's a massive locker, the biggest they sell, which shouldn't have surprised me as much as it did. I wasn't sure what to expect in terms of what is inside furniture wise. Seph had mentioned it isn't much, but the storage locker size makes me question what she considers "much."

Lifting the heavy orange metal garage door, the lights automatically flips on revealing a mostly full cement room. Everything is perfectly nestled inside, bins in a row in the far back while the furniture lined the walls to my left and right. There are about ten pieces in total, a full bedroom set complete with a mattress and box spring, all carefully wrapped in plastic.

My keys have a pocket knife attachment, so I go to work off the plastic.

Every drawer is empty, every bin is filled with seemingly female designer clothes and shoes, and every box of knick knacks seemed worthless barring their weight in memories. There are pictures of her as a blonde with her father, with his friends, and with her girlfriends out at clubs in the city. She looks happy enough, but nothing like the down to earth woman I have known these past six months.

I thumb through the luggage that was shipped from Montana, wondering if maybe she kept the "valuables" with her. Piece by piece, I pull out familiar clothes from her suitcase, occasionally pulling them to my nose to sniff her scent in. She smells like daisies, always like flowers.

Then I see it. My handkerchief tucked into a pocket of the suitcase.

Paralyzed from a strange familiarity of deceit, everything inside me goes cold with recognition. How did she have this?

I allow the white silk to skate through my fingertips while I inspect the initials I already knew were mine. I had given this to one girl and one girl only. The gorgeous blonde bombshell from Savannah. The girl whose face was blurry, but I thought about 24 hours a day until the moment I met Persephone in the diner. She had said her name was… "Steph" I say out loud to myself as I play the scene back in my head.

"She said Seph not Steph," I reasoned while diving for one of the pictures of her and her friends before a night out. It is her; the similarities didn't click in my mind, I haven't thought about that girl at the bar in months.

That night, I had texted the number on my Uber ride home and never got a response. My disappointed ego chalked it up to a drunken sleight of hand or a true write off. She seemed pretty tipsy that night (as was I) by the end. The mystery "Steph" from Savannah enraptured me that night, a night I meant to just hang with the boys. Her make-up was heavy, her clothes were skintight, her hair was tousled, bleached, and insanely long. That was not even a thread of the same woman I found in Sephy days later.

Persephone is as light as a summer breeze, naturally stunning with dark brown hair and green eyes. The bar was dark, "Steph" could have had green eyes too. I just didn't notice as much at the time.

In my head, the only thing that made sense is they are the same woman, no one else could possibly have this handkerchief with these initials and lipstick stain. It even faintly smelled like old beer.

The number Seph eventually gave me a few days later on our coffee date was not the same area code. I purposefully called Seph on my phone before I left our impromptu date to avoid the same situation, she ironically put me in days earlier. A wrong number. If it weren't for her blow off at the bar, I wouldn't have been so persistent in assuring a new girl's digits were real days later.

Once Persephone dropped into my hemisphere, I gave up and forgot the beauty from the bar that kept me up at night with her witty jokes and tantalizing lips. She was a very distant memory to the woman I fell head over heels for by date three. I hadn't thought of her since, but now the two were colliding at an astronomical rate, threatening to blow my head clean off my shoulders.

Slowly, I sink down to the floor to sit cross legged. I let my eyes stare off into nothing, open but replaying questionable moments from the past 6 months. My mind tries to conjure up a vision of "Steph" to compare it to Seph.

I realize she had to have recognized me, though, and that's when the icy feeling of betrayal set in. Again. She knew for so long and never thought to bring it up, even in jest. We could have laughed it off together, we could have made it an inside joke, but it was just another lie in the pile. Another reason to not trust the woman I loved with my entire being.

My eyes unfocus at the thought that my trust in Persephone is almost entirely broken. Hanging on by a mere thread. I find no evidence of stolen belongings, but I don't find any evidence that proves her innocence either. Harrison's accusation of theft is not made up; he had nearly killed her for whatever she took. Whether she took it willingly or not, she had to have something of his, something valuable, and nothing about her track record with the truth led me to believe anything that came out of her mouth anymore.

I have been in a default loving boyfriend mode the past few days, giving her the benefit of the doubt after she nearly died in the bathroom and a traumatic situation in Montana. I have defended her from my family and discovered the truth about the extent of her abuse, but there is also a thick thread of duplicity sewn into each truth she spun.

She neglected to mention we have met before, a few days prior, and instead hid the evidentiary handkerchief.

She has been vague but semi-truthful about her abuse but hid the proof and downplayed the severity.

She told me she has no social media but has a secret Facebook account she messages an assistant somewhere to do her bidding.

She led me to believe she is an average girl with an average job at a small coffee shop and lives in her small studio apartment, but in reality, she owns a multi-million-dollar company.

She omitted her "heiress status" and her financial standing but uses her money to help the community and the people in it.

She purposefully withheld the details of her past relationship, the reasons for her NYC departure, and everything pertaining to her old life.

She told me she would meet me back at the hotel the night of my sister's wedding but instead she ran away from me. From us. And she kept running.

She refused to tell me that my new brother-in-law was her ex-fiancè and instead carried on with the night as if he wasn't the sole reason for her leaving New York.

She shut me out when I tried to understand but allowed me only when she felt her life was in danger.

She told me she loved me, but she left me for weeks with no answers.

My eyes flutter shut and I rub them so hard that I see stars while they are still closed. It takes several moments for my vision to refocus but when it does, my rage unfolds. I shoot up and punch the side of the closest dresser. I punch it hard. Like I may have broken my hand, hard. Then I punch it again.

Then I hear a thud from the bottom of the dresser. Like something falling inside.

I bend down on my hands and knees to check underneath, nursing my fury induced injury, but nothing is there. A gut feeling makes me open the bottom drawer, a drawer I have just opened multiple times when I was begging for a shred of evidence that would either persecute or clear Seph.

There is a hard drive sitting there, with a bit of duct tape on the sides.

Where the hell did this come from?

I open the next drawer, as I have before during my sweep of the furniture, and it is empty. But from the angle I am at, I can't see much else other than the four sides of the drawer. This couldn't be the only one.

Frustrated but determined, I spent the next ten minutes carefully removing all the drawers in the dresser to get a clearer viewpoint to the back of the dresser.

With the drawers out, I know I found what Harrison claimed Persephone stole. Hard drives lined the inside walls of the entire dresser. Quickly, I close the garage door for privacy then reach into the dresser to pull out hard drives and vacuum sealed bags of memory cards. I have been searching for a lead to clear the haze around Persephone's past, a burner phone, a diary, or even a little black notebook, but I never expected to find a pile of hard drives.

The Lord only knew what was actually on them.

Financial records? Illegitimate books? Insider trading? Blaire had practically said as much.

For two hours, I took out every drawer, every false bottom, every door, or compartment that could stealthily hide a secret, uncovering at least 30 hard drives. I stood in the middle of an erratic minefield of black, plastic, and wood unsure what to do next.

Was this actually Seph's? Harrison wants it back. He is desperate for it back, and she has never wavered, even in the face of near death, that she doesn't have whatever he was convinced she stole. Perhaps it is because she didn't know she stole it at all… She didn't know her grandmother's antique furniture was the perfect vessel to hide these drives.

What I need to do is figure out what is on them. Then I could release my verdict. Even with the evidence, I don't have enough to convict my brother-in-law or my girlfriend.

Luckily, my laptop is in my car, so I ran out to grab it and bring it inside the storage unit with me. I plug in and start my investigation, preparing for whatever possible illegal activity I may find.

My guess is illegal stock trades or cooked accounting books. Harrison seems like a white-collar crime kind of guy.

What if this is Persephone's though? What would I do then? It makes me pause. Did I want to know? No. Did I need to know? Yes.

I trudge on.

The first hard drive has several video files, maxing out the storage. The drive itself is titled "Bobby." The first video pops up and shows a woman in a very compromising position with a clearly hidden camera. The edges are covered with fabric and the angle is less than stellar.

But God damn, it shows the girl's face clear as day. I don't recognize her, not that I thought I would, but she wore a large necklace, spiked heels and nothing else. I assume "Bobby" is the man who is plowing her from behind on a hotel bed. I wince the entire time shuffling through the 45-minute video to ensure it's just sex in this file.

The other ten videos on the drive are all the same hotel, different girls, but the same man, "Bobby." I only watch enough to confirm each girl is not the same face, then click out to the next one. My gut curdles with every file I open. Did they know these videos existed? Did they care?

While the illegal aspect was clear, I can't understand why Persephone or Harrison would want these. Aside from possible small dollar blackmail, what are these even worth to the average person?

I dig my way through about 10 hard drives. The videos are all filmed spanning over the last 2-3 years, each drive is titled with a male name. Most I recognize as Harrison's groomsmen; "Doug," "Cooper,"

"Austin," "Tommy," "Angelo," "Christian," "Hudson," "Giovanni," and then it came. "Harrison."

My heart rate sped to find my brother-in-law's name as a drive name, blood pulsing to my brain at an alarming rate. I knew it was possible, maybe even very probable when I saw all the other guys' names, but it was a devastating moment to confirm it. I click open the first file on his drive. This is before her dad died, before her depression, before the abuse.

The script is the same as the others, same hotel room, same angle, same view of the woman's face, exposing her in different positions. Harrison has the most videos, by far. While the other men have 10-12, Harrison has almost double.

His videos range from 2017 up until April of 2020, right before Seph left. I can feel my lip curl in disgust, watching him cheat on Seph fills me with more ire than any man should ever feel. My chest feels her betrayal for her. He is a piece of shit, lying, no good, pig.

I click through the subsequent videos until I reach the one I was most fearful of finding. A video titled 'Blaire'.

I refuse to watch it; it is from January of this year. It has to be her. I don't need to see it to know. My inquisitive mind needs to see all the videos to obtain all the facts, in order to pass final judgement, but I do not need to see my sister naked. I decided against viewing it.

I want to throw up.

The last ten drives I go through are meticulously organized by genre. Some are labeled with miscellaneous women's names, but they are all divided out in proper titles folders. Some are threesomes where Harrison is featured, others where he isn't, and it is just his groomsmen or friends. Each guy seemed to have at least one blow job video in the folder, like it was a checkbox to join this twisted boy's club.

I feel like I am invading these women's privacy by watching, so I only stop long enough to confirm which male is in the video, then take a quick note of the female's face, not like I'd recognize any. Each time I take inventory of the female on an untitled video, I beg the Lord above that it isn't my girlfriend. Each time he grants me that grace…

It isn't until the very last video on the 'Moneymakers' drive where I find a video labeled 'Persephone' from two years ago. Every muscle in my jaw tightens and the room starts spinning around me.

I knew just as well when I found Blaire's video, Persephone's was imminent as well, but I didn't know how it would affect me when I found it. She has already been through so much, so much pain and hurt. How was I ever supposed to show her this?

I can't breathe.

My eventual sigh of surrender echoes in the unit, unsure what to do next. I can call Seph to come here and figure this out together, but then I could be dragging her into this in a way I wasn't comfortable with yet. Afterall, Harrison is *my* brother-in-law. He is *my* family to deal with, but this directly affects her.

Isn't that what my sister and mother said?

Chapter 24

Brooks

———

The rest of the day crawled by, I went through the motions on autopilot, trying not to think about the horrors I uncovered this afternoon. I didn't watch the video, either video for that matter. I couldn't bear to press play. To see Seph with any other man ignited every jealousy pang on my body. It was debilitating.

The wheels in my brain are now turning, forming a plan to not only bring some peace to Persephone and I, but also figure out what my shitstick of a brother-in-law is planning on doing with all those sex tapes and why does he want them *back* so badly?

When the clock hits 6:30, I pack it up for the day and rush home. Seph hasn't texted me all day, but I am hoping she will be in bed resting. I hope she doesn't try to run again.

I let my brain shift to the other major realization of the day. "Steph" was Seph. The girl from the bar is the same woman I fell in love with these past six months.

The handkerchief from her storage unit is nestled back in my pocket, it's original docking spot from before that Saturday night at the bar. I haven't figured out how I am going to approach Persephone about it, especially since the tapes are much more important, but I know I will have to mention it eventually.

I am willing to let a lot slide when it comes to her personal affairs and her past, but Georgia is her present. It is supposed to be her future and we started off on a lie. A beautiful, incredible, *hilarious* lie. I keep asking myself the same question, "Does it really matter now?" and I keep coming to the same answer, "no." But like a dog with a bone, I can't let it go.

The drive home from work allows my mind to absently wander. *What if she did leave? I only found her the last time because Michael slipped up. Would I be able to find her again?*

The lights are on in the living room as I come up to the porch. The relief that washes over me in that moment is embarrassing. I am relieved she hasn't left my ass, again.

Slipping into the house, I find her curled up into the couch, buried in blankets, surrounded by a few empty single-serve chip bags and a mound of tissues.

Thank God she's still here.

"Hey."

"Hi."

"How was your day?"

She gives me an amused eyebrow flinch, as if I should already know by the tissues and food wrappings decorating her on the couch. I return her silent sarcasm with a tight smile and nod then toss my jacket and briefcase to the armchair.

"Can I come in?"

She flips the blanket open to welcome me into her nest while wrappers and tissues go flying. I swoop in and wrap my arms around her waist to pull her close. Nuzzling into her neck with my face, she loosens from her stiffened state to melt into me, too. This is a familiar scene and one I want to stay cocooned in with her until the end of days. I forget about the pain of the past weeks when my body is touching hers, as if nothing else matters but the warmth of her skin.

Peppering soft kisses into her hair, I move her tangled mane to the side to kiss her neck and a sound of approval slips out of her. My hands slide up her soft thighs and drift under her shirt to find more velvety skin to touch. Finally, our mouths find each other, and small intimate kisses turn into heavy lingering ones.

With every swipe of tongue, I moan at the connection. Her hands are exploring the day of wrinkles in the crotch of my slacks. Every point of contact is one I didn't have moments prior and one I'd bargain my soul to never let go of. She slips her loose t-shirt off over her head, and I take advantage of the loss by loosening my tie and unbuttoning as many buttons as I can before she plants her lips back on mine and then continues to rip the shirt off me regardless of the buttons left.

The blankets slide off us from the movement of our limbs and we frantically lose all the remaining barriers distancing us from each other. Our lips never detach when I drop the final scrap of cotton separating our fully naked bodies from each other. She squirms beneath me, trying to find the perfect spot to grind against me.

Minutes feel like hours as our limbs intertwine on the couch and Jeopardy dings are going off in the background.

"I wish it could be just you and me like this forever," I mumble in between kisses. She nods her head in agreement as we continue on our juvenile make out sesh. Tears slip from the slits of her eyes, and I kiss away the salty waterworks before picking her up and carrying her upstairs for the night. I know how emotionally taxing this is on both of us, I just cry a little bit less.

We spend the rest of the night wrestling between the sheets, mumbling sweet nothings into each other's ears, and drifting in and out of consciousness till hunger finds us late at night, and I scourge the cabinets for Pop Tarts, bottles of water and chips. Sleep eventually finds us both for the evening.

It's still dark when I roll over to reach for her and find the side of the bed cold and empty with the hall light on.

"Seph?" I call out from my half-awake groggy state.

Did she just get up to go to the bathroom?

She doesn't respond, but I hear rustling in the drawers and the distinct noise of a zipper. My chest tightens, worrying that perhaps my brother-in-law could be here finishing the job he started in Montana. I pop out of bed, whipping the covers over me and stalking into the hall to find Persephone with silent tears streaming down her face and a half-packed bag in her hand.

"What are you doing, Seph?"

She sinks down onto the toilet seat and drops the bag to cover her face with both hands. She sobs softly in one of my plain white undershirts and a pair of her ugliest underwear, still not answering my question. I crouch to her, completely naked beside boxers, and grab her hands in mine to comfort her.

"What's wrong, my girl? What's going on? Talk to me," I beg.

"I... " she searches my face in confusion while I wait for her to explain. "I mean, last night was goodbye, right? You said... and it can't be just us. I just... I thought it would be easier to leave before you woke up."

"What?" My heart free falls into my stomach at her words, she says them so definitely that I can't hide the anger rising up to my face.

"Your sister and mother... they're not going to let you continue to date me... not after everything... Hell, I wouldn't let you date me. I just assumed you were being nice letting me stay a day or two. Last night was... goodbye sex, wasn't it?" She fumbles more with the words, while I'm trying to piece together a logic that I do not wish to subscribe to.

I've been mad at her. Pissed at her actually. I've been absolutely destroyed by the lies, the constant running, and stand-offish moods, but at this moment, the thought of her leaving for good levels me like nothing else. The thought of her leaving me after all the shit we've been through the last week is more painful than anything I'd ever felt in this lifetime.

It's 3:46am on a Thursday in November when I realize none of the past matters because I cannot go on in this world without Persephone Kline.

"No. No, Persephone. Last night was absolutely everything except for goodbye sex. Fuck. Why do you keep trying to leave me?" It hurts, it hurts more than it ever should to say the words I feel so deep within me. She's locked me out of her heart, her apartment, and her head with all these secrets and all I want is to be nestled up next to her, sharing every ounce of my life with her. She keeps pushing me out and away. She's a damn flight risk and all I want to do is keep her grounded and out of harm's way.

"You left for work without waking me up… and… you didn't text me all day. I just assumed… Oh, Brooks… I don't think I should stay anyways; I don't think *this* is going to ever work itself out." She pleads with her twisted rationale. I know she is only thinking of me, of my family and how difficult it might be in the future with her by my side. But she doesn't even know the extent of her ex's vileness.

"Goddamn it, Seph," I push up from her and drop her hands a bit more roughly than I intend too. "How do I fucking love you so much and all you do is push me away? Why don't you want me, too? Why don't you want me back?"

Her face shifts from sadness into a look of pure shock. "You still want to be with me?"

"Of course, I do, Seph. I love you so fucking much, it killed me every time you've tried to leave. It kills me every time you've shut me out. It kills me everytime I find out another truth buried in your lies. I just want to live happily in this house with you, I don't even care about my sister or my mom or that dirtbag of a brother-in-law I have now. They're barely here anyways. I want you. I want the truth, no matter how ugly it is. Every damn day, I fucking want you to stay. I've wanted you to stay since the time you told me you were just 'passing through.'" I am standing, pacing back and forth in the hallway now, only stopping in the doorway incrementally for emphasis on certain words. Buzzing through every precious memory with her when I remembered the tidbit, I learned today at the storage unit.

I'm not even mad about it anymore, so I joke to help soften my aggressive admission of love, "Hell, Seph, I've wanted you to stay since you were a damn blonde giving me a fake number at a bar."

Her big doe eyes are pinned on me, now like a deer in headlights blinking at me. I can see the moment she realizes what I am talking about. Then her wheels start spinning, but I'm not sure if they are working out more reasons to leave or, finally, *a reason to stay.* The silence kills me, second by second, breath by breath until she finally speaks.

"How did you figure that out?" she breathes.

"I'm gonna take one from your playbook, 'I don't want to talk about it right now,'" I say with a hint of humor, but in all seriousness. She responds with a nod and tear streaking down her cheek. I mean it to be a funny moment, but I can see how she can't find it in her sunshine of a soul to muster up a chuckle.

"Say something, say anything, please," I whisper.

"I love you too, Brooks," she says under her breath and a small curve peaks at the corner of her mouth. "I love you so much, too, and I'm so sorry for everything. I'm sorry for feeding you half-truths and full on lies in some cases. I'm so insanely sorry for this mess I've put you and your family in." She pauses to catch her breath and shake her head. "I'm so sorry and I don't know how I will ever make it up to you, how I *could* ever. I just wanted to keep this all so far away from you as possible. I didn't want to weigh you down with my baggage."

Relief swells through every inch of my chest, filling my lungs with fresh air for the first time in days. "Stay, stay with me, Seph. That's how you can make it up to me. Stay here and let me love you. Stay here and just tell me the truth from now on," I beg now, my voice hushed and desperate for agreement. Desperate for clarity. Desperate to remove every square inch of air between us. Desperate to kiss her for the first time since all the cards were on the table.

Well, almost all the cards. I still need to tell her what I discovered in her grandma's furniture.

She nods while staring at my bare chest and I take a few large strides to gather her in my arms to bring her close. We stand hugging in the bright bathroom for several minutes before finding each other's lips and whispering more I love you's and apologies into each other's mouths.

We go back to bed and I hold her closer than I ever have before. I want to fall asleep, I want to let the newly announced love tuck me into a stirless slumber, but I can't shake the feeling that this isn't over yet.

I can't help feeling she might leave me again if I don't fix what was still broken.

Chapter 25

Persephone

——————

With things more settled between Brooks and I, it's time to figure out what Harrison was hunting me for. My heart told me to bring Brooks into the fold on this, to trust him like he'd trusted me, but I need to look for myself first. I need to do this one thing on my own, then if I can't figure it out, I'd ask him to come and look, too.

Using Brooks' house phone, I call Aisley at the office to get the most up-to-date location of my furniture, which should have just recently been shipped back to this coast. It's changed locations almost three times already, all done discreetly by Aisley, and I've hardly kept track. The furniture itself had no value to me except sentiment since the pieces were handed down from my grandmother.

To be honest, they don't mean much to me, but I couldn't bear leaving them in the apartment with Harrison. They are mine. I have so little to take away from him that emptying out both guest bedrooms felt like the only chip I had left to play in our match up. He saw the gaping hole of furniture versus if I prayed for an unfeeling man to feel.

Aisley answers, "Hades Enterprise, this is Aisley speaking, where can I direct your call?"

"Hey Aisley, it's Persephone," I say warily.

"Persephone!" She is surprised but quickly remembers to keep her voice hushed in the office. "Sorry, how are you? Did you get the furniture okay?"

My brows furrow. "What do you mean? You didn't send me the address. I was calling to ask you for it," I am confused, and my tone is unfairly frustrated at her.

"Oh, uh, I sent you a Facebook message. It said it was read. I thought it was odd you didn't reply, but I just assumed you were busy," she fumbles her rationale as I rifle through my purse for my phone to check the messenger app.

"Huh," my attention diverts to opening the message and reading it through.

She strung together a slew of words but I wasn't concentrating on her and forgot to listen.

"Does it say on your end when I read it?" I ask.

"I saw it turn from delivered to read right after I sent it at 4am. Was that not you who read it?" She sounds as worried as I feel, but my gut goes right to Brooks.

Fuck. Did he read it?

"Thanks Aisley. I gotta go," I hang up before I hear her goodbye, and I run down the stairs to sort through the last two days' worth of mail to no avail. My mind is racing, trying to figure out why Brooks would care about my storage, until it hits me.

He doesn't trust me.

He doesn't trust I'm telling him the truth about not stealing Harrison's money because I have yet to give him a real reason *to* trust me. I've lied at every turn, about my life, my relationships, my health, and my wealth.

It's time to lay everything out on the table with him, most of it is already out there anyways. It's time to stop trying to handle everything on my own and finally tackle this shit together, as a unit. If he wants me to stay, he's gonna have to run into this war/ storage unit hand in hand with me.

I hear the front door open while I stand at the island in the kitchen clutching the countertop as if I would topple over without its support. Brooks enters the kitchen with a smirk and his jacket slung over his shoulder along with his messenger style leather bag. He looks like a hot lawyer, one who had a long day and needs a few fingers of bourbon.

He saunters over to me to place a long, sensual smooch and I groan with approval. Something about asking for his help with this is calming my rattled nerves and I can't wait to dive in.

"How was your day?" He says flatly, but genuine.

"Okay, yours?"

"Had some interesting moments…" he trails off while opening the fridge to reach for a beer.

"I need to talk to you about something. It's… important," I blurt out.

Closing the refrigerator and turning slowly on his heel, he looks almost guilty but then turns curious. He raises a single eyebrow to encourage me to go on, so I do.

"We need to go through my furniture again. I checked it before my move to Montana, but I only quickly looked through the drawers, they were all empty of course, but I think with everything that's happened, we have to like, break them apart and really dig." I ramble while staring at his beer absently. He puts down the bottle and reaches for my hands.

"I don't even know how to say this…" He starts and I cut him off.

"I know I should have asked you before, but this whole thing has been so crazy. I need your help now," I pause for dramatic effect and blink my saddest puppy dog eyes up at him, "I need you."

We stand staring into each other's rounded eyes, his marred with shock, mine with exaggerated pleading, both begging each other to say what we're thinking. He breaks first.

"I did already. Let's go sit down, I'll explain," and he leads me to the kitchen table still holding my hands.

"I'm confused."

"I don't even know where to start with this one…" he says to himself. "The other night you fell asleep before me. We had been talking about your blonde hair and I was just so curious and couldn't fall asleep..." Brooks studies my face for a reaction before continuing. "I took your phone to find an older picture of you," he stops again to take another pulse check on my mood, bracing for potential anger, but I remain eerily calm despite the invasion of privacy.

"It was much more than I bargained for, what I found, I mean," he grabs both my hands again to cushion whatever comes next. "I found the photos, Seph, of what he did to you... I don't even have the words to describe how I felt when I saw them."

I keep silent but continue to rapidly blink, as if it will shut back any potential tears threatening to rip down my face right now and betray my calm disposition.

"Not that I thought you were lying before, but it was so much worse than I imagined. So, so much worse," he pawes my cheek with the pad of his thumb, and I instinctively lean into his comforting touch while memories flood into my mind. Memories attached to those pictures that were only meant for me to look back on, to remember the pain from those moments. They weren't meant for anyone else to see. The shame of them racks through me.

"When I was looking, a Facebook message popped up. I got so mad, Sephy. You told me you didn't have Facebook. Goddamn, I lost all sense of judgement in that moment and thought the worst. Thought it was a secret boyfriend or something. I felt like you had been hiding so much by not showing me these pictures and everything else. I said, 'fuck it' and read the message," he pauses for a negative reaction to which I only nod and keep steady eye contact.

We both know what message he read and the information it held, the location of my furniture.

"The key was in the mailbox in the morning like Aisley said and that's what I spent yesterday doing... Tearing apart every fucking dresser and cabinet you owned to find the truth."

I should be mad, but I'm not. Yes, he invaded my privacy, but I pushed him to the breaking point a million times and all he's ever asked of me was honesty. All he's ever gotten back was deceit. He was desperate for a modicum of truth, and I couldn't blame him for taking the crumb that was out there for him to freely grab.

My logical brain rationalizes that he saved me the time and effort of tearing that place up, and I crack a halfhearted smile. "What did you find?"

"You're not mad?" He looks at me suspiciously.

My sigh spurs me on, "I pushed you to the point of being that curious. It's my own fault you lost it at that moment." I take note of his slowly relaxing face. "Plus, I'm kind of turning a new leaf," my shrug forces a gentle smirk that he happily returns back to me. "I have nothing to hide from you anymore, Brooks. Look anywhere you'd like. I'm an open book from here on out."

The admission delights him, and he leans in to press a satisfied kiss to my lips. We stay in that mold for a few seconds, as if each moment was connected and helped to make up for each ounce of heartbreak, we have both endured this past month. He broke apart to take a deep breath and sighed.

"I found $1.5 million in cash."

"Okay, wow. Uhm, that's a good chunk." I start thinking out loud to myself, "But what would make him come after me like that?"

"There was more…"

"Drugs?"

"No," he swallows hard.

"Anything else?" I prod because it seems like he is avoiding whatever else there was.

"Yeah, uh, I don't even know how to sugar coat this, babe. I'm just going to say it… I found 30 external hard drives of… sex tapes," my mouth drops open in pure shock and he continues as if that wasn't appalling enough.

"Each drive was a different guy. I recognized a few of them from the wedding, but they each had about a dozen videos a piece, all with different women. It was… disgusting. I don't think any of the women knew they were being filmed. Every video was shot in this hotel, looked like the same room every time," he shakes his head in disgust.

My face is still flabbergasted, and my eyes still bulged from my head, trying to blink as if it will help process the information quicker.

"There was one... uhm, fuck. There was one drive labeled "Moneymakers."

"Was there a video... of Blaire?" I ignore what he says as my concern turns to his sister. Even though she was fucking Harrison behind my back for months, she was still the love of my life's sister. She was still *his* family.

His sudden stillness sends a chill down my spine and dissipates through my limbs, paralyzing me where I stand.

"Yes, I obviously didn't watch it. There was... one of you, Seph."

Like a normal anxiety attack, my vision starts to blur, time feels like it is speeding up and slowing down all at once. The walls start to move, my body and mind start to dissociate and puddle to the ground. In the distance I can hear Brooks say, "I'll fucking kill him, Seph. I'll kill him with my bare fucking hands... Seph? Are you okay? Seph?"

The last thing I see is Brooks' worried brow and his sharp eyes staring back at me.

"Seph?"

I wake up to Brooks stroking the hair along my face while my head laid on his lap and my body elongated on the rest of the couch. His own worried glare stares back at me when I crack open my eyes in confusion.

"What happened?" I moan while trying to sit up. Brooks gently keeps my shoulders down and runs his knuckles over the side of my cheek.

"You... had a panic attack, I think. Are you feeling okay?"

"Yeah, I'm fine. I just had a crazy dream," and I force his hands off me to actually sit up this time. I rub my fingers on my temples and then run my hands through my hair trying to remember the details.

Brooks doesn't reply and his lack of response encouraged me to keep talking to fill the silence, "I had this dream that Harrison had a sex tape of me or something, it was very weird." My mind is still reeling a bit from my slumber, and I risk a glance at him to see his reaction.

His face drains of color, and he immediately flops his hand from my shoulder.

"Seph…"

"He had a bunch of sex tapes, apparently. It was truly insane, I really need to take more vitamins or something," I keep blabbing on, as if speaking it outloud will force it from my head.

"Seph, that wasn't a dream, baby," the less common pet name makes me cringe. Not because I don't like it, but because he is using every tactic available to soften the blow of reality threatening to send me into another spiral of panic.

I laugh a humorless and borderline scary laugh. My brain now registers the information for a second time and still has no idea how to respond to the most humiliating invasion of privacy I could imagine. It's my own cackle that leaves Brooks concerned when my laugh turns into violent sobs. Brooks steps in to provide more physical comfort in the form of a bear hug and whispers promises of revenge in my ear. I let him hold me until the shock wears off enough to compose words.

"How…" I tilt my head up to search his tortured eyes that are mixed with rage and sympathy.

"I don't know… It was like any other video on the drives, same hotel room, same set up," he takes a deep breath and shakes his head out like it will help him get the memory out of his brain. "I didn't watch it originally. But I had to know today for sure, so I only looked long enough to confirm it was you. You were still fully clothed in the shot I saw; I couldn't bring myself to watch anything more than that." He blows out a breath, "but there was another 45 minutes' worth of footage from when I stopped."

I squeeze my eyes shut as if that will hold the tears back and I let Brooks console me. He squeezes me tight, presses kisses into my hair while I work on not hyperventilating and my water works turn on full blast.

"Wh-what w-was t-the date of the v-video?" I muster out between sobs.

"December 14, 2018."

The night we hooked up for the first time, after a holiday party. We had met while mingling with my father's friends at a mutual friend's Christmas party. I knew him from before, he had stopped by my dad's office a few times while I was in there and he had introduced himself. We were barely acquaintances by the night of the party, but not complete strangers. We got drunk, he got frisky, we went back to his hotel together.

It wasn't anything I hadn't done with 20 or so other men in my life. I was as impartial to one-night stands as I was about sleeping with a man on the first date if the date went well. Honestly, Brooks would have gotten it from me the first night if I wasn't bruised up like an old apple. Our first date was phenomenal by any conventional standards, but he was too much of a gentleman to even broach the moment. My only apprehension was the residual abuse marks, not the act of sex itself with Brooks.

Harrison and I were both intoxicated that night, so our physical dalliance was sloppy and short, if I remembered correctly. It is mortifying to think Brooks found that, found a tape I never knew existed, and then had to play it back to ensure it was actually me. It is humiliating and disgusting, I can only imagine how Brooks thinks of me now.

Defiled.

I sob harder into his arms at the thought. "I-I'm s-so sorry. I h-had no idea h-he t-took that v-video." At some point, this man needs to cut his losses from me. I'm a straight up PR and real-life nightmare. If it wasn't the lies and poor choice in ex-fiancés that would do me in, it would definitely be the impending scandal from a leaked sex tape from a millionaire heiress. It would be a shame no one would be able to withstand. Paris Hilton may have survived it, but I sure as hell wouldn't.

He shushes me while his fingers find a trail along my back to stroke to calm me. "I got you, I got you," he whispered over and over into my ear. It's as much comfort I can handle before I realize I am leaning too much on him and he needs to get as far away from me as possible, yet again.

"I should go," I start to pull away and he argues back.

"What? Persephone, I know you're upset but let's figure out a game plan before you disappear again," the last part is said with sarcasm, but he doesn't realize how literally I take it. I *should* leave again.

"What did you say m-mine was under?"

He clears his throat and all hint of amusement, "Moneymakers."

"Did he mean like they were the hottest faces, or? I don't even know what to think of that," I say half to myself.

"Not sure, they didn't seem overly exceptional looking," he slips mindlessly before he realizes the mistake he makes in wording. I give him an offended look and he quickly backtracks, "Uh, that's not what I meant, you are obviously exceptional looking, the others... uh... were just average? I guess I didn't notice their overall appearance much."

"I'd like to see the drives, Brooks," my voice rang clear and steady for the first time since I woke up. I am determined to keep boxing away my emotions slowly, one by one. I need to look at all the girls, see if there is a pattern, see if there's anyone I recognize so I can alert them immediately.

"Yeah...okay, uhm, they're in my car. Do you- do you want me to get them now?" He is nervous and stuttering.

I nod, "Please, if you don't mind. And a laptop."

He purses his lips with an apprehensive look in his eye, but gets up despite it and completes my request, no questions asked.

We silently set up a workstation from the couch, curl into each other, finding comfort in the contact of our bodies as if that will help shield away the disgustingness of this task.

"I should look through them, see if I know anyone," my fingers find the keypad and start sifting through the files from the first drive labeled Tommy.

Tommy is a man I unfortunately know well. He had always been kind to me, bought me a drink when I had an empty hand, always held doors open, tried to make small talk with me on occasion, and even went out of his way to attend my father's wake. What I knew of him did not leave me to believe he is a sexual predator, but the tapes prove otherwise.

His particular perversion was nothing more than vanilla, but disgusted me along with the other *friends* I recognized. While I didn't know *all* of the men from the tapes, I knew most, if only by name. They were Harrison's friends from college or the yacht club, some even old co-workers. Most of them I used to party with, some I'd even gone to drinks and on vacations with. It makes my stomach turn.

The recognizable girls' faces are few and far between. Some I notice are women who were around for short stints of time spanning from a few weeks to a month or so. They had rotated into our circle for a while until they were ultimately discarded for the next pair of legs. I had never thought of it much more than an awkward problem when we saw her out at a club following the breakup.

We shuttled through the tapes quickly and in silence, only lingering long enough to identify the woman in frame, then moving to the next video, then the next drive. Brooks looks as nauseous as I feel, having to watch these all for the second time.

Then comes Harrison's drive and I freeze. Brooks grabs my hand and squeezes it while placing a comforting kiss on my neck before trying to take the laptop out of my hands.

"No," I demand. "I need to check for the women," my voice is monotone, and I tug the laptop back to its original position in my lap. The dates are what kills me most, seeing them incrementally throughout our relationship stings, like this was a regular occurrence that he was doing no matter what I did for him in bed to help prevent it.

Dogs will be dogs, I think to myself before starting the process of identifying the women who he cheated on me with, and the slew of those who came before me.

I can feel Brooks watching me watch, bracing for a potential cataclysmic impact, but one never came. The anger rumbles inside my chest, but it never bubbles over. Am I just numb or did this not hurt because the hatred in my heart superseded the hurt? I skip over Blaire's video entirely, pretending it is not even there for Brooks' sake.

The last drive I notice is not inside Brooks' bag along with the others and I search my spot, patting around to see if I misplaced it. Brooks reaches into the seat of the couch, where he apparently hid the damn thing until the end.

"Why'd you hide it?"

"I don't want to watch this," he says warily. "I don't want you to have to watch it either."

My eyes thank him for his concern, but I reach over him to grab it. I grumble, "I just want to rip the Band-Aid off quickly," and snatch it from him.

We shuffle through the first four videos, all women I know and some I adored in a previous life. All have wealthy parents who own big corporations, like me. The tag Money Makers now makes more sense. We are in a class all on our own. The rich fucks, literally.

I pause before opening my file, glance at Brooks for a go-ahead, then proceed to open the file labeled with my name. We both take one last inhale before holding our breath and becoming statues. The camera cuts on, Harrison set it up to be concealed while I am out of frame, most likely freshening up in the bathroom.

We relax momentarily while Harrison makes his way around the bed to begin shedding his clothes, starting with the shoes and tie.

When I come into frame, my perfectly curled hair and green satin floor length gown brings me back to that night. It is strange to watch it from this angle when all my memories are blurred and patchy from the first person POV.

Harrison said something quick, and I laughed, but the audio itself is muffled from the unknown material shielding the camera from my view. We connect in the middle of the room, still clothed, and I feel Brooks flinch on sight of first contact. I, however, remain impassive, as if I am watching this night for the first time and the woman in the hotel room is not me. Brooks' hand slips into my own when Harrison begins undressing me, and I him.

Harrison removes all my garments before I get his off, then he moves me to the bed to kiss me more. It's disgusting how this script mirrored the other videos, too. Brooks uses his other hand to press his pointer finger and thumbs into his eyes midway through the video and I can't say I blame him. I can't imagine if the roles were reversed, I'd never be able to sit through watching another woman degrade him in this way. Watching the intimate moments between two consenting partners.

Knowing what comes next, I shuttle through the worst of it and once it's clear the deed is done, Brooks and I stare into a screen frozen on Harrison's chest. He is the first to move, to say something, while I feel the single tear escape from my eye.

"He wanted to make money off all of you from this drive. He knew your families would all pay to get rid of a sex tape," his voice is dull but confident in his assessment, working off the nickname and the specific women. I know he is right; it is what I have also considered as well.

"Perhaps," I mumble mindlessly. "Why did he wait?"

"He didn't need to use it, is my guess. You started dating right after this, right?"

"We never spent another weekend without seeing each other from that night on," my words drift from memories to our beginning.

He seemed so smitten. "Maybe he thought he'd get more from a marriage than a tape."

"He never deserved you or your love, or Blaire's," Brooks curses and forcibly stands up from our seat on the couch to pace in front of me. He tries to avoid thinking about what we just saw by piecing together all the other information. "I'm assuming by the bag of memory cards and his vehemence on getting them back, those were the only copies."

"I agree, most likely only copies."

Brooks stops pacing, one arm wraps around his lower chest, the other propping up his head with his knuckles resting under his chin. I stare at the screen, thinking about all the women on these tapes, thinking about if they know or if the men have already threatened them or not. I file through the list of women trying to think if I am close enough to any of them to reach out to call and ask right now. Only one came to mind.

"We have to tell Blaire. She has to know," I say finally.

Chapter 26

Brooks

───────

"That fucking bastard." Blaire grumbles then breathes out a slew of inaudible curses. Her reaction worries me. It isn't like Persephone's state of pure shock where moments feel like minutes and the air sucked out of the room. Blaire is *pissed,* not **surprised**.

Trying to be delicate, I say, "I watched only enough to confirm it was you."

She huffs, "Of course it's fucking me. How many hard drives of these tapes did you find?" She eyes me curiously.

I wish our Facetime connection wasn't as crystal clear as it is when I came to the realization that my sister knows about the other tapes. I haven't mentioned there are other girls or other recordings, and I definitely haven't mentioned they are on *other* hard drives. I haven't even mentioned how I found them taped to the back of Persephone's grandma's furniture, but somehow, she got there on her own.

She either knew before this phone call or isn't surprised by her husband. I'm not sure what is worse.

Harrison had gotten released from custody on bail, but everything got dropped when Seph refused to press charges. She bent for him, saying it wasn't worth the aggravation of being called a liar during trial, and having to pull me into the middle of it all.

While I appreciated her gesture, I couldn't help but feel she was giving up. Resigning to allowing this man to intimidate and manipulate her, even from a plane ride away. If nothing else, Blaire should be kissing Seph's feet thanking her for not dragging this thing out.

But it is my sister's lack of response to the tapes that I can't move past.

"How did you know there were other recordings, Blaire?"

"Well, I j-just assumed, I can't be the only dumb bitch to have gotten wrapped up in his shit," she starts getting defensive, but I can see the fear shimmering in her eyes.

"No, you're not. There were sev-"

Blaire cuts me off, "What were the dates? I want to see them."

"Blaire, I can't send out revenge porn over the internet. It's bad enough we have them and haven't given it over to the authorities."

"I need to know the dates then. Just send me a screenshot of the file names and the dates," she says quickly, unconcerned if sharing those file names will involve me further in some way.

I don't tell her the file names are the actual women's names either. The additional knowledge Blaire seems to have is making me even more suspicious of my sister than I cared to admit.

"They spanned perfectly over the last three years, no gap longer than a few months," I hear her curse again. I give her a moment then proceed, "How do you know so much about these tapes, Blaire? What are you not telling me?"

"Ugh, Brooks you're so dramatic. I am just assuming," her voice is strong, but her delivery is weak and hollow. Heat rises to the back of my neck at her unsympathetic response. All those women have had their privacy invaded, their private sex life exposed and recorded, and all she cared about was if he was cheating on her, while she was the mistress in Persephone's relationship. I am disgusted with my own sister, and I can't contain it anymore.

"I swear to God, Blaire, you need to tell me everything you knew about these goddamn tapes prior to me calling you today. I am not fucking around anymore, this is serious. I don't give a shit if he's your husband, or my brother-in-law. He has threatened my girlfriend's life and made a sex tape of my sister." I impressed myself that I left out the fact Persephone had a sex tape, too. As much as I love my sister,

I still don't trust her with that knowledge, especially as it pertains to Harrison. I let my anger get the better of me and hope my elevated mood scares Blaire to tell me more, "I need to know all the facts before I skin him alive."

Silence follows for a few seconds until she breaks it with a deep sigh.

"I can't believe I'm telling you this, but I am so pissed at him for all this shit. He told me he deleted it and that he didn't have more than a few from before our relationship. Lying bastard..." she starts, and I brace myself with bated breath for whatever she is about to dole out.

She rolls her eyes, leans far back in her chair to cross her arms. With another exaggerated huff, she admits, "He's in deep with his bookie and those videos must have been his golden ticket."

Persephone excuses herself for a while as I spend a long time interrogating my idiotic sister via Facetime, asking her every possible question that comes to mind, including if Harrison actually used any of these videos for blackmail yet. Like a wife on the stand, she remains semi-neutral despite her angry state.

"It's not something we discuss casually at the dinner table," she says succinctly.

"Oh, you didn't discuss his secret gambling habit or the fact he was planning on using sex tapes for blackmail to pay his gambling debt?" I shoot back. My patience which once could have stretched across the Pacific Ocean is now as thin as hair.

Blaire rolls her eyes for the hundredth and continues on begrudgingly. "Neither, asshole. We had more important things to do and talk about. I don't have access to his accounts so it's not like I can search for any random deposits."

Seph moseys down the stairs, like a scared doe, she eyes me asking permission to join the conversation by sitting in earshot of it. She crosses behind me with purposeful intent of making sure Blaire knows she is now joining the chat room. I know by the way Seph glances over her shoulder to look at the camera as she paces with a hardened face, directed at Blaire.

Blaire gives us little useful information except the fact he's been in debt for a while and my sister has been paying the bills since Seph left him 'high and dry'.

Blaire is more than aware of Seph's financial standing and how that plays into Harrison's plans of future matrimony, but it is a tricky topic to navigate with Seph in the room. At one point, I asked Seph run to grab us coffee in the other room while I pretended to pace around the room to set some ground rules with Blaire about what is respectful to admit to.

"Blaire, I don't want her to hear that you were in cahoots with Har-*Graham* to use her for her inheritance and I will disown you if you even so much as infer it when she comes back into this room." My voice is low but harsh, leaning in towards my sister on screen in silent command. I can barely handle the disappointment of the lack of character in my sister. I refuse to allow Seph to feel anything worse than what she needed to in this moment, or any other moment after this. "Don't be a bitch, you've already been enough of a problem in this," I add for good measure.

Her lip curls up in disdain, I can even see it over Facetime, but her begrudging nod denotes she will play nice for now.

"So," Seph steps into the living room, balancing two cups of coffee and a plate of cookies with a strained face. "What did I miss?"

I shoot a quick glance at Blaire who has begun to open her mouth but thinks better of it and quickly shuts it.

"Nothing. We have to figure out how we want to deal with the videos. Maybe we should just delete them," I half-jokingly say. My heartbeat levels out once Blaire settles back into her chair with crossed arms, a sign of disagreement.

"I'm not sure if I'd want to know or not… Blaire," Seph's attention diverted to the phone perfectly positioned to encompass us both in the shot. "Do you think you could take a look at the file names for

'Money Makers'? I have a feeling those girls weren't as random as we think."

Seph's tone gives me pause. She's onto something but doesn't mention what it is for a reason. She doesn't want to disclose her hunch in front of my bastard of a sister yet. She doesn't trust her, neither do I for that matter.

"I just texted you the list. Any names ring a bell? I recognized Tracy, Ashley, Cherie, Jacqueline, and Mia, but the other's I couldn't place," Seph's tone is more business-like than I'd ever heard before, like she is mid-negotiation. "Some I recognize…"

Blaire snatches her phone from the propped up state, scrolls to her messages to examine the names, and cuts her off, "Kathryn, Pamela… Laurie. Really? Huh…Kristin." A soft snort, my sister says half to herself, "His friends took down his client's daughters, and vice versa."

She clicks her tongue and continues, "Risky business mixing business and pleasure. How else do you catch a money-cow though?" My sister keeps mumbling to herself, inspecting the names and rattling off the daughter-father connections when Seph stealthily mutes our end.

"My dad was his client too," she looks up at me with sad eyes, defeated eyes, embarrassed eyes, and unmutes the phone.

Before Blaire finishes connecting all the fathers to their respective daughters, Seph cuts her off, "Send us a list, daughter to father. We'll handle the rest."

My sister nods, "Sure."

Like a resigned petulant child, Blaire's initial resistance is lost. Over the hours we have talked, argued, hammered out details, the fight in her slowly has receded. It is like she finally realizes how bad this truly was, finally relinquishing her role as a loyal wife.

"Please tell me you're leaving him, right?" I say, hopeful that my sister is smart enough to not stay with this idiot.

Her eyes shoot across the screen to look at Seph and she drops to almost a whisper, "I knew about her…" She takes slow a deep breath and closes her eyes for a moment, "I was dumb to think he wasn't doing it to me even though he was doing it to her."

Seph stills next to me but doesn't look up at the screen and keeps her gaze to the table.

"What he's done is sick, it makes me sick to my stomach," her voice still soft but turning harder with every word. "I can't be with someone that thinks that's okay."

The finality resonates between the two locations, hundreds of miles away but felt equally in both states. I nod, not needing to dive into it further.

"One last question," the voice beside me says, and the change in tone catches my attention. "Did you happen to sign a prenup?"

"No."

"Good."

The next few days I spent at the office were frantic, trying to squeeze 10 hours of work into 8 hours of day so that I could sprint home to Seph. She has been vague about her plan, mostly because we haven't had much time to ourselves to talk, but I was piecing it together from the bits I did know. It didn't seem like a purposeful omission or avoidance like I was used to from the Seph I knew pre-Blaire's wedding, but one I didn't necessarily recognize either.

Broken, but strong. Tired, but confident. I let those positive emotions inside her light the pathway back to her as well. I want more than anything to just get back to her each and every night, to keep moving forwards and onwards in our relationship, for this to keep being the reason to hold us back, but the path home to her heart is long and winding.

She is still sleeping in my bed every night, but we hadn't so much as kissed since she saw the videos, since I admitted to rummaging through her phone and subsequently, her storage locker. We hadn't talked about it either, the video of her, the video of *Blaire*, or any of the videos in between. We hadn't talked about what I did to find those videos either. She hadn't asked.

We are more than cordial though. Ate meals together, woke up together, went to bed at the same time, like usual. She doesn't shy away from changing in front of me which is a small victory each morning and night and sometimes I'd wake up in the middle of the night to find her sleeping on my shoulder. She hasn't run away again either, which was an even bigger victory every hour that passed.

We don't talk much though... Well, *I* talked a lot. I fill the usual gaps of comfortable silence with meaningless babble, chatting about clients or cases. Fuck, I even went into detail about the lettuce on my sandwich today just to hold her in a conversation with me. She is impassive towards it all, only offering polite crumbs in response coupled with considerate nods and close-lipped smiles. They look as painful on her face as I'd ever seen. Each one presses a pin into my heart, piercing it without effort.

The new divide in our relationship feels like we are standing on opposite sides of the Grand Canyon. I want to go back to deep conversations about the plots of shows we have watched or funny stories about her dad's pranks. I want to go back to lazy moments in my bed where she stretches her barely clad body over mine in the morning, when she presses hot kisses into my neck and chest until gentle touches caress us both to sleep.

I want to go back to days where we'd lounge on the couch cuddled up under a blanket to binge watch episodes of *The Office* or make dinners together, I handled the stovetop while she played sous-chef. I just want to go back a few days in time to crawl into the crevasse of a single minute and stay there. She didn't mind, but my intention was dishonest. I want to take back my discovery, my deceit, my own betrayal of trust.

It is my guilt that had me throwing shit at the wall hoping it will stick that night.

"So are you going to keep me at arm's length forever while living in my house, or are we going to actually talk about this?" I say it half-jokingly in my mind, but it comes out harsher than anticipated.

Her back is to me when her head whipped around mid-sentence. The only response from her incredulous eyes and a slack jaw, mouth wide open in shock. I have her attention finally so instead of backpedaling like I should have, I double down.

"You acting like nothing happened isn't going to make it go away," I cross my arms, leaning against the kitchen counter. Her glare holds my own for several moments until she tilts her head and begins to speak.

"We've both lied, both went behind each other's backs. Not much to say about that," her normally silky voice is hard and unyielding. She doesn't want to play right now, and doesn't want to have the conversation I am forcing her to have.

"Can you at least give me an idea of what you're cooking up with my sister," I wave an idle hand, "who I thought was more of an enemy in this than myself. Wouldn't be the first time I was mistaken when it came to you." My blow is low. It comes from every ounce of desperation and self-consciousness in my heart. I am not sure where we stand, if *we* stand anywhere at all, but I know Seph well enough to draw her out with an argument.

Her lips pursed in silent thought, "So you shouldn't be surprised why you're not being *briefed*."

Touché.

I shake my head and cradle my forehead in a hand, pressing my fore finger and thumbs into my temples to massage a better idea out of my head.

"I'm not icing you out," her voice is softer, gentler than before. "Brooks... you're..."

I meet her halfway, "An asshole, I know. Fuck, Seph. I'm sorry, ple-"

"A lawyer, Brooks. You're a *lawyer*, and I'm doing something questionably illegal right now."

"Plausible deniability," I blink and whisper to myself.

She is protecting me.

"I didn't want to flow back into things, make the town think we're back together, then shit hits the fan…" she shakes her head and leans against the fridge in front of me. I can't stop staring at her, in awe, in gratitude, in frustration and anger. Angry with myself for assuming the worst in her, again. For doubting her, again.

"You could lose your license. If you were all smiles again, or even seemingly normal, everyone would assume we're together again. Your naturally depressed state is working perfectly. Hope you can fake it for a few more days because if you blow it now, a week's worth of not touching each other will all be for naught," she chuckles, and I rake a shaky hand through my hair before catching her eye with my own.

A distant memory sparks in my mind while she anxiously twists the ring she wears on her right hand.

"Or you could just marry me," I keep her stare as it evolves from amusement to genuine confusion once she realizes I'm not kidding.

"Don't joke about that kind of thing, Brooks," her tone is icy as she pushes off the fridge to walk out of the kitchen. I snag her wrist softly to pull her to me, making it harder for her to walk out and leave.

"I'm not," I drop to both my knees to open the kitchen cabinet under the sink. Digging for that tiny velvet box I hid there before the wedding feels like eternity while she watches me in confusion. Her eyes are saucers, seeing every nervous clumsy fumble of cleaning supplies I pass to fish out the very expensive piece of jewelry I purchased a little preemptively over a month ago.

My hand stills when I finally feel the box. My vision spins along with me while I slowly twist to face her on one knee.

"Brooks…"

I can see the twinkle in her eye, but I'm not sure if it is happiness or pity. I am so deep in this now, I don't even care. I need to ask her. I need her in my life, by my side.

"Persephone…" I mumble and she starts to shake her head, no.

"Seph, baby," my heart plummets, begging for her to pick it up and allow it to beat again. She searches every inch of my face while I watch all the emotion drain from hers. "I knew from early on, I told you none of this matters, I'll sign your dad's prenup, I'll emancipate from my family if I have to," she snorts a bit at that.

"I'm kidding, or at least I hope it wouldn't come to that, but know, I just want you. I want you every day, every way. I wanted you when I didn't know anything about you, I wanted you when I knew only some, and I want you even more now that I know it all. Seph, marry me." I pop open the box and her hand clamps over her mouth.

The tears start streaming down her face and I haven't taken another breath since I let those words slide out of my mouth.

She shudders and cradles her face in her hands, sobbing.

"Seph, say something. Please." I slip my free hand loosely around her wrist to bring her back to focus. The moment I make contact with her, arms quickly wrap around my neck in an iron grip.

"Yes," she whispers into my ear, and air finds my lungs again. "Of course, yes."

On my lunch the next day, I scoot over to the coffee shop to pick up a muffin and an ice coffee only to find my sister sitting with my new fiancè.

"When did you get here, *sister*?" Things haven't been resolved since all the curd had floated to the top. My natural stasis with Blaire will be this until something major changes. Until Harrison's head metaphorically rolls for his crimes.

Her eyeroll forces me to curl a lip, "Busy, go away." Her hand flicks towards the door, and I capture Seph's wary gaze. My eyes drop to see an empty left hand. She isn't wearing her ring.

"Can I speak with you for a moment?" My tone was curt, but I was feeling a little too out of the loop and hurt.

"Sure. Blaire, I'll just be a second," Seph whispers to my sister while she slides out of the booth to drag me around the corner for an even more private conversation location.

"Why are you kicking up dirt here? I told you…"

"Can't you please just tell me what you're up to now? It cannot be good if it involves Blaire being here and potentially illegal activity you are so inclined to not even tell me."

"I'll ruin the surprise if I tell you now," she says with a serpentine smile, sending a wanton chill through me.

"You know I don't care for surprises," I wrap an arm around her waist and pur a few 'later tonight' desires into her ear while she tries to wiggle out of my grasp, mocking offense.

"Talk to the hand," she smashes an open palm to my face and breaks free.

With both palms open and out towards my sides, I yell one last fleeting whispered whine, "Please?"

She stops mid-stride, turns slowly on her heel, and I swear I see the flames flickering in her eyes like she was born from the fire of Hades himself, "You already know, Brooks…" Her pause and drop in octave sends another more sexual chill down my spine, "I got friends in *low places.*"

Chapter 27

Brooks

———

NYC REVENGE PORN RING EXTINGUISHED

Fifteen New York native playboys were charged Monday morning with multiple counts of revenge porn, county prosecutor's office spokesman said Tuesday. Charges to follow may include felony blackmail and bribery. Federal prosecutors also arrested one of the fifteen for drug trafficking, intent to distribute, and possession of cocaine after an anonymous tip was dropped to the police that weekend…

Shock is the only thing that registered on my face.

Over the course of five years, over 100 women's sex tapes were found in cryptically categorized hard drives and stashed alongside a pound of cocaine. There are reports of the tapes being used in previous blackmail scenarios against some of the more prolific women named in the suit.

None of the men named have attorneys who would comment on the charges.

I pick up to call Persephone, to confirm what I think I know already, but her phone goes directly to voicemail. The lack of response concerns me, but she told me she wasn't leaving the house today. She probably just isn't near her phone, I rationalize, though it goes against even instinct in me. I shoot off a text to confirm her whereabouts, not because I'm possessive but because the weeks prior have proved I'm not crazy to be worried.

The bubble is instant, which equally soothed and irritated me. She screened my call.

Persephone: Sorry, can't chat. I'm home, don't worry, you wart.
Brooks: Love you too
Persephone: *eye roll emoji*

I chuckle and toss my phone so it slides on the paper on my desk. She's smarter than I give her credit for.

Walking into the front door that night, I expected a pile of blankets on the couch with my future wife plopped in the middle watching reruns of *Gossip Girl*. Color me surprised to find the living room dark, but the dining room light bleeds into the hallway as uproarious laughter bounced around the back of the house.

"I told you 'If you can't make a stripper happy, you can't make your wife happy'", and more laughter ensues, along with a wild feminine roar of my girl. I have never heard her squeal like that before from laughter.

After discarding my jacket and bag, I make my presence known and stepped into the over 60s card night popping off at my kitchen table. I might as well have been a statue because not a single suit-clad man batted an eye at me until Seph tilts her pretty face up from her hand to acknowledge me with a saucy smile.

"Hey you," she purrs while reaching for her whiskey glass.

"Hey," I can't help but smile back, she is so cute when she drinks. And her ring is finally on her hand.

She slams a hand on the table to catch the attention of the six males around her, "Gentlemen, I'd like you to meet my fiancé, Brooks," her whiskey holding hand shot out half in a toast and half because she's lost dexterity of her other arm, which is currently slung over her chair.

The men pause momentarily to take me in, one tilts his head, "What do you do for a living?"

"I lie for people all day" I reply, hoping to win over a few grins with self-deprecation.

"Ah, so a lawyer?" One chirps and the group erupts in a quickly fading chuckle.

"Are these the uncles?" My eyes dart back to my woman and she nods with a smile.

"We're talking business, Brooks, do you care to join or-"

Seph cuts the man off mid-sentence, sober as a stone, "Brooks isn't involved in this, Rocco, he's got no skin in this whatsoever."

All the eyes floated towards her to answer her verdict with apprehension.

"Isn't he yo-"

"Don't even think about finishing that sentence Uncle G," she snaps again, but looks up at me with apologetic eyes.

The silence is cut only by ice cubes jingling in glass tumblers before one man with a nice suit says, "he'll read about it in the papers eventually." Laughter erupts again until play continues, and they forget I am there again.

Walking away, I hear the reshuffle of cards and my gut twisted. Not only am I not getting dealt into business with my future wife, but I also wasn't even invited to sit at the table.

What is she doing?

The next morning, I woke up to an empty bed. My heart lurched, not with worry, but loneliness and hurt. Did she even come to bed last night?

My feet slap against the hardwood in search of her, checking the upstairs guest bedrooms only to find them empty. Living room couch is a mess of blankets, but empty. Then I hear it, the faint cries and I know where she is.

Sliding into the bathroom, I see my feisty Sephy kissing porcelain, moaning absently before crawling into the shower stall fully clothed. Unaware of me, since her eyes have yet to flutter open. Dawned in only skimpy underwear and a tank top, she reaches for the shower knobs to turn on the water. Wincing at the initial contact of what I assume was cold water, she eventually aligns to the back corner which allows the water to cascade on her without entirely hitting her face. Her head leans back, and I can't help but laugh.

The sudden noise jolts her and her eyes snap open to the door. They soften to an almost closed state once she realizes it's just me.

"Toss your cookies all night? Or just this morning?"

"My uncles don't like when you say no to another drink," she groans, eyes closed again.

"Why were they here last night?" My voice is gentle, not trying to accuse her of anything.

"I needed their help, they came," her answer sounds short only because every word is a massive effort from her hungover head.

"Are they always like that?"

"Yes."

"Where are they now?" I lower myself to face her but with my back against the cabinets. One eye slips open to note my change in position.

"No idea. Home? Strip club? Hotel?" She breathes loudly, "Don't know, don't care."

I stare at her, taking in her distant responses as if they are filled with their normal sweetness. She doesn't wear a hangover well.

"What the hell is going on, Seph?"

"Not sure what you mean, be more specific," she groans and splashes the stream into her face.

"Saw an article yesterday, some people got arrested for revenge porn and *cocaine*?" The sex tapes were one thing, but the pound of coke was a very nice touch I am positive Seph laid with them for a reason, but I can't figure out why.

"Sucks for that dude," she smirks.

"Isn't this over?"

"Almost," she gives a breathy laugh this time. "One last nail in the coffin."

"And I can't know? Even as your soon to be husband?" I muse half sarcastically but still seriously.

"Even you, my lovely, *understanding*, wonderful fiancé," she opens her eyes to croon the compliments at me, then lowers her side to the shower floor, directly in the line of water. I get up to turn it off, grab her a towel and help her out, rolling my eyes the entire time.

"Can't have a firework show without a finale," she jokes before descending into the bed and snuggling into my lap as a pillow for her slumber to avoid more of her hangover. But to also avoid me and my questions.

Chapter 28

Persephone

It was a complicated trial. Because the cocaine and drives were found in my grandmother's belongings, which had been shipped across the country and over state lines multiple times. I spent more time on the stand explaining my strange apartment changes than Harrison's lawyer spent defending him.

They were creating reasonable doubt to the cocaine charge, trying to reduce the sentences, but I had an upper hand at every turn. Blaire had planted more drugs around the house, which was her end of the deal to hold up, and she came through. It also helped to be in the pockets of every politician and elected official in New York City, thanks to my dad's cadre.

The drives were a hook, line, and sinker, but the drug charges were contestable. They put his sentencing from zero to 2 years, most likely not even serving any hard time, to a guaranteed 5-year prison sentence for drug trafficking of a class B narcotic. Revenge porn punishment isn't indicative of the severity of the crime and how heavily it affects its victims. For most, a fine is the most that's ever brought up for sentencing, no matter how bad the situation is.

The system is broken for victims. That wasn't true justice, since the sentence didn't reflect the true crime, but maybe, just maybe, this was *vengeance* for us all.

I couldn't involve Brooks in the part of the plan that had me acquiring a pound of cocaine. Planting illicit drugs seemed like something a respectable lawyer should stay far away from, especially if they want to keep their license and practice.

That's why I called in my uncles.

Finding a couple grams here or there through old party girl connections would have been easy enough, but discreetly sourcing an abundance at that magnitude was a horse of a different color.

The cadre would have come through sooner had I asked, maybe even broken a few legs in the process, but I didn't know the severity of this all until Brooks had uncovered the drives.

The uncles weren't regular drug users, they were respectable businessmen who I'm sure dabbled from time to time in their youth, but they had contacts with other very important people. Some of which were not so respectable, but they were still *businessmen*.

Brooks' shock wore off once he figured out how I acquired it, but he still couldn't figure out the final checkmate. I could tell it bugged him, he asked about it often and rolled his eyes about it equally as much. I always assured him it was more of a surprise than anything, that the worst was over.

"What's this?" Brooks flips open a document on the desk I had set up in one of his spare bedrooms for my own office.

"Papers," I retorted, not bothering to look up because I know what file he is looking at.

My peripherals caught him thumbing through the legal document like it was the Sunday paper until he stilled at one page. I know the page; I know the verbiage listed. I came up with it myself.

An ode to my father, in my own way.

"Persephone," his tone so serious and low, "What. Is. This?"

"We gave her an offer she couldn't refuse," I say in my best Godfather impersonation coupled with a shoulder shrug and a wave of my open palm. A flawless rendition of the scene, if I do say so myself.

"Persephone…"

I try to keep my tone laissez-faire and my eyes re-focused on the documents I am still reading through, "The contract is for management of my partial ownership in the hedge fund once your sister divorces my ex-fiancé."

The silence, I assume, is him reading through the fine print stipulations of the deal. The paperwork explicitly says no duties or assets transferred until divorce is entirely final and filed.

The final move is mine, to ensure my own piece of mind in the future.

Blaire is smart and tenacious with a stable history of employment at JP Morgan since graduating college. She made her way up through the years and settled into a comfortable Senior Director position with a cushy salary, but the allure of ownership of a major hedge fund was too good to pass up. Especially in exchange for a divorce to a convicted felon.

The fallout from the trials have made their relationship contentious on top of the already weakened state it was in from the lying, the videos, and everything else. But Blaire had indicated possibly staying with him through his sentence, rebuilding, and starting over somewhere in California.

Harrison was always so good at making up and promising more than he could provide. I can't say I am surprised, and I know how much pain this would cause *our* family.

My future family.

Blaire didn't sign a prenup and Harrison found himself in a serious hole from his secret gambling habit, Blaire was essentially bankrupt trying to pay off his debt. He racked up credit card bills, defaulted on some personal loans, and sold all his stocks this past year without my account padding his life. Blaire was out of options. She had a cheating husband who dragged her down with him. My offer could have been an equally paying job as the one she had before, and I think she still would have taken it.

My intention was never to take over the 51% of my father's company, I had no interest in running it and was fully committed to breaking it off to sell it piece by piece. When my uncles came together like a pack of lions to help plant the cocaine, make the anonymous tip, and inconspicuously send the furniture back to Harrison with a well thought out email paper trail, I realized they might want to buy into a lucrative business since they had so much fun working together on this.

My uncles are entrepreneurs at heart who know how to run a business. It's not like I handed over the keys to hell without a care in the world. I know they'll take care of it as it is their own, like they take care of me like I am their own.

The rest of the board wasn't thrilled with more cooks in the kitchen, but I didn't balk at my decision because of their sourness. This was my choice, my company. I kept a chunk for myself, which was the part Blaire would manage, while I could continue to collect a paycheck, but gave my proxy vote to Rocco. At the end of the day, I wanted to be with Brooks. I wanted to stay in Georgia and live my life down there, live where our love grew and will continue to grow.

Love changes your perspective on the world. It changes how you interpret movies and books. It changes how you ingest and process popular culture or social situations. It softens you in the right places but hardens you when it's gone. It strengthens the muscles you never thought you had or ever used before.

Love changes you in the most beautiful of ways. It opens your eyes to see brighter sunsets and deeper oceans. It makes you protective and selfless.

That's why I initially left. I put my own needs on the back burner to keep him out of harm's way and it nearly broke me in the process. I protected him in my own way despite tearing my heart into shreds. It was a tradeoff I'd do a thousand more times if it kept him out of the line of fire, protected his business and reputation.

My instinct to leave was natural. I was flight and not fight, every time. When I left Harrison, it was for my own self-preservation. When I left Brooks, it was for him.

But now that I'm staying? It was for me.

"This was the final card, wasn't it?" Brooks whispered, still flicking through pages of the contract.

I swivel in my chair towards him, grinning from ear to ear, proud of the outcome from the poker game I've been playing the last few weeks. I have not only won the hand, but I beat the house.

"Pocket aces, what can I say?" Brooks' stern face makes me drop my grin and ask, "You're not mad, right?"

"No, I'm not mad my sister is divorcing her piece of shit husband and my fiancé offered her management of her multi-million-dollar company in exchange for her compliance and silence." Brooks blinks at me absently while I try to gauge his tone alongside his expression.

"I'm feeling a little lost here," I mockingly pout, "Are you mad or glad?"

"Neither are hitting the correct emotion quite *right*," he bites off the last word. I'm thinking he's closer to *mad* than *glad* on the mood scale.

"Well I'm not a mind reader, *fiancé*," I make sure to emphasize our relationship status to remind him of his undying love for me. "Please, tell *the love of your life* what is eating you."

A force grin that doesn't reach his eyes parts on his face. With each passing second of him glaring into my eyes, he is like a stick of butter in the microwave. Just melting away while time ticked by. His displeased face softened into a tenderness I've never seen before on him.

"I'm at a loss of how she coordinated a very illegal take down of this magnitude without involving me or consulting me. It's bringing up some old emotions from days where she liked to conceal truths," he confesses in parody. While no resentment lingered in his tone, the words are born from a place of historic despondency.

"You know I couldn't," my eyes softened to his hurt. "I was trying to protect you *and* your career."

"If we eloped, you wouldn't have had to. Couldn't testify against your wife."

"'Local Lawyer married heiress with drug problem', I can read the headlines now," I mock him. "I wanted to tie up these loose ends of *my past* for good, on my own. Well partially, I needed the help of the uncles for some of it," I shrug, talking to myself towards the end.

Brooks rolls his eyes, "Please tell me this is the last surprise, the last deceit, the last time I'm going to find something startling sitting on your desk or your phone."

"Would you like me to get a contract for that drawn up?" I purr, recognizing the playfulness making its way back into his tone.

"Add it as a clause in our prenup," a smirk draws across his face and the back of his knuckles drift near my face to caress my cheek.

My head naturally leans into his touch, like a cat careening into a stroke on its head. The last of it is over and we both recognize this is the end of the madness. His gaze locks with my own when a hand slips through my hair and onto the back of my neck. Standing over me while I sit still in my desk chair, his other hand's thumb strokes my cheek before his mouth slowly descends to mine.

My world contracts to the brush of his lips on my own. All the painful moments in our past were lost at sea, never to see the light of day again. The lies I have told slide away into the ocean, resetting a new landscape of sand with each wave that rolls in.

I drag my own hands through his thick mane, deepening the kiss and shifting it into something else. We are finally together without fear or question. His hands guide me up and out of my chair to have me lean against the desk. My knees might have given out if not for Brooks' arm locked around my waist and the desk holding me up.

Brooks breathes my name into my mouth, then peppers my jaw with soft kisses between whispered affections.

"'You know you had me at hello'", I mumble the half question into his neck, and he sucks in a breath then begins to chuckle at my sappy movie quote.

Brooks surprises me with one of his own, softly singing it into my ear, "*All I wanna do is grow old with you*'."

Epilogue

———————

A year later
Brooks

Persephone is bouncing down the street from the coffee shop she still works at part time towards me, who is coming from my office on the corner. All smiles, holding what I truly hope is a cinnamon scone and an iced coffee for me. The sight of her still brings me to my knees.

We are finally in a good place with my family, which took nothing short of a miracle from the Cadre to help fix.

The months leading up to and after the trial were hard, especially between my mother, Blaire, Seph, and I. I definitely utilized my mediation skills, trying to qualm Blaire's emotional state and my mother who was automatically defensive of her daughter against Seph.

Eventually, the arguing became stagnant.

Blaire was pissed that Seph had essentially forced her hand in ending the marriage, but also knew she couldn't stay married to Graham/Harrison. Seph was always empathetic and apologetic for the circumstances. She never felt great about the ultimatum she gave Blaire, but also recognized Blaire never grieved her marriage for ending. Blaire was just embarrassed about the PR aspect of the split. It wasn't a "good look" for her, as she put it.

"Neither is staying with a sexual predator", Seph would say back. She had no regret for what she did, but apologized profusely, nonetheless.

At the end of the day, Blaire's ego was wounded, and she needed time to lick her wounds, in peace. Many miles away, back in New York City. Far, *far* away.

My mom was the first to warm up even slightly, bringing a famous casserole over to the house one night for dinner. We noticed a regular cadence over time, of her dropping off food, and little by little, Mom would linger longer, until she finally accepted an invitation inside to eat with us. Months of this occurred and she finally admitted to me that she was curious about the woman her son deigned to marry.

One night, after a few glasses of wine too many, Mom admitted her initial cold treatment of Persephone was because of Celia, but then evolved into a show of allegiance for my sister. She said she was scared of Blaire's reaction if she even seemed slightly inclined towards a relationship with Seph.

When my mom's relationship with Seph was cordial and friendly, it had almost been an entire year of radio silence from Blaire. We decided to finally sit down and hash it out for good, since Blaire still didn't want to discuss anything with Seph, it was me, my mother and Blaire to try and smooth it out.

"Brooks, we understand that Graham… or Harrison, rather, was not the man we thought him to be," my mother's southern charm dripped on every syllable. She has a fascinating way of making everything sound so much more pleasant than the cold reality of it.

"No he was not," I reiterated, folding my arms across my chest in agreement.

"But neither was Persphone, she was also strangely imbued in this as well. You have to understand how…. Peculiar of a scenario this is for us all," my mom waited for a reaction but found none so she continued on. "Blaire needs an apology and a bit of familial allegiance from you. She feels like her brother is against her for a woman he hardly knows."

"She's my soon to be *wife*," I bit out and my mom nodded in what seemed like partial agreement.

Blaire was seething in the corner, glowering at me, allowing mom to be her mouthpiece no longer.

"And when Graham was *actually my husband*, you still took her side, and expected me to as well!" Blaire shot up from her chair to emphasize her rage.

Blaire had taken the bribe from Seph, half because of the salary for her new job, and half because she knew she couldn't stay with Graham after what he'd done to all those women, including herself. But Blaire had no inclination of letting go of the sentiment behind it all, that she was on the wrong side of a losing game and hated every second of it. She hated that this looked bad on her part. That she had a failed marriage on her resume now.

"I felt the video evidence was enough to convict," I mocked while turning to my mother with my palms open in a defenseless pose and I heard Blaire snort to the side of me.

"Neither of you are going to agree on this so how do we move forward? It's been long enough, don't you think?" My mom asked both me and my sister. We looked at each other, unsure of the answer. I harbored no ill will for her, I just didn't want my soon-to-be wife persecuted any longer for protecting herself and putting away a bad man.

Blaire was the one with the issue.

"I need a written apology from Persephone, an extra week of paid vacation, a Louis Vuitton suitcase set, and… and a dinner reservation at Rao's in the city!"

"Then all will be forgiven?" Mom asked suspiciously and Blaire nodded enthusiastically.

I rolled my eyes at the material list but breathed a sigh of relief that it would be a lot simpler of an atonement than I anticipated. Persephone had the money for the bags, and the week of vacation shouldn't be an issue.

"Done," my tone was pleasant, but firm and I held out a hand for Blaire to shake.

Her lips curled into a devious smile that had me worried, but she took my hand greedily to shake on it.

"Will you like the apology as an email, or sent by courier pigeon?"

Blaire pushed past me with a shove of her shoulder and a hair flip, "Obviously pigeon," she joked back, but half of me suspected she might have been serious.

My sister was superficial, but at least this elongated issue would be over soon enough.

"You WHAT?" Seph choked out.

"I promised her a written apology, by courier pigeon, then a week of vacation, a set of luggage and a dinner reservation. I thought that was not bad for the circumstances. It wasn't exactly a fair negotiation since her future ex-husband is in jail because of you. Didn't exactly have great leverage."

Seph's eyes bulged in anger, and I realized that she was still not thrilled, though I couldn't figure out why.

"What? I am lost here, babe. What is the issue?" I placed both my hands on our kitchen island, watching her slowly slip into a deeper fit of rage while wearing a very cute apron and cooking dinner.

"Beside the fact the bitch already has seven weeks of fucking vacation from her *original* deal, I have no idea how I'm going to get her a dinner reservation at one of the most difficult places to get a damn table at in the city! I don't live there anymore; I don't have the same connections…" Her eyes glazed over in a fit of frenzy before she turned around to give the pot she was nursing an obligatory stir.

"Oh, well, that would make sense why she seemed so cavalier about it. She probably expects you to never be able to get her a table, therefore, no apology accepted," I pieced together aloud.

Seph tossed the spoon on the counter next to the stove and turned to me with a shake of her head and rolled her eyes. "Hand me my phone and then start Googling courier pigeons, tough guy. I gotta give my uncle Rocco a call."

I huffed a laugh, knowing nothing was impossible if you know a guy, who knows a guy, who knows another guy.

Hi friends and readers,

I wanted to do a special shout out to all the people who helped me in the process of writing this book.

First, the love of my life, may not have any idea what makes a good romance or a suspense novel, but John sat through hours of brainstorming, reading paragraphs out loud, and talking through storylines for the good of this book. He is the one who gets dragged into all my crazy ideas of adventure and does nothing but lets me spread my wings to fly. He supports my extremely ambitious nature, feeds my curious soul, and affords me the freedom to accomplish all of my lofty goals. It's our love that inspired the healthy and jovial parts of the relationship between Brooks and Persephone in the book. It's our love that will continue to inspire me in all my future novels to come. He has given me the gift of unconditional love and I will always be grateful for him and his support.

Second, I want to thank all the wonderful people in my life that helped me proofread for grammar, strengthen story arcs, smooth over chapter concepts, and everything in-between. They read first drafts, second drafts, fourth drafts, specific chapters over and over until it was perfect. I could not have produced this book without their physical help, but even more so without their unconditional support. Thank you to my closest friends Ashley McKenelley, Tracy Ambrosecchio, Kristin Greco, Garrett Beltis, and Maria Abreu. Thank you to my family who helped proofread too because they never fail to support me in everything I do; my brother Justin DePinto, sister-in-law, Kara DePinto, aunt, Annette Slattery, uncle, Donato DePinto, and cousin-in-law, Kathryn Tippett. You are what makes up my heart and this book would not be what it is today without your efforts, love, and full backing every step of the way.

Third, I want to thank my parents, Jackie and Frank DePinto, for their continued encouragement throughout my very short 30 years of life. Ever since I was a little girl, they have always preached to me how I can achieve anything I set my mind to and I've been able to accomplish so much because of their confidence in me. Their continued belief in my abilities has formed me into the fearless and self-assured woman I am today. I cannot thank them more for the years upon years of assurances, advice, and love. It's because of them I had the confidence to pour a piece of my soul into a 90,000-word novel and broadcast it into the world for anyone to read.

I'd also like to thank John's parents, my future in-laws John and Patty Bakos, for not only raising the most incredible man I know, but for allowing me into their home during the COVID-19 quarantine when we moved out of our apartment and into their basement. Not only were we able to buy our new house because of it, but it also afforded me the peace and tranquility to write my book! I couldn't ask for better in-laws or people to have in my life.

There can't be a thank you without thanking all our followers. Books N' Betches fans are literally the light of my life right now and so many of you gave me such amazing feedback, edits, and confidence to finish this book. This book would not have been possible if not for all of you.

I'd like to thank everyone who bought this book, supports my podcast (Books N' Betches), follows me/us on social media, or has been in contact with me in the last 5 years. You've touched my heart in ways I can't fully express, and I owe my endless gratitude to you. Thank you for supporting me on this adventure, liking my pictures, buying my book, listening to my words, or just following along for the ride.

Thank you from the bottom of my heart. This book will always be one of my most major life accomplishments and I will never forget the love I felt on the way to achieving it.

All the love and light,
Erica

Developmental editor: Cece Carroll
Book cover: Fiverr artist- zakarianada

Printed in Great Britain
by Amazon

64821509R00173